THE NIGHT WANDERER

THE NIGHT WANDERER

An Aelf Fen Mystery

Alys Clare

Severn House Large Print
London & New York

This first large print edition published 2017
in Great Britain and the USA by
SEVERN HOUSE PUBLISHERS LTD of
19 Cedar Road, Sutton, Surrey, England, SM2 5DA.
First world regular print edition published 2016 by
Severn House Publishers Ltd.

British Library Cataloguing in Publication Data
A CIP catalogue record for this title is available from the British Library.

ISBN-13: 9780727895202

Severn House Publishers support the Forest Stewardship Council™
[FSC™], the leading international forest certification organisation. All
our titles that are printed on FSC certified paper carry the FSC logo.

Typeset by Palimpsest Book Production Ltd.,
Falkirk, Stirlingshire, Scotland.
Printed and bound in Great Britain by
T J International, Padstow, Cornwall.

For the Old Woo,
from OGH, with very much love

Lassair's Family Tree

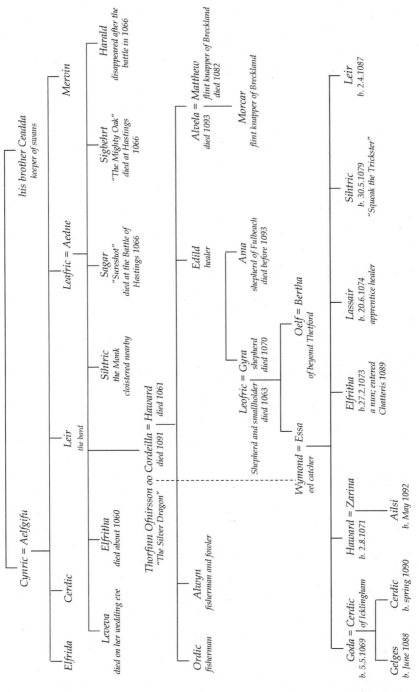

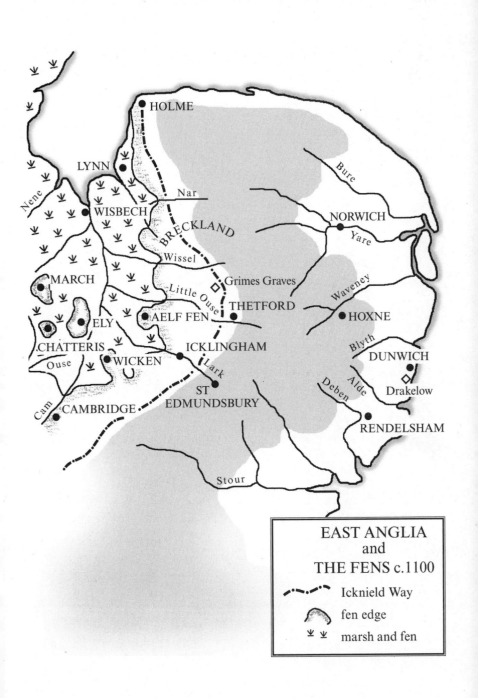

EAST ANGLIA
and
THE FENS c.1100

—··— Icknield Way

⌒ fen edge

⅄ ⅄ marsh and fen

One

The death happened less than a week after my return to Cambridge. The season was autumn, the weather still mild and the leaves just beginning to turn yellow, bronze and copper: colours which made a pleasing contrast with the bright blue sky. The first frosts were still to come.

The body was found on the river bank, on a lonely willow-shaded stretch out to the west of the town. The throat had gone: torn out as if by a clenching fist with strong fingers and sharp nails. No human hand, surely, had that sort of force.

I've no idea why anybody thought it was a good idea to send for a healer. What did they imagine I would do? Join up the severed windpipe and put a patch on that gaping, yawning hole? Had I – had anybody – the skill, such an action might possibly have restored the corpse's ability to breathe, but by then the poor man was past saving anyway because the ruptured vessels on the left side of the neck had allowed all the blood to drain out. By the time I got there, all we could do for him was pray for his soul.

And shiver with horror, for this was no ordinary death.

I had come hurrying back to the town and my studies with my mentor Gurdyman sooner than

I had been expected, because I was following hard on the heels of Jack Chevestrier. We had got to know each other back in September, trying to help a lost woman find her way home,[1] and although our time together had been quite short, already I sensed there was a strong connection between us. In my sensible moments, I found it hard to understand how two such different people – a Cambridge lawman and a village healer from the fens – could have anything in common. But the fact remained that something had drawn us together. I had followed him back to Cambridge because I wanted to find out what it was.

I had already settled back into life with Gurdyman, who, when I presented myself at his twisty-turny house hidden in the maze of lanes and alleyways behind the market square, had looked up from his workbench just long enough to say, 'Oh, you're back,' quickly followed by, 'Go out and buy us a couple of pies, it must be long past noon,' before diving back into whatever was absorbing him and ignoring me for the rest of the day. I was used to him, though, and I didn't mind. Once we'd eaten, we got straight back into our work together; he'd been instructing me in the Nine Herbs Charm a few weeks back, before we'd been interrupted, and it soon became apparent that this was merely the first in a long list of powerful charms he was planning on teaching me. I reflected with considerable pleasure that I was exactly where I wanted to be: deeply involved in the studies that I loved with a mentor

1 See *Blood of the South.*

2

I greatly admired, and with the prospect of an intriguing friendship to pursue as soon as I had some free time. Life, I thought as the days went by, not without a little complacency and self-congratulation, couldn't be much better, and happily I looked forward to the weeks ahead.

Which just goes to show that it is a mistake to take for granted the pleasure of calm, peaceful days where nothing much happens other than what you're expecting will happen. As soon as I stared down at that throatless corpse, I sensed the presence of evil and, somewhere deep inside me where intuition counts for a great deal more than logic and reason, I knew the calm, peaceful days were gone.

I waited with the body while a lad ran to find an officer of the law. It had been discovered by a courting couple, who had slipped away to this quiet stretch of the river once their day's work was done to enjoy some private time together before the cold of oncoming autumn made such outdoor assignations uncomfortable and imprac-tical. The lad had come along shortly after the discovery, together with the boy who had dashed off to fetch me. He was now sitting hunched up some way down the track, as if determined to get as far away from the corpse as he could. He and his companion had been looking out for a shady place to fish.

I felt very sorry for the courting couple. They'd described to me how they found the body, or rather the young man had, for the woman was still too distraught to speak. She was only a girl,

3

really, and apparently she'd fainted. The young man looked scared to death, watching her with anxious eyes, presumably in case she keeled over again. *He really loves her*, I thought. It was a strange thing to have noticed under the circumstances – probably I too was suffering from shock – but, nevertheless, I was heartened by that demonstration of the young man's love. He hadn't brought her out here solely to explore the plump young body, although that he definitely *had* done, for her gown was still unlaced. I would make sure to point that out tactfully, before he took her back to town. Perhaps she had wanted the intimacy as much as him, I mused, for men make a mistake if they think they always have to coax a woman, and . . .

My rambling thoughts were interrupted by voices and the sound of footfalls. Five men were coming along the path that ran along the river bank, one of them carrying a hazel hurdle. I recognized the man in the lead; he was, like Jack Chevestrier, one of the sheriff's men.

My heart sank. It was only then, when I knew it wasn't Jack who'd been sent to investigate the death, that I realized how hard I'd been praying it would be.

The law officer was a tall, skinny man with narrow shoulders, a prominent Adam's apple and a face that came to a point, with a long, protuberant nose above a receding chin. His eyes, small, intensely dark and rather close together, increased the resemblance to a rat.

'What's all this about a body?' he demanded belligerently. He looked at the young couple, a brief, lascivious grin twisting the small mouth as he took in the girl's dishevelled gown, and then turned to me. 'I know you,' he said, jabbing an accusing forefinger at me. 'You're that healer girl. Did you find it, then, and reckon you'd try to save it?' I noticed he hadn't yet looked at the corpse, lying beneath the willows.

I paused to calm myself, then said quietly, 'I didn't find the body, no. This young couple did.' The girl had made the discovery when, lying on her back, she had flung out her hand, then, wondering why it seemed to have landed in a sticky puddle, raised her head to have a look. That was when she fainted, and, as she started to come round, she'd been copiously sick. 'Then these two boys came along.' I pointed to the pair, standing a little apart and clearly trying to melt into the background. 'One of them came running to find me.'

The lawman nodded, a sarcastic smile on his face. 'Right, and you reckoned you'd act the hero and save a life? Is that it?'

He managed to make what would surely have been a laudable action into something faintly risible. I began to dislike him profoundly.

'Saving lives is indeed what I am trained to do,' I said, just about managing to sound polite, 'but I realized as soon as I got here that there was no possibility of doing so in this case.'

'Beyond your competence,' the lawman said. He glanced at the two skulking lads. 'They should have sought out someone with more experience. Some *man*,' he added.

I made myself count to five, fighting down the

hot, furious words. When I was pretty sure I could speak without spitting, I said, 'The most experienced man in Cambridge could not have saved that poor soul.' I hesitated, wondering if it was wise to show him up in front of his men, but then I thought, *He deserves it*, and went ahead. 'As you would have seen yourself if you had bothered to look, the corpse has no throat.'

The girl moaned, bent over and threw up again.

The lawman went very white. I watched him, the struggle going on in his head clearly visible in his face. He took one step towards the body, saw the blood and hastily stepped away again. 'Dead,' he said, too loudly. Then, turning to the man holding the makeshift stretcher, 'Go on, then! Pick it up! Don't just stand there gawping, you've got a job to do!'

The man with the hurdle glanced at his companions and they all moved reluctantly towards the body. I took pity on them. It was hard to be expected to show courageous indifference to violent death, especially when your commanding officer so obviously couldn't. I stepped between them and the corpse, and, bending down, took up a fold of the blood-stained cloak, draping it over the head and shoulders so that the dreadful wound was invisible.

The man with the hurdle gave me a grateful smile. 'Thanks, miss,' he muttered.

The four of them bent to their task. They handled the corpse with gentle hands, as if it could still feel.

The lawman was already striding back towards the town.

I waited until the men and their burden had gone. Then I turned to the two lads. 'Save your fishing for another evening,' I said. 'Go home now.' The lads needed no further instruction, and, as one, broke into a run and headed off; not, I noticed, in the wake of the officer and his men but up another, lesser-used path. It was a less direct route, but had the advantage of allowing them to avoid any further attention from the law. It was a sensible precaution.

I met the eyes of the young man and said quietly, 'Can you look after her by yourself or do you want me to come with you?'

He stood up a little straighter. 'I can manage.'

I nodded. Then, holding his gaze, I indicated the lacings on my own gown. For a moment he looked puzzled, then realization dawned and, turning to the girl, hastily he tidied her up. He glanced towards me and gave me a quick grin. 'Thanks,' he mouthed. Then, his strong arm round her curvaceous body and her head leaning trustingly against his shoulder, he took her away.

At last.

I stepped over to the place where the body had lain and began the careful search I'd been itching to do since I got there. The lawman should have done it – of course he should – but fate's hand had sent a man who was squeamish around blood and dead bodies, and his one desire had been to get the corpse back to town and hand over responsibility to someone else. If Jack Chevestrier had been dispatched to the scene, matters would have been very different. I knew, for I had already seen him at work and—

With an effort, I made myself stop thinking about Jack and got on with my task.

I knelt on the grass, careful to tuck my skirts up to avoid the blood, and slowly walked my hands, palm down, all over the area where the body had lain. It was quite easy to identify, for as well as the mind picture I had concentrated on committing to memory while the corpse was still in situ, the grass had been bent and flattened.

The ground held no warmth. This poor soul had been dead some time.

Next I studied the pool of blood. It, too, was cold, and congealing, brownish in colour. Then, on hands and knees with my arse in the air and my face close to the grass, slowly and meticulously I went over the whole area. I didn't find a thing.

I sat back on my heels. Closing my eyes, once more I conjured up that image of the body and listed everything I knew about it.

It was that of a man; in late middle age, well-fed, plump-faced and clean-shaven, with neatly cut grey hair styled in a bob. He was clad in a costly robe of good wool in a bronze shade, faced with embroidered panels at the collar and the edges of the openings. He wore a hat, pulled down firmly over his brows so that even the violence of his death hadn't knocked it off. Around his waist was a wide leather belt on which hung a purse and a short dagger in a gold-tooled sheath. His boots were of chestnut leather, supple and new, and there had been divots of muddy grass on the soles, as if he had dug in his heels to stop himself being dragged backwards.

I got up and went to check. Sure enough, a couple of paces away I found two indentations in the grass.

Reluctantly, I pictured the fatal wound. Death would have been pretty quick, and I supposed that was some consolation for the horror of its manner. The man had, I thought, been approached from behind. Feeling himself grabbed in strong arms, he'd have fought briefly, but futilely. Had the assailant turned him round to kill him? I had no way of knowing. The wound was deeper on the left side – where I'd noticed the severed blood vessels – so it had probably been done by a right-handed person, either reaching out as he stood before the victim or curling his arm round the front of the throat if he had stood behind him.

Finally, feeling more than a little queasy, I thought about that murderous hand. *Was* it a hand? A *human* hand? I shook my head, for it was dreadful to contemplate. The wound had looked huge as my horrified eyes had gazed down at it, and briefly I'd had wild visions of some nightmarish animal straight out of ancient legend, its murderously long, sharp claws spread on a huge paw, a hybrid of wolf, bear and lion.

But my sensible mind knew that such creatures had no existence outside the old fireside stories.

Did they?

All at once I was struck by the frightful realization that I was standing all by myself at the very spot where a chubby and wealthy townsman

9

had met his appalling death. I was quite a way out of town, and it was rapidly getting dark.

I gathered up my skirts and fled.

Gurdyman was waiting for me when I got in. I was panting hard, sweaty, dishevelled, and still suffering the after-effects of my panic. I was touched to see a swift expression of relief cross his face; he'd been worried about me. Worried enough, I thought, to have abandoned his experiment down in the crypt and come up into the house.

'I'm quite all right,' I assured him as he shepherded me along to the little kitchen, where a pot of water was simmering over the hearth.

'Sit.' He pointed at the stool in the corner, and I did as he ordered. It was a great relief to rest. He poured water on to the contents of a mug he had set ready – some herbal mixture . . . I smelt valerian and chamomile – and handed it to me. 'Drink.'

I blew on it and took a sip. He'd put a lot of honey in it, too. I sipped again.

After a moment, I said, 'You're treating me for shock.'

He nodded. 'Quite so.'

I met his bright blue eyes. 'How did you know?'

'I sensed a great upheaval . . .' he began in a soft chant. But then he grinned. 'No I didn't. But, child, you were summoned at twilight by a lad in a blind panic who said there was a body lying soaked in blood and the healer had to come as fast as she could, so obviously you weren't summoned to pick daisies.' He spoke lightly, but

10

his eyes, still on me, were watching me with anxious intensity. 'Was it bad?' he asked softly.

I nodded. I went on sipping. The brew was wonderfully comforting, and I was already beginning to feel sleepy. Gurdyman stepped towards me and briefly rested his hand on my shoulder. 'Go to bed, Lassair. I shall return to my workbench.' *And that's where I'll be if you need me*, hung unspoken in the air. He trotted off along the passage. 'We shall talk in the morning,' his voice floated back.

'In the morning,' I repeated softly. Then, my eyelids drooping, I finished the drink, made my brief preparations and then clambered up the ladder that leads to my little attic room above the kitchen. I took off my boots and my outer garments, then fell into bed. Whatever soporific Gurdyman had put in my drink, he'd added it with a generous hand. I was asleep within moments.

The sound of voices woke me. I opened my eyes to see sunshine pouring in through the windows that overlook Gurdyman's sheltered little inner court. It was full day; my mentor had kindly left me to sleep on.

Voices . . . Two male voices, Gurdyman's and another.

Shocked into wakefulness, I leapt out of bed, filled the bowl with water from the jug beneath the window, washed my face and hands and then, putting more water in a cup, took up one of the little twigs I cut specially and cleaned my teeth. My herb-induced sleep had been heavy, and my mouth felt as if it was lined with fluff. I pulled on my gown, re-braided my hair, tied on a clean head band and arranged my small coif, trying all the time to keep my movements restrained and quiet; I really didn't want to give the impression that I was taking particular care with my appearance, even though of course I was. Then, boots in my hand, I climbed barefoot down the ladder.

My attempt at nonchalant sophistication was somewhat spoiled by the fact that I missed my footing and slipped down the last few steps, landing in a heap on the floor.

The conversation out in the court abruptly stopped and Gurdyman said, 'Are you all right in there, Lassair?'

'Fine!' I said, my voice a squeak.

There was a pause, then he said – and I could *hear* he was smiling – 'Aren't you coming out to join us?'

So I did.

He and Jack sat opposite each other on wooden benches, with Gurdyman's portable working board set up between them. Gurdyman was smiling at me indulgently. As for Jack, when I nerved myself to meet his eyes, I saw with a lift of the heart that he looked as glad to see me as I was him.

He got up as I approached and gave a sort of bow. He said quietly, 'I heard you were back.'

I nodded. 'Yes.'

Gurdyman endured a few moments of Jack and me looking awkwardly at each other, then said firmly, 'Lassair, I expect you can guess why Jack is here. Come and sit down, for he wants to talk to you.'

I hesitated. If I sat next to Gurdyman, Jack might think I didn't want to be near him, and if I sat next to him, it might make me appear too forward. So I pulled up a third bench and sat on that. Gurdyman shook his head in exasperation. Then, turning to Jack, he said, 'Go on, then.'

Jack was watching me closely. 'You were called out yesterday evening to attend to a wounded man down by the river, Gurdyman tells me.'

'He was dead. The wounded man, I mean. I think the people who found him panicked, and sending for a healer was the first thing they thought of.'

'He had been dead some time?'

'Yes.' I explained about the cold ground and the congealing blood.

'I've taken a team out there this morning and organized a proper search,' Jack said with a frown – of criticism for the inadequacies of the colleague I'd met yesterday? – 'but we found nothing.'

'I looked, last night,' I said quickly. Had that been the right thing to do, or should I have left it to Jack? 'I didn't find anything either.'

'What of the others who were there?' Jack asked. 'There were some lads, and a young couple, I believe. Would any of them have noticed anything, or picked up some object?'

'I doubt it,' I said. 'The two boys had barely got to the scene before one of them raced off to fetch me, and I don't think it would have occurred to either of them to start searching; they were far too shocked. As for the courting couple, before they found the body they were only interested in

13

each other, and afterwards, his sole concern was to take care of her.'

'You don't think it would be worth my while to find them and talk to them?'

'No.' He'd learn nothing, I was sure of it, and I would save them from the ordeal if I could.

Jack seemed to accept that. Still watching me closely, he said, 'What are your thoughts?'

'Er – What do you mean?'

'Tell me what you observed, and what you conclude from it.'

I paused, trying to sum up my impressions and work out how to express them in a way that would be helpful. It wasn't easy, especially when he was staring at me so intently. I had forgotten the clear green of his eyes. *Get on with it*, I ordered myself.

'The man was wealthy and enjoyed a rich life, with plenty on the board and in the larder,' I began. 'He could afford good clothes, and he had recently treated himself to a costly robe.' The wool had had that distinctive, new-cloth gloss and smell. 'He wore fine boots, although he wasn't much of a walker, for the wear on the soles and heels was uneven, and he probably turned his toes out at quite an awkward angle. He had a purse attached to his belt, as well as a dagger in a nicely decorated sheath.' I stopped, thinking. 'Whoever attacked him didn't do it to rob him, because the purse was still bulging, and they took him by surprise. He didn't have time to get his dagger out.' I paused again. 'The assailant jumped on him from behind and he dug in his heels as whoever it was pulled him over backwards. The killer tore out the throat, I would guess in one savage movement and probably with the right hand, destroying the windpipe, the gullet and the blood vessels on the left of the neck. The man would have died instantly.' Suddenly I could see that awful wound again. I swallowed, fighting the light-headedness. 'I can't begin to imagine the weapon,' I said. 'You'd think it was the huge paw of some wild creature, only I don't know anything that comes that big.'

Silence. I heard my last words, over and over in my head, like a fading echo. *Anything that comes that big. Comes that big. That big. Big.* How stupid I sounded.

Then, after what seemed hours, Gurdyman stirred and addressed Jack. 'You have seen the body?' Jack nodded. 'Do you know who he was?'

Jack sighed. 'Yes,' he said. 'His name was Robert Powl. As Lassair surmised, he was indeed a wealthy man, building himself a fine new house out to the north-west of the town, not far from where the quayside starts to peter out.'

'He was a merchant?' Gurdyman demanded.

Jack shook his head. 'No. He had a fleet of river craft, and his business was the transportation of cargoes – goods, livestock, people – around the fenland waters and up and down the rivers between here and the coast.'

'A lucrative business,' Gurdyman observed.

'Yes,' Jack agreed. 'He seemed to be doing very well.'

'Has he family?' I asked, somewhat sharply. It seemed more important to ask about the people

15

left behind to grieve than about the poor man's prosperity.

Jack met my eyes, and I sensed he knew exactly what I was thinking. 'He was a widower,' he said. 'His wife died five years ago, and they had no children. He lives with a small household of staff, who have been informed of their master's death and the manner of it, and are deeply shocked.'

'And can any of them suggest why their master was killed?' Gurdyman asked. 'Had he enemies? Somebody he had crossed in business?'

'We are enquiring, but it appears not,' Jack replied. 'Robert Powl liked to make money, and he was keen to use that money to make more, but then so do all successful men of affairs.'

'Why, then, was he killed?' I asked in a small voice. *And in such a terrible manner . . .*

Jack looked at me, his face full of sympathy. 'I don't know, Lassair.' *But.* I could hear the *but*, although it wasn't spoken.

So could Gurdyman. 'But you have your suspicions?' he said.

Jack looked from one to the other of us. 'I have—' he began, then stopped.

'Go on,' Gurdyman urged. He glanced at me. 'You won't scare Lassair. She is made of stern stuff.'

Jack drew in a breath. Then very quietly he said, 'This death is not entirely unexpected.'

Gurdyman saw what he meant before I did. Leaning forward, he said, 'There have been others, killed in the same manner.'

But Jack shook his head. 'No – not people,' he

16

replied, in the same barely audible voice, as if he feared eavesdroppers out in the alley on the far side of the high enclosing wall.

'Not *people*?' Gurdyman echoed. 'What, then?'

'A rat, then a cat, and finally a dog. The rat was found by St Bene't's Church, under the tower. The cat was on the quayside, hidden under a pile of wood shavings left by a shipwright. The dog was curled round the lip of the Barnwell spring.'

I shivered suddenly, for all three locations seemed to be significant. St Bene't's has a well, said to be very old, in its churchyard. The tower, built by the Saxons, soars above it, and people say it's haunted. The river can appear deeply sinister when you're there alone, with the dark waters flowing silently by. And the Barnwell spring – the name is a corruption of bairns' well, for traditionally boys and lads met there on the eve of St John the Baptist's Day to wrestle and play – is very, very old. Legends abound concerning its origins and although nowadays it has lost much of its old magic, if you go there at sunrise, when the mists are gently floating above the grass, there is still an atmosphere; a whisper of ancient things.

And now dead animals had been left at each place.

'Were they killed like the dead man?' I asked.

Jack turned to me. 'Yes.'

'Throats ripped out as if by a sharp-clawed hand?' For some reason I needed to hear it confirmed.

'Yes.'

'Have you any idea why?' Gurdyman spoke quietly.

17

'I—' But Jack stopped, shaking his head.

'Theories, then,' Gurdyman snapped with uncharacteristic impatience. 'I cannot believe you haven't got a theory.'

Jack straightened up, gazing over Gurdyman and me at the wall beyond. 'I understand that something similar has happened before.' He didn't want to tell us. You could clearly hear the reluctance in his tone.

'When?' Gurdyman spoke the single word like a bark.

'A long time ago,' Jack said. 'But the pattern was the same. A mouse first, savagely killed and left in a churchyard. Then a hare, left by the river. The dog was found in a well that used to exist at the corner of the marketplace.'

'And then a man? Precisely as has just happened?' Gurdyman demanded.

Jack snapped his full attention on to him. 'Yes, exactly the same,' he said slowly. 'As far as these present events have gone, it appears that this is an exact copy of what went on before.'

'As far as—' Gurdyman was saying.

But I didn't need to listen to the rest of his exclamation, nor to Jack's answer.

For I already knew.

The brutal murder of Robert Powl would only be the first.

Two

I walked with Jack to the door. For all sorts of reasons, I didn't want him to go. He stepped into the alleyway, looking up at me as I stood on the doorstep, and I felt glad because I realized he felt the same.

Then I sensed there was something he wanted to say. 'What is it?' I asked.

'Don't—' he began, then stopped.

'Don't what?' I felt fearful suddenly. He wasn't hanging around purely for the pleasure of my company.

He didn't speak for a moment. Then, in a quiet, urgent voice, he said, 'People are already scared. The fear will get worse as the news spreads, and that will happen very swiftly.' He frowned. 'Otto's a fool. He ought to know better than to go drinking and allow his tongue to run away with him.'

Otto must be the officer I'd met yesterday. 'It shook him,' I said gently. 'It was an awful sight, and he was unmanned. He couldn't get away fast enough, and no doubt he thought a few mugs of ale would restore him.'

Jack's clear eyes stared up into mine. 'Otto is an officer of the law,' he said sternly. 'He has no right to be unmanned by dead bodies.' Then, more kindly, '*You* weren't.'

'In general, I am used to death, and I don't fear

19

it,' I replied. 'But yesterday's discovery was ghastly. If you think I was unaffected, you're wrong.'

'I'm not wrong. Of course you were affected, but you didn't allow your emotions to overcome you.'

'How do you know?' I countered. I was starting to feel quite sorry for Otto.

'I know,' Jack said softly, 'because you obviously kept your head. In there just now' – he nodded towards Gurdyman's house – 'you gave me the sort of careful, detailed, observant description of the body as it lay that I should have had from my own officer.' He glared at me, although I knew his anger was with Otto. 'I don't believe he even looked at the corpse.'

He didn't, I could have said. But I held back. Otto seemed to be in enough trouble already this morning, and he was probably nursing a drinker's headache and queasy stomach into the bargain.

There was a brief silence. Then Jack said, 'Lassair, I was about to say that there will soon be rumours spreading, and people will vie with each other to come up with the most lurid version. They'll – well, you know what people are like when they're frightened. There's an almost irresistible need to talk about the thing that scares them, and everyone exaggerates. They'll link these events with what happened before, and every last man and woman will draw parallels which may not necessarily exist.' He hesitated, then, in a carefully casual tone that didn't fool me for a moment, added, 'No doubt the old grandfathers and grandmothers will be in great demand as their

20

younger kin demand to hear the old legends and stories, and they'll all make the most of their brief popularity and indulge every request.' He tried to smile, but it wasn't up to his usual standard.

I heard several things that he hadn't actually said. That Otto's tongue had run away with him in a tavern full of avid listeners, and so by now everyone was talking about Robert Powl's terrible death. That already the story was being embellished, as people used their own fertile imaginations to furnish the details they hadn't been told. That, with typical pessimism and determination to see the very worst in a situation, people were already anticipating more deaths, no doubt describing them in increasingly sensational and dramatic detail.

And, most frighteningly, that there was some horrific legend in the town's past which was even now being resurrected . . .

'I'd like to—' I began.

But he interrupted me. Leaning closer, his face tense, he said, 'Please, don't listen. Close your ears to the gossips and the storytellers.'

'But—'

'If we lose ourselves in dread and terror, how can we act with good sense and logic?' he demanded. 'Some of my men are already worrying about leaving their homes undefended while they're on duty, especially the night watch. I've had to reorganize the rosters, and few are happy about it. I need you to—' He stopped.

I need you to keep your head because I depend on you. Foolishly, I hoped that was what he'd been about to say.

21

'I can't promise not to hear the rumours,' I said carefully, 'but I have taken your warning to heart, and I will do my best to put them in the context of a frightened populace trying to comfort themselves with a bit of exaggeration and sensationalism. Will that do?'

Now, finally, he smiled properly. 'I suppose it'll have to.' Then he turned and hurried away.

Gurdyman and I got straight down to work. He set to with single-minded absorption; he was instructing me on the four elements, earth, water, fire and air, and the mysterious fifth one known as quintessence, the spirit that fills the world and the heavens with life. He had drawn the symbol for this concept, which was a circle divided into four by a cross. This had led him off into one of his customary side roads, and now, as he compelled my attention in the wake of Jack's departure, swiftly he filled an old, much re-used piece of vellum with other symbols. 'For this is a secret art, child,' he said, pausing from his work to look up and fix me with a penetrating blue gaze. 'Whether we are referring in our work notes to an element, a substance, a metal, a plant, an animal, or one of the tools of our trade' – he indicated the workbench, crowded with vessels of all shapes and sizes, jars and pots, a crucible set on a tripod above a flame, a still and alembic – 'we never use the name, but instead employ a symbol whose meaning is known only to us.' He had been drawing the objects' secret symbols as he spoke. 'You'll have to learn all these,' he added offhandedly.

I was fascinated. He knew, of course, that I would be, and that was undoubtedly why he had embarked on teaching me something so mysterious. He's got a kind heart, old Gurdyman, and he wanted to distract my thoughts from that wrecked, brutalized body.

We stopped at some point to go upstairs and eat bread and cheese, sitting outside in the inner court. From the position of the sun, I thought it was a little after noon.

We returned to the crypt, and I pleased my mentor by drawing a set of twenty symbols with adequate accuracy and reciting – very softly – the name of each one. Then, taking me utterly by surprise, Gurdyman said, 'Enough of that for now. Go and fetch the shining stone, child, for it is time you told me of your progress with it.'

I obeyed him, but only because I had to. That day of all days, close involvement with my magical stone – the heirloom handed down to me by the huge awe-inspiring old Icelander whom I have only quite recently known is my grandfather – was the very last thing I wanted.

The shining stone is made of a strange substance that I had never heard of before encountering it. Gurdyman told me it is formed out of the red-hot, white-hot matter that is hurled out of the depths of the earth when a volcano erupts, and the heat is so tremendous that the very rock turns liquid. That is the first change. But then, when this newly molten substance cools – when, for example, it meets water – it turns to black glass. That is the second change.

No wonder there were strange, arcane forces at work inside the shining stone. It was, it seemed to me, the epitome of the sort of achievement men like Gurdyman strived for: one substance turned, or, as he would say, transmuted, into another. In the case of the stone, it wasn't just the one transmutation.

Sometimes when I look deep inside it – at first glance it is plain, glossy black, but then after a while you can make out sinuous, winding strips of brilliant green and fiery gold – I find myself speaking to it. *You were once rock*, I say, *and you lived in a place so far away that I can barely imagine the distance.* My grandfather Thorfinn told me the stone came from a land beyond the sunset, where men's skins are dark and they wear feathers in their long black hair. *Then the earth caught fire*, I continue, *and the heat melted you, but your agony stopped and you grew cool again, and found yourself changed out of all recognition.* I always feel sorry for the stone when I think about that. *How does it feel, to be here with me so far from your home? Are you happy?*

It may sound foolish to ask an inanimate object if it's happy. Unless you had actually held my shining stone in your hands, you couldn't understand, but there is life inside it, and I know it. It has the power to make you see the truth; it is ruthless; if you have the strength, it will enable you to reach out to the spirits and ask for their help. Of course it's alive.

Understandably, I think, I'd been in awe, not to say terrified, of the stone for quite a long time after it came into my hands. But gradually, over

24

the weeks and months, curiosity had overcome fear. What had really prompted me to stop being such a coward and get on with it had been when someone else – my grandfather, to be exact – had tried to make me use the stone to find out something he needed to know. Then I had been hit by a powerful combination of anger, indignation, resentment and possessive pride: *You would have me use the shining stone for your own purposes*, I yelled at him the last time I saw him. *If you had a use for it, you should have held on to it.*

I have regretted my cruel outburst ever since. I know my words hurt him deeply, for he loves me, as indeed I do him. I hope very much I shall see him again, and soon, in order to apologize and make things right between us.

But oh, he did me a favour. The power of my emotions that day acted like a cleansing fire, and afterwards I knew, as plainly as if it had told me, that the shining stone was truly mine. I had risked one peep into it since coming to this wonderful realization, and what I saw then shook me to my core. That had been back at home, in Aelf Fen, and I had resolved not to make a further attempt till I had Gurdyman beside me.

I found that I had wandered through the house to the foot of the ladder leading up to my little attic room, where I keep the stone concealed. *Well*, I thought, *it looks as if the moment has come.* Squaring my shoulders, I climbed up, knelt down and reached under the bed to the loose board beneath which the stone lay, safe in the soft leather bag that I had made for it. I took it out, held it briefly to my heart, and went back to the crypt.

With Gurdyman's eyes on me, I took the stone out of its wool wrappings and laid it on the workbench. He had already cleared a space, as if perhaps he felt that the shining stone was too awesome an object to be placed among the clutter of the working day. Reluctantly I lowered my eyes and stared at the stone.

Perhaps it picked up that I wasn't in the right mood to be allowed a glimpse into its depths; I don't know. I hope that was the case, because I like the thought that we are becoming close, the stone and I, and that it is aware of my feelings as I try to be aware of its own. Whatever the reason, I saw nothing. I went on staring, but the stone didn't allow me in, and all I saw was my own faint reflection in its glossy black and, today, impenetrable surface.

After a while Gurdyman said quietly, 'Why are you unwilling, Lassair?'

I raised my eyes and met his. Was it so certain that it was my reluctance that was not allowing anything to happen? Why did he not consider that the blame lay with the stone, shutting itself away from me?

There didn't seem any point, however, in arguing. 'I don't know,' I muttered.

'I think you do,' he countered, although not unkindly. 'I can think of three reasons. First, you have been badly affected by the body you were summoned to look at yesterday, and your sensitivity has been temporarily blunted.'

'No!' The response was instinctive; I didn't like

26

to think of my sensitivity being blunted, even if it was only temporary. Besides, although seeing the body had been a shock, it wasn't true to say that it had badly affected me.

'Very well,' said Gurdyman. 'The second reason is that it is I who am asking you to look into the stone, and you are no longer willing to do so at anyone else's behest.'

Again, I met his cool gaze. I wondered if he knew about what had happened between my grandfather and me. It was quite possible. My aunt's lover Hrype – another mystical figure who is almost as powerful as Gurdyman and, at times, far more threatening – had been present when I'd yelled at Thorfinn, and Hrype also knew Gurdyman. I found that the prospect of Gurdyman knowing how I'd behaved was both something to be pleased about – because he'd know that at last I'd stood up for myself – but at the same time a little shaming. It wasn't right to treat people you loved in that way.

But Gurdyman was waiting for me to answer.

'Er – it's true that I'm not prepared to use the stone to find out things for other people now.' I sought the right words to explain. 'It seems a betrayal of the stone, or perhaps of the relationship we're building between us.'

Gurdyman nodded. 'I think that is right,' he remarked.

'But this, now, isn't quite like that,' I hurried on. 'I don't believe you want me to find anything out on your behalf. I think you want to help me, and, indeed, I do need your help.'

'And you shall have it,' he replied. 'So, we

come to the third reason, which is that, some time recently, you have looked into the stone by yourself, for yourself, perhaps with the tentative purpose of finding something out, and been somewhat shocked by what the stone showed you.'

He had found the truth, as I suspected he would. Very little escapes Gurdyman. I had indeed looked into the stone, a few weeks back, just after I'd walked out to the place where my grandfather's boat had been moored and found him gone.

I saw a ship, very like my grandfather's beautiful longship, the original *Malice Striker*. Yet I didn't believe it was Thorfinn's ship: somehow I knew – perhaps the stone told me – that this was a craft that flew over the dark blue waves there and then, at the very moment that I was watching it, and so couldn't be my grandfather's craft because that was a wreck on an Iceland beach. I knew that was true because I'd seen it there.

I also knew because on board that ship I perceived within the stone – or I assume that's where he was – I saw Rollo.

Rollo is a secretive Norman, and, for want of a better description, I suppose you could call him a spy. He finds things out for the very important and the very wealthy of the land – I dare not think just how important and wealthy. He is my lover, or I should say he was, for a while, a year ago. Since then he has been away, presumably on some mission or other, and I have had no word from him.

The stone showed him to me, though, on that swift, beautiful ship. He looked straight at me, and then turned away.

I have wondered since whether he did that because he knew I had met Jack Chevestrier. That I liked him; admired him; enjoyed his company and had come hurrying to Cambridge to seek him out.

I didn't feel I could say any of that to Gurdyman, so I just muttered, 'Yes, that's what happened.'

He waited. 'You saw something that frightened you?'

'No, I wasn't frightened. I—' But then I thought, *I do not need to reveal this to him. It is not his concern.* I looked at him and said, 'I don't wish to tell you, Gurdyman. It's private.'

His eyebrows shot up, and just for a moment I thought I saw admiration in his face. I was tempted to feel proud of myself, but then I realized, with a thrill of awed respect, that it was undoubtedly the stone's strength, not mine, that had prompted that firm refusal.

Gurdyman had turned aside. 'Put the shining stone away, child,' he said evenly. 'We'll try again when you wish to.'

It might have been my imagination, but I thought I detected a faint emphasis on *you*.

We were eating a late supper, sitting beside the hearth in the cramped little kitchen, when there was a knock at the door. I made to get up, but Gurdyman shook his head, already on his feet and, still chewing, heading off along the passage. I heard the heavy bolts being drawn back, and the door creaked open. Voices: the same ones I'd heard that morning as I awoke.

Gurdyman came back to the kitchen, and Jack

29

was behind him. He nodded a greeting, looking slightly abashed.

'Jack has come to ask our help,' said Gurdyman.

'I didn't say Lassair!' Jack protested. 'She doesn't have to come.'

Gurdyman turned calm eyes to him. 'Lassair is my pupil,' he said in the sort of voice you don't argue with. 'It is my duty to share every aspect of my work with her, including that which is distasteful.'

Distasteful?

Gurdyman turned back to me. 'Jack will escort us to the room beneath the castle where the body of Robert Powl has been taken,' he said. 'The castle is quiet now, with only the night watch on guard, and very likely we can slip in and out again without being seen.'

There were many thoughts flashing through my mind, most of them to do with the fact that I really didn't want to look at that mutilated body again, but I said, 'Why mustn't we be seen?'

Gurdyman bowed to Jack, as if to say, *Go on, tell her.*

'Sheriff Picot is dismissing the death as the result of a wild-animal attack, and he has made it clear that he does not wish anybody to question this,' Jack said, his voice carefully neutral and not giving away what he must obviously think of the sheriff's absurd conclusion. 'He is trying, I believe, to stop the rumours; hoping, by supplying a reasonable explanation, to halt the rising panic.'

'But it's not reasonable!' I protested. 'No animal exists that could have made such a wound!'

'Not so,' Gurdyman corrected, 'for I have heard tales of savage creatures like enormous cats that roam the mountains far to the east, and other, similar beasts that live in the hot lands to the south. There are huge white bears, too, in the permanently icy lands to the north.' Jack caught my eye for a moment and we both smiled. Gurdyman must have noticed. 'But it is, I agree, unlikely that any such animal should be found hereabouts.'

I looked at Jack, for I had guessed why he was here. 'You want us to investigate the damage to the corpse, and suggest how it was done, don't you?' I demanded. 'Is that it?'

Jack winced at my words, but he nodded. 'Pretty much, yes. I'd really value your opinion,' he added.

Gurdyman looked at me enquiringly. Filled with a mixture of fearful apprehension and a growing excitement, I got up. 'I'll go and fetch my shawl.'

Three

It was not long after sunset, but already the streets were deserted. Lights flickered in some of the windows as we hurried along between the huddling houses, and at one point someone who had presumably heard our approaching footsteps reached out and firmly closed the shutters.

The body had only been discovered last night, and already fear was spreading like a contagious miasma.

As we crossed the Great Bridge, the quays stretching out on either side of the river down to our right, Jack, who had been pacing ahead, fell into step beside Gurdyman and me. 'Sheriff Picot is talking of imposing a curfew,' he said, keeping his voice low, 'but I think there will be no need.'

How right he was. Glancing down at the river, I noticed that even the ships' captains and crews, usually sociable in the evening and often to be seen assembled around a makeshift hearth or a brazier, drinking, sharing their food and chatting, were nowhere to be seen. The craft that lined the quays were closed up, their occupants safely inside.

Jack led us on past the new priory on our right and shortly after we turned off the road towards the castle, up on its hill. Well, we call it a hill, but by any other than fenland standards, it's more of a shallow rise. The main entrance was imposing, leading over a wooden drawbridge to a gateway with a heavy iron grille and a couple of guards outside. However, we were not, it seemed, to go in that way. Jack dived off down a narrow little alleyway that ran around the base of the rise – it was bordered by the huge rampart surrounding the castle hill on the left and by stone walls on the right, and was in fact more like a tunnel than an alley – emerging after fifty or sixty paces into a small open space surrounded by hovels, animal pens, storerooms and a ramshackle stable.

'This used to be the workmen's village,' Jack said softly. 'When the castle was built, the masons, carpenters and their teams lived here.'

Gurdyman nodded. 'And this is where Sheriff Picot has instructed that the corpse be stored,' he murmured.

It made sense, I realized, for a man determined on stopping gossip and rumour in their tracks to remove the source to a place where men didn't have to walk past it, look at it and smell it every day. Nevertheless, it seemed a little hard on the unfortunate Robert Powl.

'He's not in one of the pig pens, is he?' I asked with a nervous laugh.

Jack turned to me. 'No,' he said. 'There's a little chapel. I put him there.'

He paused to strike a spark and set the flame to the lantern he had brought, and set off again, Gurdyman and I following close behind. It was very dark in the deserted village, the looming, overhanging walls blocking out what remained of the last light. The chapel crouched over on the north-east side of the settlement, slightly apart from the nearest row of hovels. Jack shouldered open the wooden door – it had warped, and stuck on the stone of the step – and, holding up his light, ushered us inside.

Not only had he managed to find somewhere that was in itself fitting to receive a corpse, he had also given the place a good clean. At least, I supposed it must be he who had tidied the accumulated detritus of years into a neat pile in the corner and swept the floor. From what I knew of Sheriff Picot, such an action would not have occurred to him.

The body lay on planks draped with white cloth and set on two wooden trestles. Another, similar cloth had been drawn over it, covering it entirely. Around the throat, the cloth already bore dark stains.

Jack went over to the walls on either side of the corpse – the chapel was only about four or five paces wide – and lit flares stuck in brackets. Light flooded the small space, and, as if taking this as his cue, Gurdyman stepped up to the body. With calm, efficient movements, as if he did this every day, he folded back the sheet and smoothed it across the chest.

Robert Powl's dead face stared up at us. He looked different, and I realized it was because someone had taken off his hat. The top of his crown was quite bald, and rounded like an egg; perhaps that was why he had worn his hat so determinedly drawn down across his brow.

Gurdyman beckoned me forward, and I went to stand beside him. I looked into the dead eyes. They were wide with horror, and a muddy hazel in colour. One was a little bloodshot.

'Could we not shut his eyes?' I whispered to Gurdyman.

He leaned down over the body, peering closely. 'There is a theory,' he remarked, 'that a murdered person's eyes reflect the face of the killer, but I do not subscribe to it myself.' With a deft touch of his thumb and forefinger, he lowered the eyelids. Straight away I felt better. Not much better, but a little.

Gurdyman was inspecting the wound. Instinctively I had stepped away, but he reached for my hand and drew me back. 'Come and look, Lassair,' he said gently. 'There is nothing here to harm you, and I am beside you.'

His calm voice gave me confidence. Gathering my courage, I looked right into the wide, open, bloody wound.

It was no wonder they'd all been saying some ferocious animal did the damage. As well as the sheer size of the gaping hole, I now made out the clear marks of five sharp claws, or talons, four over to the upper left, where the worst damage had been done, and one coming in and up from the lower right. It really did look as if a giant hand, or paw, was responsible. Dread went through me, and a sort of superstitious shiver, as if, once I'd admitted the possibility into my mind that such a creature existed, it followed that it must be lurking outside, waiting . . .

I moved a little closer to Gurdyman.

Jack had gone to stand on the opposite side of the trestle table. He, too, seemed to be transfixed by that wound. 'Could it—' He stopped. Then: 'I am not saying I support the theory of attack by some large wild animal, but *if* this were so, could the damage have been done by teeth?'

'Interesting,' murmured Gurdyman. 'So, instead of talons having made the marks, we are suggesting it was teeth? A row of four incisors and canines in the upper jaw, let us say, and one protruding fang in the lower?' He leaned right down over the body, a hand holding back his garments to keep them out of the gaping throat.

'It wasn't a serious suggestion,' Jack said.

Gurdyman didn't answer. After a moment, he said, without turning round, 'Will you hold up your light, Jack? Yes, yes, that's right, just like that.'

For what seemed like an age, there was silence, other than some faint squelchy noises as Gurdyman, who had extracted a small pointed silver instrument from some hidden pocket inside his robe, probed. I felt ill, and I had the strange sensation that the middle section of my legs wasn't there. I think I made some soft sound, for Jack's head flew up and instantly he was hurrying round the table, one arm around me.

'Step outside,' he said, 'you've gone deathly white.'

'No, I'm all right.' *I will not faint*, I commanded myself. I managed to give him a smile.

He didn't look convinced. He stayed exactly where he was, at my side, where he could catch me if I fell.

So total had been Gurdyman's absorption in his task that he had missed the small drama. Looking up now, an expression of mild surprise on his face on observing that Jack no longer stood where he had before, he said, 'I cannot support the teeth theory, but nevertheless I am very glad you raised it, Jack, for it compelled me to investigate more closely.' He held out the silver instrument, on the tip of which was a tiny object, stuck to the fine point with a gout of flesh, or perhaps dried blood. 'And look what I found inside the deepest cut!'

I made myself take a couple of deep breaths. 'What is it?' I managed to say.

'I don't know yet,' Gurdyman admitted. 'I need to examine it back in the crypt.' He frowned at it thoughtfully, then carefully wrapped both instrument and find in a small piece of linen and stowed them away. 'Now, what else is there for sharp eyes to observe?'

The faintness was passing, and now I took on the role of student, helping my mentor as he stripped off the garments and carried out a careful inspection of the rest of the body. Not that we learned anything, for, other than the normal scars, swellings, and marks of ageing that can be seen on anyone past youth, there was nothing to see.

We dressed the corpse again, and Jack drew the sheet up over the dead face. We turned to go, Gurdyman and I waiting by the door while Jack extinguished the torches. At the last moment, Gurdyman looked back at the body. 'No other marks,' he said very softly.

'Yes, we have just established that,' I said.

'Do you not see the significance?' he said, his face eager as he waited for my response.

I visualized the body. One great wound, nothing else . . .

'He didn't struggle,' I said, appreciating all at once what Gurdyman meant. I had already suspected as much – and mentioned it to Jack – on the grounds that Robert Powl hadn't drawn his dagger. 'He didn't have time to put up his hands or his arms to protect himself. He didn't try to run away, for there was no bruising or marking to indicate that his assailant held on to him.'

'And so?' persisted Gurdyman.

'He was taken completely by surprise,' I said.

'Which suggests?'

Now I saw the scene in my mind. 'It's likely he was jumped on from behind. Either that, or else the killer was so well concealed that his victim didn't see him until he was right there on the path in front of him, claws reaching for his throat.'

'Well done,' murmured Gurdyman.

As we followed Jack's light back through the deserted village, round the castle's foot and back towards the great bridge, Jack said quietly, 'I wonder what business took Robert Powl out to that lonely stretch of river bank?'

It was a great relief to be back in the twisty-turny house. Jack left us at the door – it had been fully dark for the return journey and he had drawn his sword – and urged us to bolt it. We didn't really need to be urged.

Gurdyman wandered off along the passage that leads down to the crypt. 'Go to bed, child,' he said over his shoulder.

'Don't you need my help?' I knew what he was going to do, for already he was reaching inside his robe for the cloth-wrapped pick and whatever was stuck to its point.

'No,' he said firmly.

With some relief, for, despite my resolve to be

the ever-alert pupil, I'd really had enough for one night, I slipped away.

'It is a fragment of horn, or claw,' Gurdyman said in the morning. We were standing in the little inner court, the early sun pouring in, and he held up the object for me to look at. He had cleaned it, thankfully, and I saw a small pointed piece of hard matter, shaped somewhat like a steeply sided cone. It did indeed look just like the broken-off tip of a horn or a claw.

'It's a great shame,' mused Gurdyman.

'But isn't it just what you expected?'

'Yes, precisely!' he said eagerly. 'I *expected* it to be what it is, but I *hoped* it would be made of wood, or even metal.'

I thought for a moment. 'Because then you'd have had proof that this killing was the work of a human hand, wielding some frightful weapon, and not a savage animal.'

'Yes, yes,' Gurdyman agreed. 'We might even have gone on to conclude that our killer had designed and manufactured his weapon purely with this murder in mind, to make us think an animal was to blame.'

'But he was too clever,' I said slowly. 'Instead of satisfying himself with sharpened wood spikes or metal blades, he used a substance that has animal origins.' I looked at Gurdyman. 'You are quite convinced a human is behind this?'

'Oh, yes,' he breathed. 'Now we – or, rather, your friend Jack Chevestrier – must begin to work out the motive.'

'He—' I began.

But Gurdyman held up his hand. 'Enough, Lassair. We have done what he asked of us, and already I have sent a message to tell him of my findings.'

'A message! But surely the whole aim is not to spread panic, and if the messenger tells anyone else that you found a bit of horn in the body, it'll only fuel the gossip!'

Gurdyman sighed. 'Child, it was a written message, not a spoken one. For one thing, I very much doubt the man to whom I entrusted it can read, even if he would be so foolhardy as to break the seal. For another, I was very discreet, and only said that my discovery did nothing to help the situation.'

'And Jack will know what you meant?'

'Of course he will,' said Gurdyman robustly. 'He's a thoughtful and intelligent man, which is more than you can say for anyone else in Sheriff Picot's organization, including Sheriff Picot.' Before I could respond, he said, 'To work! We have much to do.'

We worked hard all that day and the next. I hoped constantly that there would be a visit from Jack; wouldn't he want to discuss that fragment of claw, and the mind behind the creation of the dreadful weapon it had come from? Surely he would have found out much more about Robert Powl, and want to talk over with us what lay at the heart of the killing.

He didn't come.

On the third day, the killer struck again.

* * *

40

Very early the following morning, before Gurdyman and I had had a chance to put our noses out of doors, Jack came at last. Any pleasure I might have derived from seeing him was quickly subsumed by fear; I knew just by looking at his expression that something terrible had happened. He wouldn't go out into the sunny little court – I guessed he feared being overheard, although the high walls made it unlikely – but spoke to us in the dark, narrow passage behind the closed door.

'There's been another death,' he said shortly. 'Same method.'

'Who is the victim?' Gurdyman asked.

'Someone who works at one of the lodging houses on the quayside.'

Lodging houses was the polite description. They were drinking dens and brothels, there to fulfil the needs of sailors a long way from home, although by no means used exclusively by them. My healer aunt Edild, my first teacher, had enlightened me on the subject of the diseases that spread in such places, and on occasions I had treated townsmen who had come to seek me out under cover of night, bitterly regretting the brief pleasure that had led to such painful and humiliating consequences. Not that it was for me to judge, and my aunt had always impressed on me the importance of courtesy and kindness, no matter what the ailment. I had also learned to be extremely discreet; it was a healer's first duty, and I would have kept my mouth shut even without the extravagant payment some of the town's leading citizens pressed upon me.

'Where was he found?' Gurdyman was asking.

'On the river, perhaps half a mile downstream from the quay.'

Near to the road that led off towards Ely and the fens, I calculated. 'Close by water again,' I said softly.

'Yes, that's what I thought,' Jack agreed.

'The man was known to you?' Gurdyman asked.

Jack hesitated. He glanced swiftly at me, then away again. 'It wasn't a man.'

Neither Gurdyman nor I spoke.

'It is an even worse abomination, I think,' Jack said eventually, 'for a woman to have been killed in this brutal way.'

'And why?' Gurdyman said. 'Robert Powl was a wealthy man, and, although we assume he wasn't robbed, it is reasonable to postulate that his murder is somehow connected to his business affairs, or his importance in the community. But of what significance can a lowly tavern maid have been?' It was chivalrous of him to assume that the woman had been a maid and not a prostitute, and for all I knew, he was right in that assumption.

'I can think of nothing that links them, yet,' Jack agreed, 'save for the vague fact that both earned their livings from the river traffic; Robert Powl by providing a fleet of transport, Gerda by what she offered in the lodging house.'

I wondered if he was being deliberately ambiguous.

'Perhaps,' I said hesitantly, still working on the thought, 'all that they have in common is that both were out by the river, alone, unobserved, when their assailant felt the compulsion to kill.'

Both Jack and Gurdyman turned to stare at me. Gurdyman's face wore a thoughtful, appraising expression. Jack looked horrified.

'You appear to support the wild-animal theory after all,' he said, 'for isn't that – an opportunist attack on a vulnerable victim – just what such a creature would do?'

I shrugged. 'Perhaps.'

'What *were* they doing out on the river bank, alone?' Gurdyman asked. 'Robert Powl's presence there I can understand, for, being the first victim, there was nothing yet to fear. But this Gerda must have known about the first murder—'

'They talk of nothing else down by the quay,' Jack said lugubriously.

'—and so why, then, would she be so foolish as to venture out?'

Neither Jack nor I could come up with an answer.

'I intend to go straight down there now,' Jack said after a short pause. 'I'm hoping someone will be able to tell me something: she had a message summoning her to go and meet someone, perhaps, or a man she was with asked her to venture outside, or she heard a noise and went to investigate, or—' He shrugged.

He had, it seemed, come to tell Gurdyman and me about Gerda's murder before we heard a doubtless far more lurid and inaccurate version elsewhere. It was good of him, and I thanked him as I saw him out.

He turned to look intently at me. 'Please, don't go out unless you have to.'

'We have to eat,' I pointed out gently.

'Of course, but keep to the well-frequented

43

places.' He paused. 'And I know I've said this before, but don't listen to the gossip.' He went on looking at me for an instant, then gave me a sort of salute and strode off up the alley.

When, in the mid-afternoon, I went out for food, I found the marketplace humming. Probably everyone was out doing their provisioning while it was full daylight, and while there were plenty of people about. The pie stall on the corner was doing a brisk trade, and I was lucky to find anything left to buy. Not that it amounted to much; not enough, anyway, so I ventured further into the throng and managed to purchase a loaf, cheese, a string of somewhat soft onions and a small bag of apples.

I had turned for home, resolving to do as Jack had urged and not stop to listen to what everyone was saying. But then there was a minor mishap – a little boy managed to evade his mother's grasping hand, and, revelling in his sudden freedom, he sped away through the crowd and tripped up an elderly man, who fell heavily and banged his head. Lots of the stall-holders know me by sight, and I couldn't have escaped even if I'd wanted to. Even as I put down my basket and crouched down beside the old man, someone was yelling, 'Find that healer girl! She was here a moment ago, I just saw her!'

The elderly man had a lump on his head and was a little dazed, but otherwise unhurt. I sat with him for a while, holding his hand, and presently helped him to sit up.

'Oooooooer, I feel dizzy! I need to rest here a bit longer!' he moaned, clutching on to me and managing to squeeze my breast.

I bet you do, I thought. But he was my patient, he probably did feel dizzy, and the squeeze could have been accidental.

'You mustn't get up until you feel better,' I said. 'I'll stay with you.'

'Will you?' He looked at me with trusting eyes, and I could see how grateful he was.

'Yes,' I said. Then, leaning closer so that only he, and not the small circle of goggle-eyed people standing round us, heard, I added, 'But just you keep your hands to yourself, or I might change my mind.'

He gave a delighted chortle of laughter. But, all the same, he folded his hands chastely in his lap.

The small drama was over and our audience melted away. So it was only then, as the throng cleared a little, that first I saw the man standing on a box in the middle of the market square and then, as he flung his arms wide and launched into his tale, heard him.

I knew him by sight. He was one of those who earned a crust with their storytelling, turning up on feast days and market days, wherever there is a crowd to be entertained, and acting out the old tales, myths and legends. I'd often stopped to listen to him, for he was good, and had the ability to hold his audience's rapt attention.

I had a feeling I knew precisely what today's tale would be about; there was, after all, only one thing people would want to hear.

Jack had told me – warned me – not to listen. But, detained there still tending my randy old man, it seemed I didn't have a choice.

This was the story I heard.

Four

'There was once a greedy merchant who had been born with every privilege yet, as is often the case with such men, always wanted more,' the storyteller began, launching straight into his narrative. A fat-bottomed woman in front of me shifted, and I saw him more clearly. He wore a new coat – business must have been rewarding recently – and he had been freshly shaved and barbered. His eyes were dark and shiny as a robin's in his lean, tanned face, and he let them roam over the audience, making sure we were all attending. We were. Moreover, as soon as his light, carrying voice had begun the tale, more people had stopped what they were doing and joined the listening crowd.

'The greedy merchant bartered and bargained,' the storyteller continued, 'he bought cheap and sold dear, and his fortune grew and grew, but still he wasn't satisfied. He married a beautiful woman, and she gave him an even lovelier daughter' – he paused to run lascivious eyes over the young women in the audience, some of whom simpered and giggled – 'but he wanted more. He wanted more precious daughters to marry off to wealthy men who would reward him well for the privilege, and he wanted sons who he would force to work for him so that his enormous wealth increased still further. But his beautiful wife grew sick, and she died.' A dramatic little pause, the storyteller's face assuming an expression of deep sorrow.

'Some said her death was from a weary, broken heart, for she knew her husband did not love her for herself but only for the children he wished to father on her. And then do you know what happened?' He glanced around the intent crowd, eyebrows raised. A man said, 'No! What?' and there was some laughter. 'Well, I'll tell you,' said the storyteller with a smile. 'The greedy merchant was left all alone, for, no matter how many women he flattered and courted and tried to impress with his fine house and its rich furnishings, his elegant horses, his gorgeous raiment, his jewels and his gold, none would have him. He was growing old now, and his character showed in his face, and the ladies he wooed knew better than to accept him.'

'Serve him right!' a woman's shrill voice observed in an indignant tone.

'His beautiful daughter grew towards womanhood, and he put her in a costly litter lined with goose-down mattresses and pillows and the softest woollen blankets and hung with silken curtains, and he scoured the land with her, displaying her to all the richest lords and noblemen. Most of these fine men offered for her hand, for as well as a lovely face she had a sweet, gentle manner, and it was easy to fall for her, and so the greedy merchant decided that the only thing to do was to set up an auction, and let the competing suitors bid for her hand.'

There were several mutterings, and someone said, 'The bastard!'

'The day of the auction came,' went on the storyteller. 'It was summer and the sun was out, shining with a smiling face in a deep blue sky, yet right on the eastern horizon there could be discerned, for those who troubled to look, a small dark cloud. However, few could tear their fascinated eyes away from the spectacle of the greedy merchant's daughter, up on a high wooden platform in the middle of the market square—'

Suddenly he paused, then, looking around, his eyes wide as if only then noticing his surroundings, he said, 'Very like to this square, if not the self-same one!'

There was a gasp from someone at the front.

'There she was, the beautiful daughter' – he picked up the tale – 'sitting on a silk-covered throne and dressed in the most gorgeous gown in a shade of sea-green which exactly matched her eyes. The marketplace thronged with people, and the suitors had a job of it, elbowing their way to the front so that their bids could be heard. Meanwhile,' he added, lowering his voice dramatically so that as one his crowd all leaned forward to hear, 'the dark cloud on the eastern horizon had grown bigger and closer.'

Several people looked nervously over their shoulders.

'The bidding began. The opening offers were modest: the price of a good horse, or a golden circlet. Steadily they increased: the price of a manor, a small army, invading a neighbouring state. Still the greedy merchant was not satisfied, still he stood on the platform beside his beautiful daughter, yelling, sweating, exhorting, calling out again and again, *More! More! It is not enough!*'

The storyteller paused, just for an instant, raising his eyes and gazing into the distance, a faint frown on his face. Then, with a little shake as if forcing himself back to the present, he went on.

'The black cloud now hovered over to the east of the market square. It had grown huge, stretching right to the far horizon. But still the bidding went on. *I offer my patrimony,* called out an eager suitor who stood right at the front, beside the steps leading up to the platform. *My castle, my estates which are wide and varied, the men and women on my estates, the animals, the crops, the badgers, the squirrels, the deer and the hares, the birds and the bees, the spiders that spin and even the flies that buzz and bother.'*

The storyteller's eyes were wide with wonder at this wondrous list of treasures beyond belief.

'*It is not enough,* screeched the greedy merchant. *More! More! I must have—*'

Abruptly the storyteller broke off. Then, arms spread over his head, voice raised, he cried out, 'Suddenly the vast black cloud blossomed out like some foul fungus and it blotted out the sun. The crowd, the majority noticing the cloud for the first time, went silent, gazing up into the lowering sky with expressions of doubt, fear and apprehension. *More! More! It is not enough!* cried the greedy merchant into the sudden stillness.

'There was a bass growl like thunder, and out of the cloud a deep voice spoke. *I will have your daughter*, it said, *and what I offer in payment you will willingly take, for it is beyond your*

49

wildest dreams. The greedy merchant looked all around with avaricious eyes that sparkled with the anticipation of wealth beyond his dreams. *Where are you?* he demanded. *Show yourself!'*

The storyteller stopped. He let his gaze roam all over his audience, huddling together now, for word had gone round and the market square was packed. 'And out of the dark cloud stepped a strange figure,' he said in a soft, awed, yet penetrating voice. 'Tall, thin and imposing, he was dressed in a long flowing robe with a high collar that stood up around his ears and framed his face. He was clad all in black, save for the faintest ruffle of white at his throat. His grey hair was cropped close to his finely shaped head. He was pale – as pale as death – and the long, straight nose was as an arrow, pointing to the wide, well-shaped, downturned mouth. The eyes were invisible under the heavy protruding brow ridges, and they looked like deep, empty black holes in the stark whiteness of the face.'

A woman, perhaps a girl, gave a little shriek.

'The greedy merchant stepped forward, his face wreathed in smiles. *What will you give me for my daughter's hand?* he demanded. *Speak swiftly, for many others are desperate to have her and the bidding is keen!'*

The storyteller frowned his disapproval. 'It was clear that the empty-eyed figure did not like those words. There was another soft growl of thunder, and a sudden chill breeze ruffled the garments of the crowd, as if in the midst of a sunny day a wind had come straight out of a snow-bound, ice-frozen land. As the thunder died away, the figure spoke. *In exchange for your daughter's hand*, he said, *I offer you my world.*

'A faint cry burst out of the beautiful daughter, who sat cowering on her throne, eyeing the black-clad figure with horror in her face. The greedy merchant ignored it. *Your world?* he echoed. *What do you mean, your world? Which world have you to offer me?*

'The hollow-eyed figure shrugged his bony shoulders. *A world I rule, as your kings rule this one,* he replied. It was an ambiguous answer,' the storyteller observed – several people muttered their agreement – 'but the greedy merchant's blood was up and he only heard what he wanted to hear. He stared at the strange figure, eyes narrowed as if he was trying to penetrate to the secret heart of the matter. As he stared, it seemed to him that he was cold suddenly, and he thought he saw a few flakes of snow fall and settle on the empty-eyed man's grey head and black-clad shoulders.'

The storyteller's eyebrows drew together, rising in a caricature of puzzlement. 'Snow? On a bright, sunny, summer's day? But the greedy merchant ignored the sinister warning. *Done!* he shouted. The crowd – who knew better, and many of whom were already slipping quietly away – gave a low, collective moan of distress.'

I tore my eyes away from the compelling figure of the storyteller. Nobody here was slipping away.

'The hollow-eyed man moved towards the platform. The greedy merchant, thinking that he had come to climb up, shake hands and seal the bargain, hurried towards the steps to greet him.

51

But the pale man had no need of steps. He stopped right in front of the platform and he began to grow. Taller, taller, till he was as tall as a house.' Someone gave a moan of horror. 'Taller, taller, till he was as high as a tree. Then he stretched out his arms, wide, wider, the long, drooping sleeves of his black robe sweeping right across the market square and freezing those who had been too slow to run away even as they stood there, so that they turned to ice on the spot and fell with a ringing chime to the ground. The greedy merchant screamed, again and again and again, belatedly remembering his daughter and scrambling back to protect her, his most valued asset, from instant death.'

He paused for breath. There wasn't a sound from the rapt crowd.

'The hollow-eyed figure gave a dreadful laugh. *Do not fear for the lady, for she is mine*, he said, and he swept her up in one huge arm, easily supporting her frail weight as she collapsed into a swoon. Now the greedy merchant's terror was all for himself. His mouth opened in a silent howl, for the air was now so cold that his lips, his tongue and his throat were already frozen into immobility. As his eyeballs crackled with frost, he stared up at the huge dark figure towering above him.'

The storyteller raised his own eyes, staring up into the sky, becoming the terrified merchant.

'And even as he watched that dread figure,' he said, returning his gaze to his audience, 'it changed. The black garments seemed to melt away, revealing deadly white translucent skin.

Then the skin began to tear, and the shape of head, shoulders, limbs and torso subtly altered . . . and there before the greedy merchant stood a figure straight out of the most hellish nightmares.' Several people screamed, not all of them women. 'It was ice-blue, scaly, with a long forked tail and slender, curving and impossibly sharp horns extending from its head. It held out an arm that curled and twisted like a snake and ended in a huge clawed hand. Then, slowly, slowly, oh so slowly, it extended those dreadful claws and reached for the greedy merchant's throat. There was a moment of terrible agony, and blood gushed out. The greedy merchant closed his eyes, for death was welcome.'

A pause. 'But it wasn't death. The merchant opened his eyes again, to see the devilish figure standing calmly regarding him. *Not death*, it murmured, *nothing so merciful. For I always keep my bargains, and did I not promise you my world?*

'The greedy merchant could not answer, for he had no throat,' said the storyteller calmly. But abruptly his tone and his very demeanour changed and, in a storm of passionate words, he cried, 'Then all at once the ice-blue devil's eyes flashed red fire, and a fierce, terrible anger contorted its entire body. It shouted some words in a strange, unknown, unholy tongue, and at the same time it stamped five times upon the ground. The solid cobblestones of the marketplace opened in a great chasm, out of which both ice-blue and red-hot flames flared up and from which a frightful stench arose. The wooden platform tilted forward and the greedy merchant fell on to hands and knees, desperately trying to cling to the rough planks, but he could get no grip. Slowly, slowly he slid forward. The platform tilted further, further, until it hung right on the lip of the chasm. Then there was a sound as if the whole earth had exploded, and the platform and the greedy merchant were pitched down into the abyss. Flames rose up, roaring, crackling, and from the gaping wound in the greedy merchant's throat there came a scream that stopped the heart.

'There was a great *crack!* and the chasm closed up. In the blink of an eye, the devilish figure and the greedy merchant's daughter were merged into a vast dark cloud, which evaporated like a teardrop on a hot stone. The surviving townspeople crept out of their hiding places and surveyed the after-math. Seventeen lay dead in the market square, but otherwise there was not a sign to show what had happened. In shock, they melted away.'

As if in echo, his voice faded.

'Time passed,' he went on after some moments of absolute stillness. 'Memories are long, but this was an event that nobody wanted to recall. Nevertheless, recall it they were forced to do, for the ice devil had enjoyed his taste of life in that fair region, and he came back. Not often: perhaps only once in two or three life spans, and the intervals were long, so that people forgot what lay beneath the disguise and only remembered the black-clad figure. Then the rumours would begin again of the sinister stranger who wandered the dark streets and alleyways by night, looking for a woman as beautiful as the daughter with the sea-green eyes, looking for another merchant so greedy that he would sell his own flesh and blood. It would start quietly . . . a rat or a cat or a stray puppy would be found in the morning in some out-of-the-way spot, lifeless, drained, its throat torn out. But then the horror would escalate, and next would come human victims. Men, women – for women too can be avaricious and cruel – and then the people would cower inside their homes, seeking what safety they could, for they would know that once again the Night Wanderer was abroad, and he was hungry.'

I had been aware of a disturbance over to my right, behind the storyteller on his box. I'd assumed vaguely that it was the storyteller's assistant, whom I'd noticed starting to circulate with his upturned cap in his hands, but I'd been too enthralled by the tale to take much notice. Now, though, there were raised voices, and someone cried out in pain. People started moving away, walking at first, then, as they reached the maze of little streets and alleyways around the square, bolting like startled hares. Among them ran the nimble, light-footed storyteller, his box in one hand, easing his way through bigger, slower people, smiling, apologizing, and soon out of sight.

The assistant wasn't so lucky. As I turned back from watching the fleeing storyteller, I saw him standing, blood on his face and his arms pinned behind him by one of Jack's larger deputies. There were three more deputies, pushing and shoving their way through the rapidly disappearing crowd, yelling, 'Where is he? Which way did he go?'

I felt a movement beside me. My randy old man, who had sat in silent captivation to hear the tale, was struggling to his feet. 'I'm off,' he muttered. 'I don't like the look of them deputies.' With an agility surprising in one who had so recently been complaining of dizziness, he skipped away across the square and shot off along one of the smaller alleys.

I too stood up, reaching down for my basket of groceries and brushing down my skirts. It seemed prudent to follow my old man's example and melt away, and I had almost reached the dark entry to the maze of passages that leads to Gurdyman's house when one of the deputies called out.

'*Oi!* You there, healer girl!'

I stopped. I heard pounding feet, and a hand grabbed my arm.

I reached up and pushed it off. 'There's no need to grasp hold of me. I'd stopped, or didn't you notice?'

His brutish face clouded. Apparently he was sensitive to sarcasm. 'None of that lip!' he shouted. 'I want to know what's been going on and you'll stay right here till you tell me!'

'Certainly I'll tell you,' I replied. I thought I sounded cool; a lot cooler than I was feeling. 'The market has been busy today, and a storyteller took advantage of the fact and set up his box to tell us all a tale. It was a very good one,' some imp in me made me add, 'you missed a treat.'

His colour darkened. He looked furiously angry, and he raised a clenched fist as if he yearned to punch me. Then, just about managing to control the impulse, he said harshly, 'Storytelling's forbidden.'

'Since when?' I demanded before I could stop myself.

He put his sweaty, greasy face right up close to mine. 'Since Sheriff Picot said so,' he spat. 'It's rumour-mongering, that's what it is, and it's bad for – for—'

'Morale?' I suggested. 'Is that the word you're fumbling for? Come on,' I said furiously and very unwisely, 'you can only just have heard the word and, although it's clearly new to you, you can't have forgotten it already!'

The blow came so swiftly that I didn't have time to duck. His big fist caught me on the side of my jaw, and I saw blackness shot through with brilliant stars. As I fell, the agonizing pain began.

I was aware of running feet, loud voices, a scuffle, a shout of protest and a shriek of pain. Heavy boots rang out on the stones, quickly fading. Someone was holding me – tightly – against a broad chest, and I made out bare arms thick with muscle crossed over my chest. I leaned back, thinking no further than how much my jaw hurt and how wonderful it was to feel safe.

Someone muttered something – a question – and, right up close, a deep voice said, 'No need, I can manage her.'

I was lifted up off the ground. 'My basket!' I managed to say, although it sounded more like *mrssskt*.

'I have it,' said the deep voice.

I closed my eyes, and Jack Chevestrier carried me home.

We were halfway along the alley leading to the house. I was rapidly returning to myself, so much so that, although it was very pleasant, I was beginning to feel embarrassed at being carried. 'I think I can walk,' I said. *Inkicnllk.*

'I'm sure you can,' said Jack. 'But I'm enjoying carrying you.'

He reached out and banged on Gurdyman's door. After some time – Gurdyman must have been down in the crypt – it opened. He took in the spectacle of Jack and me and I'm quite sure there was a swift smile on his face before he managed to smooth it away.

'Oh, dear,' he said, standing back so Jack could bear me inside, 'an unruly crush at the pie stall?'

Jack had taken me along to the kitchen and was already pouring cold water into an earthenware bowl. He wrung out a cloth and pressed it gently to my jaw. For such a powerful man, his touch was light.

'Ow,' I said.

'Is she all right?' Gurdyman was leaning round Jack's bulk to peer at me.

'She can talk for herself,' I protested. It came out as *shkntlkhslf*, which rather countered what I was attempting to say.

'One of my deputies thumped her,' Jack said. He dunked the cloth back in the cold water, then returned it to my face. I had done much the same many times for others, and only now did I discover how comforting it was.

Gurdyman sighed. 'Oh, dear me! It is not the first time she has suffered such a blow, and I fear she has not yet learned to watch her tongue in the presence of mindlessly brutal men.'

Gurdyman was quite right. I would have grinned, but it hurt. Jack, however, wasn't smiling.

'She shouldn't have to,' he said. 'It's far too easy for men to hit women, being almost universally bigger and stronger and in no fear of reprisals.' There was bitterness in his harsh tone.

Gurdyman noticed too. 'I agree with you,' he said gently. 'I wasn't condoning it. Far from it.' He paused. 'Why did the deputy hit her?'

'Sheriff Picot decided that storytellers are banned, and when word came that one of them was in the marketplace, he sent Peter – one of his more bone-headed men – to enforce the order, together with the band of bullies he normally leads.'

'And these men became violent?' Gurdyman asked. Jack nodded. 'It seems unreasonable to enforce so roughly a law that people don't even know exists,' he remarked.

'It's unreasonable all right,' Jack muttered. He glanced at Gurdyman. 'Peter and his men will be taken to task. The one who did this' – he touched my jaw with his forefinger – 'is already regretting it, I'd say.'

Good. I hoped someone had punched him as hard as he'd punched me.

Jack knelt down, looking into my face. 'I don't believe your jaw is broken,' he said. 'Can you move it from side to side? Gently now!' he added as very tentatively I began to articulate my lower jaw.

Without that kindly, caring invitation, I'm not sure I'd have had the courage to try.

'It's not broken,' I said. *Itnbrkn*.

'It's not broken,' said Jack. He frowned. 'I did warn you not to go listening to the tale-tellers, but it wasn't because I thought you'd get hurt.'

No, I thought. It was because he'd already heard that scary old legend, and didn't want me to. I wanted to tell him that I'd had no option, since I'd been looking after my randy old man when the storyteller began, but given the state of my jaw, I'd never have made him understand.

He stood up, still staring down at me. 'I must go,' he said. I thought – I hoped – I detected reluctance in his voice.

'Of course,' Gurdyman said. 'I'll see you out. Don't worry,' he added, 'I'll look after her. I'll let her off washing the crypt floor, just for today.'

I knew he was joking. I hoped Jack did, too.

There was an experiment that Gurdyman had to proceed with but, true to his promise to Jack, he insisted on my coming down to the crypt, where he made me comfortable on the bed down there, fussing round me with pillows, a soft blanket, cool water to drink and with which to bathe my face. I didn't feel like eating, so I watched, amused, as Gurdyman absently worked his way through the contents of my basket, devouring my share as well. The pain in my jaw had eased considerably, but the swelling was severe. I'd have a huge bruise tomorrow.

I was deeply relaxed, enjoying the luxury of lying with my feet up, warm and cosy, safe with Gurdyman and entertained by watching him work. For long spells there was a peaceful silence down in the crypt, and I lay watching the candle-light play on the ancient walls.

Ancient walls. Old settlement . . .

Perhaps it was because for once my mind was idling, and not crammed with the day's usual quota of things to learn, things to memorize, plans to make for the necessities of life, that something floated to the surface, and I understood how it was that Jack had known his way around the workmen's village so well.

In all probability, he'd been born there.

He had told me, back in September, about his father, who had been a carpenter with Duke William's army during the conquest of England. His father had worked on the construction of the wooden castles that William ordered to be built, whose purpose was to threaten the defeated foe with their looming presence and keep us under the Norman thumb. He had been sent here to Cambridge in 1068 and that was where he'd met Jack's mother. It seemed highly likely that the family home had been in one of those lowly dwellings we'd passed. No wonder Jack had known about the chapel.

I dozed for a while, my mind rambling in that half-world between thoughts and dreams where the two flow easily into one another. I saw Jack as a boy, earnest, honest, protective of his mother; he'd told me he was only a boy when his father died. I saw his mother harassed, bullied, forced to do work that demeaned her. I saw Jack use his big fists to protect her. *It's too easy for a man to hit a woman.*

I saw him leaning over her, his boy's face full

of distress at her hurts. The same expression he'd worn earlier, when he'd looked at me.

I wondered if he still lived in or near the workmen's village. Had he perhaps restored one of the more sound houses? The one where he and his parents had lived, perhaps? I couldn't remember if he'd mentioned any brothers and sisters . . . He'd said something about being the man of the family after his father's death, but family could have meant just him and his mother.

I realized I'd very much like to ask him.

I was awakened by Gurdyman, gently shaking my shoulder. 'Bedtime, Lassair,' he said. 'Up you get, and I'll help you.'

I did as he bade, smiling to myself. Gurdyman can't even climb the ladder up to my little attic without puffing and panting and going red in the face, so I very much doubted he'd have been able to shove me up it. Not that he needed to; all he was called upon to do was to watch from below, with obvious relief, as I clambered into my room.

'Call out when you're safely in bed,' he said.

I hurriedly took off my outer gown and boots, then fell into bed. I sang out something that sounded like *mminned!*

'Goodnight, then,' came back Gurdyman's retreating voice. He was already returning to his work.

Smiling, I turned over and went to sleep.

Five

I was awake very early, probably because I'd dozed and slept for much of the previous evening. My jaw was still sore and stiff, but my fingertip exploration suggested the swelling had gone down a little. I tried mouthing a few words, and was encouraged to think I stood a chance of making myself understood today.

I lay thinking about the dream I'd just had.

It was about Rollo. He stood up on a high promontory, looking down at a bay with deep blue water which sparkled in bright sunshine. There was an air of steely determination in his expression, as if he was making up his mind on a course of action he didn't much want to take. He held a horse by the reins: a fine horse, big and powerful, with alert, pricked ears and intelligence in its face. It stood shifting from foot to foot, and in the dream I remarked to Rollo, *You may not be eager to start but the same cannot be said for your horse.*

Rollo smiled absently. Still he wouldn't meet my eyes. Presently he sighed, and swung himself up into the saddle.

I wondered, as I lay reflecting, whether the strange and mystical process which operated my connection with the shining stone was also affecting my dream self. Or was it perhaps nothing more than my conscience, making images of Rollo turning away even as my interest in Jack Chevestrier deepened?

Did I want Rollo to turn away?

I had imagined, when I fell in love with him so swiftly and so thoroughly, that our future lay together. I'm not sure I envisaged marriage, although I once had a sort of vision of the child I would bear him one day. But it was a year and more since I had seen him, and Jack had held me in his arms only the previous day. Admittedly he'd had to do so in order to carry me home, but, no matter what the circumstances had been, I had found joy in being so close to his big strength.

Realizing that there was no point in distressing myself with my anxious and guilty thoughts, I decided it was time to get up.

Gurdyman was very kind and considerate, and would probably have let me spend an idle day had I not insisted I was fit to work. I could make myself understood now, more or less, and soon we were immersed in the astrological chart that he had drawn.

He didn't let me go on working into the evening, however, sending me away and commanding me to sit out in the court and enjoy the last of the sun before retiring for an early night. I've no idea how he knew the sun was shining – you certainly couldn't tell down in the subterranean darkness of the crypt – and perhaps it was just a lucky guess.

I sat in Gurdyman's chair, eyes closed, feeling the sun on my face and thinking that in a little while I would prepare some broth. If I dipped my bread in it till it was soggy, I ought to be able to manage it. When I heard a knock at the door, I knew who it was. I had, I think, been expecting him.

'Do you want me to come and look at another body?' I said, forming the words carefully.

He understood. 'There's no real need,' he said. 'It is the same method of killing as with Robert Powl.'

'I am willing to look,' I replied.

He seemed pleased. 'In that case, I'll take you to see her.'

'I'll tell Gurdyman.' I hurried off along the passage and down the steps, and quickly, before Gurdyman could ask any questions, explained where I was going and who with. He nodded, barely looking up.

The streets were not quite as deserted as they had been five days ago, but it was a good deal earlier and dusk would not fall for a while yet. We hastened round the foot of the castle hill and through the workmen's village, and Jack led the way inside the chapel.

I stepped up to look at the dead woman.

Only she wasn't really a woman; she was scarcely more than a girl.

'She's beautiful!' I exclaimed in surprise. 'I thought—'

I thought she'd be a haggard old whore worn out by the life she has led, I almost said. But something in Jack's expression stopped me.

'She was a prostitute,' he said neutrally. 'But I don't think she had been for long.'

I studied the face, then, folding back the sheet, the plump young body. I tried not to look at the savage wound. 'Is there anything in particular you want me to look at?' I said after a while.

'No,' he admitted.

Both of us stared silently down at the dead girl. I wondered why he'd wanted me to see her; then, straight away, I answered my own question. I'd been very surprised to find that she was young and beautiful. Like probably the majority of the people of the town, once I'd known what she did for a living, I'd leapt to the conclusion that she'd be the very opposite. Did Jack think, on finding I was wrong, that I'd be more shocked at her awful death?

I didn't like the idea of him believing that.

'It wouldn't have made any difference, you know,' I said quietly.

'What wouldn't?' He sounded cagey.

I turned and met his eyes. 'I admit it took me aback to see she's not as I expected. I'm not closely acquainted with any prostitutes, and I didn't know they started so young. They tend to keep away from healers, probably because they don't want the lecture that goes with the remedy. But if you think I wouldn't have been just as horrified, or not have the same urge to avenge her, had she been old and ugly, then you're wrong.'

He looked away. 'I'm sorry.'

'Jack, we all do what we have to in order to put bread in our mouths,' I went on. 'I work hard for my living, so do you, and so did she.' I rested my hand on the smooth young skin of the cold forehead. Gerda, I reminded myself. Jack had said her name was Gerda. 'I know which one of our three occupations I'd want least.'

My voice had risen a little, and I made myself calm down. 'So,' I said after a moment. 'What do you want of me?'

He met my eyes again, perhaps to make sure I'd finished with taking him to task. 'What I'd really like you to do is come with me down to the quayside. I need to find out more about her, and I believe the men and women who have their livelihoods there would be more likely to talk to you.'

'Of course I'll come.'

We left poor Gerda lying as still and silent as Robert Powl, on the adjoining trestle.

The quay was busy; it seemed to be the only part of town that was. Perhaps the boatmen, the sailors and the tavern-keepers were harder to scare than the law-abiding townspeople. I kept close behind Jack as he made his way between the groups of men and their female companions, noticing the courteous way he addressed them as he asked them to let him through. He was clearly not a man who felt the necessity to lean on the authority imposed by his position and throw his weight around.

He led me to a building at the far end of the quay. Its doors were open, and lantern light and a babble of voices flowed out. It was a sizeable place, and what looked like a fairly new exten-sion had been constructed to one side. It was raw and cheap, and I guessed it was for the use of the women and their clients. From within I heard someone crying out repeatedly – short, sharp cries – and then a burst of raucous and, I suspected, drunken laughter. Jack walked round this extension and, at the rear, we came to an entrance, the ground churned to mud by the passage of many pairs of feet.

I could see small doorless rooms – cubicles, really – leading off a main passage. The light was poor, and some of the recesses had curtains strung across. I didn't want to look. It seemed an invasion of privacy. Here was evidence of a basic human urge being fulfilled; male demand, female provision of service provided; it was a business exchange. I just hoped, unavoidably overhearing, that some of the women really were enjoying themselves.

A little further up the passage, Jack had stopped and was speaking to a woman coming towards him, carrying a pile of soiled bedding. She pointed over her shoulder, muttered, 'Margery's in there,' and then, shoving him aside, went on her way. I flattened myself against the wall to let her past.

Jack had gone into the furthest recess, and creeping in behind him, I saw an enormously fat woman reclining on a bed, propped up by a stack of cushions and pillows, the wide, full skirts of her brilliant purple gown spread out as if in expectation of admiration. The colour was indeed gorgeous, and I wondered what sort of dye had achieved it. It wouldn't have come cheap, that was for sure.

She was watching Jack from small dark eyes set deep within rolls of fatty flesh. It was a shrewd look, yet at her mouth I saw humour lurking. She noticed me, and glancing swiftly back at Jack said, 'Brought me a new girl, have you?'

I caught sight of Jack's expression and smothered a laugh. Margery spotted my amusement, however; I had the impression she didn't miss much. 'This is Lassair,' Jack said. 'She's a healer.'

'I know who she is,' Margery said. 'What do you want?'

'I need to find out more about Gerda.' At the mention of the dead girl, Margery's face fell into sorrow. 'I've brought Lassair with me because I reckon—'

'You reckon my lasses will be more likely to open up to a slip of a girl than a hardened old man of the law,' Margery finished for him. 'And I dare say you're right.' Again, she studied me. 'No trying to persuade them away from their work, mind. They're here of their own free will, and I look after them as well as I can.'

'No, I won't do that.'

She nodded. Then, surprisingly, 'How's that disreputable old wizard who's teaching you his tricks?'

How on earth did she know Gurdyman?

There was a sound like a distant rumble. Margery was laughing. 'Oh, don't you go jumping to conclusions,' she said, still chuckling. 'He has no use for what's on offer here. Wizards are celibate, didn't you know? Tell him I was asking about him.'

'I will,' I replied. Oh, of course I would! I could hardly wait, although I had no idea how I was going to raise the topic . . . On second thoughts – I felt my face flush – maybe I wouldn't.

'You can go along to the room off the taproom,' Margery was saying to Jack. 'There'll be four or five of the girls in there having their break. They all knew Gerda.'

'Thank you, we'll—' Jack began.

Margery reached for his hand, grabbing it. 'Be kind to them,' she said softly. 'They all loved her, too.'

Jack nodded. Giving Margery a sort of bow, he turned and strode off along the passage, and I followed.

We returned to the entrance and then went back round the extension to the main building, going on to a small room with a lively fire and an appetizing smell of stew. Six women sat around the hearth, talking in soft voices. They looked up as we came in. 'Hello, Jack,' one said.

'I'm very sorry about Gerda,' he said, eyes roving round the group. 'I'm going to investigate her death, and I'll do my best to bring her killer to justice. I've brought Lassair with me, who is a friend of mine. If you are prepared to tell her everything you know about Gerda, it will be a big help.'

The women muttered to each other. One or two were eyeing me suspiciously. I made myself stare back, keeping my expression bland. 'She's not going to be all high and mighty and get holy on us, is she?' one asked.

'No,' I said.

More muttering. Then the one who had first addressed Jack said, 'Very well. We don't like outsiders, but if it'll help hang the bastard that killed Gerda, we'll do it.'

'Thank you, Griselda.' Jack pushed me forward. 'I'll wait outside,' he murmured.

The women shifted their positions and, sitting down, I was admitted into their circle. For some time they just looked at me. I was starting to find their frank and distinctly hostile eyes disconcerting when one of them – a thin, nervous-looking girl with stringy blonde hair and poor skin – leaned in close to Griselda and whispered in her ear, the sibilance of her soft words rising into a shriek.

'Hush, Madselin,' Griselda soothed, wrapping strong arms round the girl and hugging her close. Madselin was crying now, harsh, jerky sobs that seemed to well up from some terrified core.

Griselda turned to me. 'I'll make a bargain with you,' she said, her eyes still hard. 'We'll all share everything we know about Gerda, but only if first you persuade Madselin here, and these other frightened little kittens' – she waved an arm, indicating two other youngsters huddled together in the corner – 'that the killer isn't the Night Wanderer come back to haunt us. He's no monster out of the old legends, but flesh and blood just like the rest of us.' She raised her head, her chin jutting out aggressively towards me.

It appeared that at least one of the girls had been in the marketplace earlier. I could just imagine her: rushing home, filled with a mixture of excitement and horror, breathlessly pouring out her own version of what she'd just heard to her avid audience. And now the image of a mythological devil out to get them had become fact . . .

No wonder old Margery had been willing for me to come and talk to her girls. It could hardly be good for business to have them all quaking in a huddle when they were meant to be on their backs for the paying customers.

'I can only tell you what I believe to be true,' I began, my voice sounding far more confident than I felt. 'I've heard the storyteller, and he's good, I admit. But why do you think he tells such a convincing tale?' I glanced round the circle.

'Because it's all true!' hissed a chubby young woman who had crept forward to sit at Griselda's other side.

'Because it's how he makes his living,' I corrected her. 'He tells his stories, weaves his magic, and his accomplice goes round with the collecting cap. If the tale's good, if it's convincing and makes his audience laugh, cry or gasp in terror, the storyteller eats that day.'

I let that sink in. Griselda gave me an approving nod. Madselin sniffed and wiped her nose on her sleeve. Her tears had stopped.

'Do you think it was a monster what killed her?' asked a dark, dusky-skinned woman sitting at the back.

I looked at her. 'I don't believe in monsters.'

'Who was it, then?' the dark woman persisted.

I hesitated. Would they know about Robert Powl? If not, would it matter if I told them? No, I decided.

'For what it's worth, this is what I think

72

happened,' I said. 'There was another killing, a few days ago, when a man called—'

'Yes, we know about him,' Griselda interrupted.

'The storyteller was already in the area when Robert Powl died' – I was sure of it, for hadn't Jack warned me after that first death not to listen to the gossip and the stories? – 'and he leapt at the chance to increase his takings by resurrecting the old legend of the greedy merchant. Robert Powl wasn't a merchant, but he was rich. Then Gerda was killed, a young and beautiful woman, and the storyteller instantly altered his tale subtly to emphasize the beauty and the youth of the greedy merchant's daughter.' I had no idea if this was true, for I had only heard the latest version of the tale, but it seemed more than likely.

'So you're saying the storyteller altered the tale to fit what's happened?' Griselda demanded. 'To increase his takings?'

'Yes.'

She nodded. Far from reacting with indignation, her expression suggested she approved of the storyteller's good sense. 'And you reckon our Gerda was killed by human hands?'

'Yes.'

There was quite a long pause. Then Griselda began to tell me about Gerda, and presently the others joined in.

Much of what they said was probably irrelevant. Her sweet nature; her cheerfulness; her refusal to allow the life she led to alter her optimistic outlook and her affection for her fellow human beings. 'But then she hadn't long been here,' added the woman who had told me this.

She wasn't a local girl but had come to Cambridge after the deaths of both parents. The family had lived out in the country somewhere – the women were vague – and had just about made ends meet trying to farm a few strips of poor-quality land. Gerda had been the youngest child by some years, remaining at home when the older siblings had gone, and none of those siblings had been willing to take her in when she was left alone. She had made her way to the town and, as countless millions of women had done before her since the dawn of time, sold the only thing that was hers to sell. It was, I realized, a stroke of good fortune that she had come across Margery's establishment. If you had to be a prostitute, it didn't seem a bad place to be one.

As gently as I could, I interrupted the women's chatter. They were eulogizing Gerda now, and I didn't think I was going to hear anything useful. 'Have you any idea why she went out the night before last? You say you all knew about Robert Powl's murder, so wasn't it strange that she should go out in the dark all by herself?'

I sensed a swift movement over to my right. Turning, I saw that Madselin had covered her mouth with her hands, perhaps to stifle a gasp of horror at the thought of Gerda venturing outside alone when there was a killer about. But there was something else, I thought; something in her eyes, some strong emotion which, in that swift impression, I didn't think was only fear. But then she dropped her head, and the moment was gone.

'She wasn't the only one to risk it,' the

dusky-skinned woman said. 'Madselin, I saw you scurrying back indoors the other night, didn't I?'

'*No!*' The single word emerged as a horrified shriek. I turned back to her, my senses alert. But one of the other women chuckled briefly, breaking the tension. Madselin, I guessed, was being teased.

Griselda met my eyes. 'Gerda's not likely to have been by herself, not to start with,' she said baldly.

I realized that my assumptions about the girls' daily routine needed a bit of adjustment. I'd imagined they'd have taken their clients to one of the little recesses off the long passage. It appeared I was wrong.

Griselda was watching me, a faint smile on her face as if she was following my thoughts exactly. 'Caught on, have you?' she said. 'The weather's still mild, and some of the men prefer a bit more privacy.'

Gerda had been found beside the river, downstream from the quay. I knew the area, for my route home to Aelf Fen took me along the track that ran along the opposite side of the river. There were places on both banks where the road bent away from the water, where it would be possible to slip in beneath the trees that lined the river and find a spot where you would be unobserved.

'Did the man who was with her have anything to say?' I asked. I was finding it hard to believe that he'd have taken her out there, done what he'd gone for, paid her and left her to find her own way back.

Could it have been he who killed her?

My shock at the sudden thought must have shown in my face. Griselda leaned forward and patted my hand kindly. 'You're not the first to wonder if he decided to follow a spot of love-making with an act of violence while his blood still ran hot,' she said. 'Your friend the lawman grilled him for a whole morning, or so we're told, but it seems the fellow's guilty of nothing worse than letting Gerda walk back by herself.'

Under the circumstances, that was bad enough.

Griselda evidently thought so, too. 'We also hear,' she said, lowering her voice, 'that the chap won't be visiting us for a while. Seems he had a mishap while he was scurrying away after Jack had finished with him. Fell down some stone steps and knocked a couple of teeth out. He's in a bit of a sorry state, it seems.'

I wondered if Jack's hard-muscled arms had orchestrated that fall. I'd seen Jack lose his temper before and lay into a man. He'd had justification then, too. But it was something to set against the image I was forming of an upright, principled man who always followed every last letter of the law.

'When can we bury her?' the dark woman asked.

'I don't know,' I admitted.

'Is she safe?' whispered the plump woman sitting beside Griselda. One of the others sniggered.

But I knew what the chubby woman meant. 'She is,' I said gently. 'She's lying in an old chapel, covered up with a sheet, and no further harm will come to her.'

Soon after that I stood up, thanked the women and left them. Margery, I reflected, had been patient, indulging me, or rather Jack, with quite a lot of her girls' time. I ought to go now.

Jack was standing at the edge of the quay, looking down at the river flowing silently past. He came to meet me as I emerged, and we fell into step as we headed back to the town. I told him what the girls had said, distilling it to its essence, which wasn't really very much.

'I hear you spoke to the man she was with shortly before she died.' I tried to make my tone casual. 'They said you were convinced he didn't kill her.'

'He was with her much earlier,' he said shortly. 'She was slain after dewfall, because the ground beneath her was wet. He was back home with his mother by then.'

'His mother might have been lying,' I suggested.

'*She* might, but it's unlikely all the other guests round her table were, especially as one of them was a priest.'

'Oh.'

I thought for a while. 'She must have stayed out there, then,' I said slowly. 'Do you think she was meeting someone else?'

'I don't know. Yet.' Jack looked at me; a quick, assessing look. 'What I do know is that had he walked back to Margery's with her and seen her safely inside, perhaps she wouldn't have been out on the river bank when the killer came by. Which is why,' he added, 'I shoved him down the steps.'

Six

Rollo Guiscard was heading north-west through Normandy. After months of travelling over both land and sea, on foot over deserts, mountains and the roughest, wildest terrain, he was mounted on a good, sturdy horse on a much-travelled and well-maintained road. He was not far from Rouen now, and only some thirty miles beyond the town was the coast. He reckoned he was almost on the last leg of his long journey back to England.

Even after so many days in the saddle, it was still a relief to be on dry land. He had spent weeks at sea on the sleek ship *Gullinbursti*, and although the voyage had been exhilarating, and an experience he was pleased to have had, nevertheless the gradually worsening conditions as autumn came on had steadily become harder to endure. The days of sunshine and calm deep-blue seas as they left Constantinople had become nothing but a memory, and even that was clouded for the ship's crew by the tragedy that had befallen them at the mouth of the Dardanelles.[2] They might have been led by a madman, but he had been their captain; they had shared in his impossible dream, and to a man they grieved for him.

By the time *Gullinbursti* reached the port of Marseilles, nobody except Rollo had possessed

2 See *Blood of the South*.

the strength or the heart to sail any further. Rollo, desperate to get to England, had pleaded and shouted, reminding Brand, the ship's new master, of his obligation to his passenger. But Brand had simply looked at him out of sad blue eyes and said, 'Your bargain was with Skuli, and he's not here to honour it. We stop here, and we don't sail on till spring.'

Accepting the inevitable, Rollo had enjoyed a fierce-drinking farewell celebration with his brothers in endurance and hardship, then bade them goodbye.

He set out the next day, having utilized the modest facilities of the tavern by the port where he had put up to wash himself and his garments, and generally refresh his gear. He counted his money. His purse was worryingly light, but he reckoned he ought to have enough to see him back to England. He spent as much as he could afford on his horse. It was going to have to bear him a long way, and as swiftly as possible.

More than once he had been tempted to make use of the chain of contacts which he had personally set up over the years; men and women who lived their mundane lives in towns, villages and isolated settlements up and down the land, going about their quiet business with no outward sign that they had another, clandestine role in the employ of a man whom they barely knew except as a good paymaster. In exchange for information, the passing of messages, the occasional requirement of a bed for the night and a hot meal, or the production of the small bag of gold coins they kept hidden for their mysterious stranger, Rollo paid them handsomely. Not that the money came from his own pocket: the King of England was the provider of the bounty, and he always paid well for good, loyal, trustworthy service. Such was Rollo's network that he could have travelled right up to the northern coast, and spent barely more than a handful of nights in inns or taverns. His contacts never turned him away; it was in their interests to help him in any way he required, since his was probably the easiest money they would ever earn.

Rollo trusted his men and women; he wouldn't have selected them for his service had he not. But he preferred not to let anybody know where he was, even his own spies. For he wasn't going straight back to King William in England; there was another place he intended to visit first.

William had sent Rollo to discover the state of affairs in the Holy Land: specifically, what truth there was behind the rumours that Alexius Comnenus of Constantinople was going to appeal to the lords of the West to help him resist the terrifyingly swift advances of the Turks. After a long and arduous journey, and at considerable risk and one grave injury, Rollo now had his answer. He would deliver his information first to William – his life wouldn't be worth a silver coin if William were ever to discover he had done anything else – but Rollo had decided that there was nothing to stop him then proceeding to sell what he had discovered, at such personal cost, to another interested party: William's brother, Duke Robert of Normandy. If William was right – and he usually was, being shrewd, intelligent and an excellent judge of men – Duke Robert would be among the first to answer the call from Alexius when it came. Unlike William, Robert was a romantic, and would not be able to resist the appeal of adventure in the East. But, being perpetually short of funds, Robert would have to look to his brother in England for the cash to pay for his expedition, and the only collateral he would be able to offer was his dukedom. With any luck – for how likely was it, William reasoned, that Robert would come back safe and sound? – William would acquire Normandy without so much as raising a sword.

The journey up from Marseilles had been long and lonely. Rollo had ridden north along the banks of the wide, slow-flowing Rhone, leaving behind the Mediterranean and the fascinating southern city of Arles, with its ancient Roman buildings gently crumbling in the golden light. At Lyons he had crossed the river, after which he struck out north-west towards Orleans and Chartres. Then he had slipped unobtrusively into Normandy.

Now Rouen was only a few miles ahead. Rollo's purpose there was not to seek out Duke Robert, but to hunt around for the sort of snippets of information that gradually built up into a full picture.

King William would, Rollo hoped, be impressed to learn that his spy had ventured right into Duke Robert's home territory. As far as the king was concerned, this part of the mission would have been purely with the intention of discovering the current trend of his brother's thinking. Only Rollo need know that there was a second purpose: for him to find out where to go, and who to speak to, when he went back seeking the duke's ear.

Sometimes, tiring of the incessant intriguing and plotting, Rollo rested his mind by thinking how good it would feel to be back in England. He had been too long in the hot, dry, dusty south, and he longed for soft rain and mist rising in the mornings, and a pale yellow sun shining through the whiteness like a distant candle flame. His thoughts turned always towards the fens; to Lassair, whom he loved.

But she may not still love me.

He couldn't banish the fear. It was irrational, and without real foundation. He and Lassair had become lovers, had exchanged tokens – he never took off the leather bracelet she had woven for him – and he knew she was not the sort of woman to give her affections to someone else just because he wasn't there. But he had been away a long time; it was a year and a half since he had held her in his arms, and he had deliberately – cruelly? – refrained from sending any message to her, even though it would have been relatively easy to do so.

And sometimes, when he concentrated all his thoughts upon her, it seemed to him that she turned away.

Jack saw me back to Gurdyman's door. Once inside the house, I was about to say goodbye, but, before I could do so, he said, 'Can I come in?'

'Yes, I suppose so.' I realized it sounded grudging. 'I mean, yes, of course.' *But why?* I could have added.

He grinned, coming in after me and shutting the door. 'Will Gurdyman be about?'

'Probably not, but it doesn't matter if he is, since he appears to quite like you.'

'I'm really not that bad,' Jack said modestly.

I led the way along the passage, past the kitchen and into the courtyard. There was no sign of Gurdyman. Although it was dark now, the air still held some of the day's warmth, so I said to Jack, 'Sit down out there and I'll bring a mug of ale.'

He settled down on one of the benches. It wasn't all that robust and gave a squeak as he lowered his considerable weight. I poured ale into a couple of Gurdyman's best pewter mugs and went to sit opposite.

'Any thoughts?' Jack asked when he'd taken the top off his ale.

'Only one,' I said. 'I'm sure it must have occurred to you too, but I wondered if Gerda might have made a habit of going outside with her – er, clients, and if so, whether she was unlucky enough to have witnessed Robert Powl being killed.'

'Yes, I did think of that,' Jack said. 'Robert Powl was murdered some way from Gerda's usual haunts, but I suppose it's possible that a client insisted on some particular spot from where she might have seen or heard something.'

'Wouldn't—' Just in time I shut my mouth on the question. I'd been about to say, *Wouldn't the client have seen or heard the same thing?* but I realized that a man in the throes of passion probably didn't see or hear anything.

'I should have asked the other women,' I said instead, hoping my face wasn't too red. 'Gerda might have said something.'

But Jack was shaking his head. 'I don't believe she would have. She was new to the life, and she'd probably have thought that venturing further away than the nearest piece of river bank would be against the rules.'

Silence fell. I was thinking about poor, pretty Gerda, and I thought Jack probably was too. Soft light spilled out into the courtyard from the lamp I'd lit in the kitchen. The air was still. I was just reflecting on how quiet it was, and how, although we were in the midst of a town, you'd have thought we were right out in the countryside, when a terrible scream ripped the peace apart.

Jack was on his feet, already racing for the door. 'That came from the market square, unless my sense of direction has deserted me,' he muttered as we fell out into the alley. He stopped, head spinning left and right, angry frustration making his face dark. 'Which way?' he demanded. 'Lord, I can never find a path through these back alleys!'

I grabbed his hand and we raced off, twisting, turning and apparently doubling back through the maze, until we emerged in the square.

Unsurprisingly, we weren't the only ones to have heard the scream. A small crowd had gathered, and more people were emerging from their houses and from the other passages that gave on to the market square. Jack pushed forward into their midst.

'Go back inside!' he shouted. The deep voice of authority seemed to have the desired effect. 'Go on, before I arrest you for obstructing the law!' he yelled at a stubborn old man dressed only in his chemise, whose chin was thrust out defiantly.

With a last glare at Jack, the old man shuffled away. Jack muttered something under his breath, his eyes roaming the square. 'Where?' he asked.

I'd been looking while he dispersed the crowd. I pointed over to the south-west side, where the better houses back on to the grounds of St Bene't's Church. Outside one of these a figure crouched low to the ground, and in front of her there was a huddled heap.

Jack and I ran across the square and in an instant we were kneeling beside the crouched figure. It was a woman, well over middle age, and she was moaning and sobbing, gasping for breath. 'Oh, no, no, no, *no*!' she wailed, her rising tone suggesting hysteria was imminent. Jack muttered, 'Can you deal with her?' I put my arms round her, murmuring soothing words, and got her up, gently leading her away from whatever lay at her feet. 'Come with me,' I said, 'we'll go back inside, and I'll make you something hot to drink, with plenty of honey, and wrap you up in a warm blanket. Would you like that?'

'Y-yes,' stammered the woman.

I led her back into the house. I knew who she was, which probably meant I also knew who was lying in the square. Dead, for surely nobody could go on living after losing the huge quantity of blood that was soaking into old Adela's white apron.

I settled Adela on a bench by the hearth, poking up the fire and swiftly mixing a drink of chamomile sweetened with a lot of honey. I swaddled her tightly in a blanket, first removing her soiled apron. It was a very beautiful blanket, of soft and pale-coloured wool, for this was a prosperous household. Then, feeling very guilty at deserting old Adela, I went back outside.

Jack looked up. 'I was just coming to fetch you. She's dead, isn't she?'

I knelt down beside him and stared down at Mistress Judith. She was – had been – a handsome woman, entering her mature years but with a grace and dignity that had kept her carriage upright and her head held high. She was wealthy, having taken over upon his death her late husband's shop, supplying materials for apothecaries and healers, and making a much better job of it than he had ever done. Mistress Judith was a born businesswoman, and I knew from personal experience that she drove a hard bargain.

She lay on her side, her carefully laundered and starched headdress awry, her fine wool veil crumpled beneath her head. Her eyes were wide open, and her face bore a look not of terror but of surprise. Her throat was a dark, gaping gash.

I bent right down over her, turning my cheek so that I would have felt any breath. There was none. Gently I felt for the beat of life beneath her ear. Nothing. Her flesh was still warm but she was dead.

'She's gone,' I said quietly.

Jack reached for the veil and spread it out over Mistress Judith's head and neck. 'We must move her inside,' he muttered. He glanced up and, following his eyes, I saw that people were once more creeping out to look.

'I'll take her feet,' I said, getting up. He looked doubtfully at me. 'She's tall but she's not fat,' I added impatiently. 'I've carried far heavier weights, and it isn't far.'

He nodded. Between us we bore Mistress Judith's body back inside her house, and laid her down beside the hearth. Jack closed the door – very firmly – and I went to sit beside Adela, whose sobs were escalating again at the sight of her mistress's body.

Jack came to kneel in front of her. He took both her hands and, looking straight into her eyes, said, 'Now I need you to help me – what's her name?' he demanded, turning to me.

'Adela.'

'You can provide one last and very important service for her, Adela,' he went on, 'by telling me everything you can recall about what happened this evening.'

Adela's spine straightened a little. 'I – I can help?' she whispered.

'Yes,' Jack assured her. 'You're the only one who can.'

It was the right thing to have said, for who doesn't like to feel important in an emergency? 'Well, let me see,' Adela began slowly. 'We'd had a busy day, with a load of new supplies to sort and store, and I was a bit late with the meal, and the mistress was short with me. She had every right to be!' she insisted, as if her mild criticism had breached some rule of correct behaviour regarding the recently dead. 'Anyway, we'd eaten, and I'd cleared up, and I was settling for the night out in my place behind there' – she indicated a small cubicle beside the storeroom – 'when I heard the mistress get up and open the door.'

'Had somebody come to call?' Jack interrupted. 'Did you hear a knock?'

Adela slowly shook her head. 'I don't believe I did,' she said, 'although I might have missed it. I was that tired,' she added, 'and I reckon I might have already been pretty nearly asleep.'

I met Jack's eyes. 'It's quite likely someone did come knocking at the door,' I said softly. 'You may not know, but Mistress Judith sold herbs and other apothecaries' ingredients, and although she wasn't really a healer, people tend to visit in an emergency to ask advice, purchase supplies and make remedies up for themselves.'

Jack nodded. He had a way, I was noticing, of absorbing information without comment. Turning back to Adela, he said, 'So your mistress opened the door. Then what happened? Did she go outside?'

Adela frowned. 'Yes, she did. She stepped out into the square, just there' – she pointed – 'where the roofs overhang and make that colonnade, and I heard her . . . heard her . . .' Her frown deepened.

'Heard her what?' Jack only just had his impatience under control. 'Did she speak? Cry out?'

Adela looked up at him. Slowly she shook her head. 'No,' she whispered. 'She laughed.'

I waited in Mistress Judith's house while Jack went for help, and sat with my arms round Adela as we watched a trio of Jack's men put the body on a hurdle, cover it and bear it away. A quick inspection of Mistress Judith's shelves provided what I needed to prepare a second, stronger sedative for Adela, and I left her warm, snug and snoring in her little cubicle. Jack set a man to watch the house for the rest of the night and then took me home.

He saw me safe inside, then hurried away, calling softly over his shoulder, 'I'll come back in the morning. I need to talk to you.'

I closed and bolted the door. I went down to tell Gurdyman I was back, and found him fast asleep on his cot down in the crypt. I made a warm, calming drink for myself – I kept seeing Mistress Judith's terrible wound – and, at long last, went up the ladder to my little attic and fell into bed. As I fell asleep – I'd put a pinch of valerian in my drink and it was quick to take effect – I wondered for at least the twentieth time what on earth had made Mistress Judith laugh . . .

Gurdyman's whistling woke me early in the morning. I hurried to wash and dress, then went down the ladder to join him.

'Another death,' he remarked as he handed me a bread roll still warm from the oven. 'I've been out,' he added, smiling, 'and it's all they're talking about.'

'I was there,' I said quietly. 'Oh, not when she was killed' – his face had paled in shock – 'but soon afterwards. Jack and I were in the inner court, and we heard her servant scream when she found the body.'

Gurdyman quickly recovered himself. 'Same method as the other two, I understand.'

'Yes.'

'And it was Mistress Judith?'

'Yes.'

I'd forgotten that Gurdyman knew her, but of

course he did: before I'd become his pupil, and during the times I was back home in Aelf Fen, he would have to do his purchasing of supplies for himself.

'Jack's coming here this morning,' I said after a moment.

Gurdyman gave me an enigmatic smile. 'Naturally.' Before I could ask him what exactly he meant by that, he went on, 'Unless either of you needs me, I'm off down to the crypt.'

'Very well.'

He picked up another couple of bread rolls and shuffled away. His mind already caught up in whatever he was working on down in his cellar, he resumed his whistling, Mistress Judith, apparently, forgotten.

Well, I thought, trying to excuse his callousness, *he didn't know her very well.*

I put more water on to heat and set out the ingredients for a stimulating, reviving drink. There were a few of the rolls left, so I organized them on a platter and took them into the courtyard. I didn't think I'd have long to wait for Jack and I was right.

'So,' he said a little later, when he had put away two mugs of my drink and the rolls were no more than a memory, 'what do we know?'

'Three deaths in a week, two women and a man,' I began. 'Two wealthy, or at least relatively so, and one an impoverished orphan in a whorehouse. Two connected to the river; one because his business was river transport, the other because she lived and worked beside it. One—'

'Mistress Judith could also be said to be

90

connected with the river,' Jack put in, 'because she bought supplies which arrived by boat.'

'So do many people,' I replied. But then something struck me: 'Adela said they'd had a delivery yesterday.' *A load of new supplies to sort and store.*

'Indeed she did,' Jack mused.

'Do you think her goods were brought in by one of Robert Powl's boats?' I felt a rising excitement; had we found a link between the deaths?

But Jack shook his head. 'Robert Powl's boats are all lined up on the quayside,' he said. 'I've just checked.'

I had already leapt up. 'But one of them could have come in yesterday!' I cried. 'Who would know?' I was reaching for my shawl, slinging my satchel over my shoulder. 'Who's running his affairs now?'

'He was a widower, and childless' – Jack had also got to his feet and was following me along the passage – 'but he had a household of several servants and employees.' We were out in the alley now, and I slammed the door. 'Who, it seems,' he said, laughing softly, 'we're about to go and talk to.'

From habit, I turned right outside the house, to head for the marketplace as I usually did, but Jack stopped me. 'I think we should stay away from the square,' he said quietly. 'If you can show me how we can get out of this warren of little streets and into the fields to the west, between here and the river, that would be very helpful.'

I did as he asked, thinking on my feet, utilizing my sense of direction, and, more by luck than anything else, soon emerging in roughly the right place. '*Good,*' said Jack with a smile, striding off towards the river, 'now we'll be able to make our way round to Robert Powl's house without anyone seeing us.'

'Why,' I asked as we hurried off, 'did you want to avoid the square and make sure nobody sees us?' *You're a lawman,* I might have added, *surely you go where you like?*

He didn't answer immediately. Then he said, and it sounded as if the admission was painful, 'I'm not investigating the murders, which of course means I have no business going to Robert Powl's house, or even, come to that, being out and about in the town, and I don't want any of my fellow officers reporting what I'm up to.'

'You're not investigating the murders?' I screeched. I could hardly believe it. 'Why on earth not?'

He smiled wryly. 'Because Sheriff Picot is extremely angry that I've allowed two of the town's citizens to be brutally slain.'

'Three,' I corrected.

He turned to look at me, no longer smiling. 'Sheriff Picot only counts the wealthy and well-known ones. He doesn't concern himself with the deaths of prostitutes.'

I opened my mouth to shout my protest, but there was no need; Jack's expression told me that.

'So who is in charge now?'

'Gaspard Picot.'

Sheriff Picot's nephew. I knew him; I'd *met* him. He was a bald man, tall, slim, habitually dressed in black, and not long ago he had sent a man to kill Jack. Jack had got the better of him and left him tied up on the fringes of the ferns; clearly, he had escaped.

'*Him*,' I breathed.

'Yes, him,' Jack agreed.

'So – so he's trying to find out who's doing the killing?'

'He is.'

'And he now has all your men at his disposal and you don't?'

'Yes.'

'And it's his uncle's doing, of course.'

'It is.' Tiring finally of his monosyllabic answers, Jack added, 'Sheriff Picot has had the brilliant idea of forcing people to stay indoors unless they have permission to go out, apparently in the belief that this will prevent any further killings, which of course it won't since people with businesses to run and lives to get on with will find ways to circumvent the sheriff's commands, and, since by definition the killer has no respect for the law, he'll ignore the order, go out and about just as he pleases, and if he wishes to strike again, he will.'

'That's absurd,' I said dismissively. 'Making everyone stay in, I mean. Apart from what you just said about people disobeying, such an order means all the lawmen and deputies will be fully engaged trying to make people stay inside their houses, whereas what they *should* be doing is trying to find out who's doing the killings.'

'Succinctly put,' said Jack, 'and distressingly accurate.' Then he grinned down at me. 'Come on, let's see what we can discover at Robert Powl's house.'

93

Seven

We trudged on across the wet grass. The fields looked very beautiful in the soft mist that was slowly rising off the ground as the sun rose and a little heat warmed the air. There was nobody about. Maybe the townspeople, frightened and uneasy at the latest brutal murder, had been only too willing to obey the sheriff's new dictate.

Presently the last of the buildings stretching along the south side of the river came into view. Quite a few were churches, endowed by the rich merchants, and some of them had been there for decades. In pride of place, however, closest to the water and with gently sloping grass-covered banks leading to the river, was a row of new houses. It was, I reflected as we drew closer, a beautiful place to live. We were only a short walk from the town – the Great Bridge and all the busy, noisy commerce of the quays were only about half a mile ahead – yet here it was peaceful and quiet, the area possessing that indefinable quality of aloofness that is typical of rich men's dwellings. Jack pointed to the second-to-last house, and muttered, 'That's it.'

I studied Robert Powl's house. It was timber-framed and thatched, with a solid-looking oak door and windows either side, both tightly shuttered. Set against the left-hand wall, and built in the same style as the house, was a large barn, its tall doors barred. For a widower, it seemed an unnecessarily large amount of space.

'Why did he need that huge barn?' I asked. 'It's not as if he was a merchant, needing space for his goods. Robert Powl only provided the transport for other people's stuff.'

Jack stood staring at the barn. 'I wondered the same thing. Perhaps he had occasionally to store cargoes until they could be collected?'

'But surely he'd have had a warehouse down on the quayside for that? Why bring boatloads of goods out here to his house?'

'He did have a warehouse,' Jack said slowly. 'We're going there next.'

He marched up to the house and banged on the door. Quite soon, it opened a crack, to reveal the long, cadaverous, pale face of an indoor servant, well past the first flush of youth. 'Yes?' the man said in a faint voice.

'Jack Chevestrier,' Jack said. 'From the sheriff.' Strictly speaking, it was true.

'Your men were here before,' the old man said plaintively. 'Wanted to know if he had any enemies.' He gave a dismissive sniff. 'Well, of course he did. Somebody tore his throat out.'

'I realize how distressing his death must be for you and the household,' Jack said gently. 'I would like to come in and have a look round.'

The old man stared at him, his expression hopeless. 'Well, you're the law,' he muttered, 'so I don't reckon I have a choice.' He stood back, opened the door wide and beckoned us inside.

The other servants, apparently having heard the exchange, had gathered in the room into which the door opened. Three women, a man and a youth, they were huddled together, managing to appear both shocked and keenly interested in what would happen next. The room was warm from a generous fire burning in the central hearth. Archways in walls to right and left led through into further rooms. 'Master slept through there' – the old servant jerked his head over to the right – 'and saw to his business affairs in there.' He pointed to the room on the left.

Jack strode beneath the arch on the left into the space beyond, and I followed. Boards had been laid across trestles, and on them were many rolls of parchment, horns of ink, quills and a small silver-handled penknife. Several stout wooden chests, bound with iron, stood against the walls. A chair with carved back and arms had been placed exactly halfway along a large table, in front of it a wooden writing slope on which there was a piece of vellum: the very last document on which Robert Powl had worked, perhaps. All was neat and orderly.

'Has this room been tidied up?' Jack asked.

The old man shook his head. 'No. This was how the master left it. He liked things tidy.'

Behind the table, hanging on the wall backing on to the barn, I noticed a heavy tapestry. Going over to have a closer look – it was a forest scene of huntsmen and a hart, beautifully done in vivid wools – I realized that it was in fact a curtain, covering a low, narrow door.

I went to stand beside Jack, who was intent on the document on the writing slope. 'There's a door through to the barn,' I said, so quietly that only he would have heard.

His head jerked up and he looked round. In a swift couple of paces, he was beside the tapestry, pushing it out of the way. He raised the latch on the little door, but it didn't open. Jack turned to the servant. 'Is there a key?'

The old man shook his head. 'Master always carried it on him.'

Jack began to say something, then, with a curse, broke off. He reached into the leather purse hanging on his belt and extracted a silver ring with two keys on it, one big, one smaller. He looked sheepishly at me. 'I took these from his body myself,' he said quietly. 'I should have remembered.'

He fitted the larger key in the lock, turned it and the door opened. He pushed me through, following hard on my heels, then closed the door in the old servant's face.

'We need to do this without an audience,' he said.

We looked round the barn. It was a big space but there wasn't very much in it: stacks of empty wooden crates and chests, standing with their lids thrown back; a handcart whose broken shaft someone was in the process of mending; a ladder with one rung replaced, in bright new wood; a stack of something beneath a cover that proved to be bales of wool of indifferent quality. 'Perhaps someone changed their minds and didn't want it after all,' I remarked, looking at the wool.

Jack was prowling round the barn, peering into corners, reaching behind bits of the wooden framework. I wandered over to the wall that I calculated must back on to the river, where I'd noticed a small edifice in stone which I thought was a shrine. It was a little over waist-height, with a door set into one side. I touched the door, and to my surprise it was cold: it wasn't made of wood, as I'd thought, but of iron.

'Have you got that smaller key handy?' I called softly.

I was still staring at the shrine, and sensed Jack come to stand beside me. 'What is it?' he asked.

'It looks like a shrine, or a sort of miniature chapel,' I said. 'But it has an unexpected door.' I tapped it and it rang out a low, clear note.

'Why lock a chapel so carefully?' Jack wondered. He put the smaller key in the lock, and it turned with a definite click of some hidden mechanism.

He pushed the door open and we bent down to look inside.

It wasn't a chapel or a shrine. It was a small stone-built, iron-doored and very secure storage area, lined with neatly made wooden shelves, the flagged floor covered with straw.

And it was empty.

'What did he keep in here?' I asked. 'Gold? Jewels? Coins?' Any or all seemed likely.

Jack had forced his broad shoulders through the low, narrow doorway and was feeling round the shelves. 'It's very clean,' he observed. 'Not a speck of dust or dirt.' He pulled himself out again. 'You try,' he said. 'You're smaller than me so you can get in further.'

I knelt down and crawled inside. Once I was

right in, I was able to turn so that my body was no longer blocking the light. I went over every shelf, but there was nothing to be found. I was about to crawl out – it was a little as I imagine being buried alive would feel like in there – when my knee struck something sticking up out of the floor.

'Ow!' It hurt, a lot, and I felt blood well up as my skin split. Jack reached to help me out, and we looked at my cut knee. I was quite touched by his evident concern, but then he said, 'Whatever could have done that?' and I realized he wasn't actually interested in the wound.

We both reached back inside the stone edifice. One of the flags was sticking up very slightly; you wouldn't have noticed it underneath the covering of straw, and we'd only discovered it because my knee had struck it. Jack put both hands to it and began heaving it up, and, after a great deal of sweaty effort and quite a lot of cursing, finally it gave. The flagstone would have thundered right over backwards on to the floor had Jack not had the presence of mind to put his forearm under it. It obviously hurt, and he'd have an awful bruise, but at least the household servants wouldn't have heard anything.

We stared at the dark, narrow, earth-smelling hole that had appeared beneath the flagstone.

'He made this hiding place so secure, with its stone walls and roof,' Jack said softly, 'but, assuming it wasn't he who dug the tunnel, he forgot it has six sides, not five.' He looked at me. 'Fancy going down there?'

I didn't, not at all, but one of us had to if we

99

were to find out where it went, and clearly Jack was out of the question. I wriggled across the floor on my stomach, and, with my arms above my head as if I were diving into water, forced myself down the hole.

The tunnel was truly horrible, and I only went on because I didn't think I had a choice. There was no way I could have turned round, and I was so terrified of finding I couldn't wriggle backwards that I didn't dare put it to the test. The earth pressed all around me, sometimes crumbly and choking, sometimes slimy with things I didn't want to think about. The tunnel's sole virtue was that it was quite short: after heaving myself only perhaps five or six times my height, the tunnel started to climb steeply, then level out, and I saw daylight filtering through greenery. I shoved my head out through a patch of dense undergrowth beneath hazel trees on the river bank, and, observing there was nobody about, dragged myself into the open. I was about to dance with relief when it struck me that if we were not to advertise the tunnel's existence – and I just knew Jack wouldn't want to do that – then I was going to have to return by the same route. I took a quick look round to see exactly where I was, then, not pausing to think about it – there was only one way to do it and that was quickly – I took a deep breath, dived back down the tunnel and wriggled back to Jack.

'It comes out on the river bank,' I whispered as I crawled out of the stone room and stood up, 'and I've memorized the place where— What's the matter?' I added crossly. Jack was trying unsuccessfully not to laugh.

'You are absolutely filthy,' he replied, already reaching out to brush off the worst of the dirt and the smears of mud. Then he extended the white sleeve of his undershirt and carefully wiped my face.

For a moment we stood looking at each other. His touch had been tender – caressing, almost – and it had affected me with a shock whose force took me by surprise. I tried to say something, but my throat was suddenly dry.

'We should get on and check the warehouse,' he said eventually. 'We . . .' He trailed to a stop. He was still staring at me, his clear green eyes intent on mine, and whatever was running through his mind seemed to distract him.

I reached for his hand, striding off across the barn and pulling him with me. 'Come on, then.'

One of us had to make a move.

Robert Powl's warehouse stood at the end of a row of similar buildings, although it was small in comparison to the others. As we drew nearer, it became clear that it was a workshop as much as a storage facility; the side facing the river had an open area beneath an overhanging roof, and was presumably where repairs to the boats in his transportation fleet had been carried out. Between it and its neighbour a narrow little passage ran back, away from the riverside, and right at the far end of the passage, overshadowed by the large buildings on either side, there was a low door, presumably giving access to the adjacent warehouse.

The quayside was not as busy as it usually was on a fine morning, although quite a lot of people had apparently managed to persuade Sheriff Picot that they had good reason to be down there, and thus avoid the strictures of the new law. None of these people – and, more crucially, none of the handful of sheriff's men who were lounging about and watching the watermen and the quay workers – had eyes for Jack and me as we approached, keeping as much as possible under cover of the trees and shrubs that grew along the river bank.

We slipped in beneath the overhanging roof and Jack tried the door leading inside the warehouse. It opened. Jack turned to look at me. 'I don't believe Robert Powl would have left this door unlocked,' he said.

Hurriedly he pushed the door open. It was clear, from the most cursory glance, that the space within had been searched. Far from being neat and tidy like its owner's house, office and barn, it was in total disarray. A stack of planks had been toppled over; a pot of what looked like congealed pitch lay on its side; the cinders of the hearth had been kicked apart; a set of shelves against the far wall had apparently been swept with a brawny forearm, and the contents were now jumbled together in heaps at the far end of each shelf, sundry objects spilling on to the floor.

'Of course,' Jack said heavily after a moment, 'with everything disturbed like this, we cannot know if the thieves found what they came for, and, if so, what it was they took.'

'No,' I agreed. 'It would have been a lot more helpful to have discovered one vacant space on

102

those shelves, with a neatly written label telling us what was normally stored there.'

'And yet the stone vault in the house was empty,' Jack mused.

'Did they come here first, do you think?' I asked eagerly, following his thought. 'Then, not finding whatever it was – probably because this place isn't secure enough for something very valuable – they went on to the house?'

Jack nodded. 'It looks like it.' He swung round to look at me. 'Very determined, weren't they? Imagine them, finding a way to get inside the house, then discovering that whatever it was they wanted was locked away in that stone crypt thing. And that can only have been conjecture, yet what trouble they then went to, digging a tunnel from the river bank and managing to come up in exactly the right spot.'

'That part would have been easy,' I said absently, my mind on the effort it must have taken to tunnel through the earth. Admittedly the distance wasn't great, and the soil was easy to penetrate, but—

Jack was staring fixedly at me. '*Easy?*' he echoed incredulously.

I realized what I'd just said. Staring down at my feet, feeling myself blush, I muttered, 'Some people have a talent for knowing where things are hidden.'

'I had forgotten,' he murmured. I looked up. He was smiling. '"It has happened, on rare occasions, that I've managed to locate lost items",' he said.

He was quoting exactly what I'd told him when

he first had occasion to ask me to use the strange ability I have to find things. My embarrassment increased, and I dropped my head.

He picked up my unease. He said calmly, 'If you say it's easy, I'll take your word for it.'

We looked all round the warehouse, but to little point other than an appreciation of how thorough the intruders' search had been. Then abruptly Jack said, 'What exactly did Mistress Judith sell?'

I had my back to him, investigating a pile of old sacks. 'Apothecary's and healer's supplies. I told you that yesterday.'

He didn't answer. I turned round, to see that he held a package in his hands. 'Such as this?'

I jumped up and went to look. The package had been torn open at one end, but even before I saw the contents I knew from the smell that it contained olibanum resin, also known as frank-incense. The oil derived from it is used, among other things, to help with coughs and breathing difficulties, but it's so costly that healers like me rarely see it. Mistress Judith kept a small stock of it, and now here it was in Robert Powl's warehouse . . .

'Yes,' I whispered. Understanding what he was thinking, I hurried on, 'But I'm sure Robert Powl's boats weren't the only ones who brought such items to the town!'

He threw down the package, grabbed my hand and we ran out of the warehouse.

It took all our combined ingenuity to find a way from the quay back to the market square without being spotted by Sheriff Picot's watch. And when we arrived at the square, it was to the realization that we stood no chance of getting into Mistress Judith's house unobserved, since a guard of two stood right outside.

'Is there a back way in?' Jack whispered as we peered out from the shadows at the end of one of the many narrow alleys giving on to the square.

'There is, but won't that be watched too?'

'Perhaps.' Jack paused, frowning. Then, looking up into the sky, he said, 'It's not far off midday now. You should go home, and I'll call for you once darkness has fallen.'

'But I—' There was no point in finishing the protest, since he'd already hurried away.

I reached Gurdyman's house without drawing the attention of the watch, although it was a relief to close the door behind me. Guessing Gurdyman was down in the crypt, I went along to the kitchen. Absent-mindedly, I tore bread and put out cold meats and some cheese. I was hungry after the morning's exertions, and Gurdyman might well emerge at any minute looking for something to eat.

I'd finished by the time he arrived, so I sat with him in the little inner court while he ate. I thought he might suggest some work for us to get on with, but he didn't. He was preoccupied, and although he responded when I spoke to him, did not initiate any conversation. Finally I said, 'Is there anything you want me to do this afternoon?'

He looked up with a start, and after a moment smiled benignly at me; I had the strong sense he'd forgotten I was there. 'No, child,' he said.

'I am – I'm busy with a thorny little problem, and better left alone.'

'Can't I help?'

His smile broadened. 'A kind offer, but no.' He got to his feet, a hand to the small of his back, and shuffled off along the passage. As he turned the corner towards the steps leading down to the crypt, I heard him muttering to himself.

It looked as if I'd been given the afternoon off. It was bad luck that it happened to be on the very day when our sheriff had just imposed a law ordering us to stay in our own houses unless we had very good reason not to.

I made profitable use of the time. I gave the kitchen, court and passage a very thorough clean, tidied my little attic room, washed out some of my personal linen and baked a batch of the sweet cakes that Gurdyman loves. Then – for I reckoned I had a busy night ahead – I went up to lie on my bed and soon fell asleep.

I was awake and down in the kitchen some time before Jack's soft knock on the door. It was fully dark, and there had been no sign of Gurdyman. I debated over whether or not to tell him I was going out, but decided not to. He wouldn't welcome the interruption.

Jack had pulled a dark hood up over his head, throwing his face in deep shadow, and I had arranged my shawl similarly. The pale flesh of a face shows up in torchlight, as does the glint of eyes. Jack nodded approvingly at me. 'I see you've been out on secret missions by night before,' he observed.

'Yes.' *More times than I care to remember*, I could have added.

'There are a handful of Sheriff Picot's watch about, but they don't seem to be taking their duty very seriously.' He gestured. 'Lead on.'

I had worked out in my head how to get round to the rear of Mistress Judith's house without crossing the square, and I managed to follow the route with only a couple of doublings-back. Quite soon Jack and I stood in a narrow little passage hemmed in on either side by high walls and, indicating the one on my left, I said very quietly, 'That's the one.'

'What's on the other side?' Jack's warm breath right in my ear gave me a strange sensation; not at all unpleasant.

'A small knot garden where she grows a few herbs,' I whispered back. 'Then there's a rear door into a sort of scullery, and then the living quarters, and the shop facing the square.'

'I hope old Adela is a sound sleeper,' he remarked.

'She may wake up,' I countered, 'but I'll say I've come to check on her after her terrible experience yesterday.'

He nodded, looking up at the wall. There was sufficient light from the moon to make out its rough surface, and, in one swift surge of strength, he stuck his fingers into niches and hauled himself up. In a couple of fluid movements, he was sitting on top of the wall, holding out his hand to me.

The jump down on the far side could have been done more elegantly – for me, anyway, although, irritatingly, Jack landed like a cat – and in single

107

file I led us between the low box hedges of the garden and up to the rear door. I opened it, as quietly as I could, and we stepped inside.

The crowded little scullery was where Mistress Judith had made her preparations, and fortunately the moonlight pouring in through the door made it possible to move without barging into things. The smell was very familiar, and for a moment I was back in my dear aunt Edild's little house. Jack was leaning over a bench and, presently, I heard the rasp of flint as he struck a spark to a candle. Soft light filled the little room, and we could see that none of Mistress Judith's many items of equipment seemed to have been disturbed.

But then it was most unlikely that jars, small glass vessels, funnels and weighing scales were what the thief would have been after.

We went through to the storeroom and Jack held the candle aloft so that we could look along the shelves. I wasn't all that familiar with their usual appearance, but it definitely looked as if someone had disturbed the pots, jars and vessels on them; in addition, they didn't look as crowded as I remembered. 'I think they've been—' I began.

Then Jack tripped over something on the floor.

As one we crouched down to look. The light shone on Adela, lying in a huddle just inside the door through to the living quarters. I called her name and reached for her hand, my other hand feeling around for injury. There was a huge bump on her head, and she seemed to be deeply unconscious.

'Is she dead?' Jack whispered.

'No, she's breathing, and the beat of her heart is steady, although it's very slow.' I was continuing my investigation as I spoke and, as far as I could tell, the bang on her head was the only injury.

'He must have stood behind the door,' Jack said, 'and when she came to investigate – maybe he made some small noise, and perhaps he hadn't realized there was anyone in the house – he stepped forward and hit her.'

'She's old,' I said quietly. 'He didn't need to hurt her so badly.'

'Will she live?'

'I don't know. We need to get her to her bed, warm her up, and somebody should be with her.'

'We can at least do the first task,' Jack said. Very gently he lifted Adela's still form, and, holding the candle, I led the way through to the little cubby-hole beside the storeroom where she had her bed. Jack laid her down and I tucked several blankets round her, chafing her cold hands to bring some warmth back.

Jack had wandered through to the front of the house, and through the doorway I could see him, peering out through the closed shutters on to the market square. Then he walked soft-footed through the house and stared out over the dark garden. I turned my attention back to Adela. But then I heard Jack give a soft exclamation.

'What is it?' I hissed.

'There's a light flickering, over the roofs of the alley behind us.'

'Well, lots of people live there,' I said. 'Probably someone—'

'It's too high for a house,' he said.

In my mind I tried to see a plan of the town. What could he be looking at?

'St Bene't's tower,' I said. 'The church is over there, behind us.'

He didn't reply. I looked at him, and he seemed suddenly tense. 'It's probably the priest keeping a vigil or something,' I suggested. 'Maybe he's praying for the murder victims.'

Still Jack didn't speak. Finally he muttered, 'It doesn't look right . . .' Then, spinning round, he said, 'I'm going to look.'

I leapt up. 'I'll come with you.'

'What about your patient?'

'I've done all I can for now. I'll come back to check on her later.'

He nodded. It was kind of him not to suggest that the reason I was so keen to go with him was because I was afraid to stay in a place where a violent killer had so recently struck. He'd have had every justification in doing so, since it was absolutely right.

We slipped out of the house and once more climbed over the wall. Now I, too, could see the flickering light, and it could only have been coming from the church tower. Jack took my hand, and we hurried through the network of passages until we came to the rear wall of St Bene't's churchyard.

We ran across the wet grass, both of us affected with the same dread. Something *was* wrong; in that holy place, it felt as if dark, cold fingers were reaching out, crushing the light . . .

The church door was ajar, and we slipped

inside. A lantern had been lit at the base of the tower, and it was its light, shining through high small windows overhead, that Jack had seen from Mistress Judith's house. The brightness threw the interior of the church into deeper darkness, and at first it was impossible to make anything out.

But I could hear well enough.

From somewhere near the altar there was a muffled gasping, as if someone was fighting some obstacle as they fought for breath. Then there was a shriek, and a low, rumbling voice muttered some words I didn't catch. Jack took off, running towards the altar, and I went after him.

Two figures were struggling together. One was small, thin and youthful – I recognized one of the junior clerics – and the other loomed over him, hooded, dark, big, tall, strong and powerful. For an instant the intense movements of the struggle twisted him round, and the light fell on him: his face was deathly white, and instead of eyes he had two big black holes . . .

I wanted to scream, but if I did he'd know I was there and he might pounce.

Jack, far braver than I, hurled himself on the pair, trying to grab at the bigger figure and pull it off the young priest. But whatever it was, it knew how to fight. It jerked an elbow into Jack's ribs, in precisely the right spot and with such violence that I could hear the breath being driven out of the lungs. Then it spun round and landed a savage blow straight to Jack's jaw, and he crumpled to the floor.

I cowered in the shadows. I knew I should do

something, but I was so terrified that I couldn't move.

Then the young priest managed to wriggle free. He came running straight for me, and hastily I crawled out of his way; the last thing he needed was to trip over me.

I thought he was going to get away, for he was fast on his feet and driven by terror.

But the hooded figure took off as if some diabolic force drove him. He seemed to fly down the aisle after the priest, and I'd swear his feet didn't make contact with the ground. He leapt on the poor young cleric from behind, and there was a sound like the cry of a bird of prey.

The light of the lantern caught the glint of metal.

I didn't want to look, but I couldn't tear my eyes away.

The hooded figure had extended one arm – one heavy, thick arm, clad in something that looked like scales. But there was no human hand at the end of that arm: instead, there was a set of long, shining, curved and viciously pointed claws, horrible yet strangely beautiful in their shape and substance.

The young priest turned, and I saw the whites of his eyes, wide with horror as he saw death descend.

There was a whistle as the silvery claws ripped through the air and a dreadful sound of ripping, tearing.

A desperate cry came, turning into a gurgle, swiftly cut off.

The dark shape seemed to gather itself up, and then suddenly it was no longer there.

I was frozen with terror. But then from somewhere deep within me a voice said reprovingly, *He may still be alive.*

On hands and knees, trembling and shivering, I crawled down the aisle to where the priest lay. I could smell the blood, metallic and tangy, long before I reached him, and soon I could see it, spreading out in a huge pool.

I took his limp, warm body in my arms, cradling his head on my lap. His wide eyes stared up at me, but I knew he couldn't see me. In the single, frightful movement, impressive in its deadly savagery, his throat had been torn out.

I bent my head over him, wishing I knew the right words. I found myself whispering, over and over again, 'I'm sorry, I'm so sorry.'

After a time – a long time, a short time – I felt Jack's warm hands on my shoulders. 'Come away now, Lassair. We will fetch help, and he will be looked after.'

I tried to stand up, but my legs shook too much to hold me. Once again, Jack picked me up in his arms and, cradling me to his chest, murmuring soft words that didn't seem to make any sense, he carried me away.

I took one last look. The young cleric – the Night Wanderer's fourth victim – lay like a patch of deeper shadow in the darkness.

Eight

'I can stand!' I hissed urgently to Jack as we emerged into the market square. I could willingly have let him go on carrying me – just then his solidity and warmth were things to cling to in the desperate night – but officers of the watch had already spotted us and were hurrying over.

'Are you sure?' he whispered back.

'*Yes!* Please put me down!'

He did, and my wobbly legs just about held me up. Jack stepped in front of me, shielding me from the pair of officers rapidly approaching us.

'What do you think you're doing, breaking curfew?' the first man said. He was squat and angry-faced, and already his hand was on the cudgel stuck in his heavy leather belt. Then, making out Jack's face, he said, 'Oh, sorry. Didn't recognize you.' He made a sort of bow, and his colleague did the same; they were, it appeared, subordinate to Jack.

Wild thoughts ran through my mind as I wondered how on earth Jack would explain our presence. He didn't even try, simply saying curtly, 'Another death. A young priest, in St Bene't's. You' – he pointed at the man bringing up the rear – 'go and watch over him. You' – the first man – 'go back to the castle, report the death and bring men to remove the body.'

The two men repeated their sketchy bow and

hurried away. Their footfalls echoed eerily through the silent town. 'What should we do?' I asked Jack.

He turned to me. 'I'll take you home. You shouldn't be out on the streets.'

I heartily agreed with him. 'I should check on Adela first.'

He nodded. 'Of course.' He reached for my hand and we ran across the square to Mistress Judith's house, where we found Adela just as we had left her. She was deeply asleep, and short of sitting with her for the rest of the night – which I really didn't want to do – there was nothing more I could do for her.

So Jack escorted me back to Gurdyman's house.

I don't believe I could have managed the journey alone. It was so familiar – I walked it at least once a day all the time I was in Cambridge – but the shock of the night's events turned it into a nightmare scene where every dark corner held a savage animal with long blood-stained claws and every tiny movement in the shadows was a ruthless, deranged killer out for my blood. I clung to Jack's hand and it was all I could do not to whimper in terror.

At last we stood before Gurdyman's door. I opened it, careful to make no noise, and Jack and I slipped inside. 'You don't need to come in,' I said. I wanted him to, very much, but I knew he must be aching to return to St Bene't's. He and I had been eyewitnesses to the murder; surely he *had* to be there.

But he said, 'I will wait. Go and find Gurdyman and tell him what's happened.'

'He'll be working, or asleep,' I protested.

'*Go.*'

I spun round and ran along the passage, turning off to the right into the corridor leading down to the crypt. There was something slightly amiss, and I noted distractedly that the door which was usually folded back flat against the passage wall had been moved slightly. It was a clever device of Gurdyman's – or perhaps of some previous inhabitant of the ancient house – in case he ever needed to hide, for when the door was closed it fitted so well, and was such an exact copy of the walls on either side, that you just couldn't detect that there was a door there at all.

I ran on, stumbling down the steps in my anxiety, my feet sounding noisily. In a part of my mind I registered Jack's heavy tread up above, as he moved along towards the rear of the house. It was good to know he was still there.

I burst into the crypt. Briefly there was light – dim, flickering – and then suddenly it was gone. In the dense, impenetrable darkness, it was exactly as if I'd been struck blind.

I screamed.

I don't know how Jack managed to reach me so quickly. He was there, arms round me, muttering soothing words, big, strong hands stroking across my back. Then, pulling away a little, he said, 'I have brought a light.'

He struck a spark, once, twice, and then it caught the oil-soaked rag wound round the head of the torch and a blessed, golden illumination flooded out. I stared frantically round, again and again. The crypt was uncharacteristically tidy, with the blankets neatly folded on Gurdyman's little cot, the normal disarray of the crowded shelves rearranged so that glass bottles, pots, dishes and vials were standing in ordered ranks, and the surface of the long wooden workbench was quite empty and scrubbed clean.

And there was nobody there.

I shook my head and rubbed my eyes. What was the matter with me? Had I been more affected by witnessing the poor priest's murder than I thought? Was I in shock, so that my eyes had seen what I wanted to see and not what was really there?

'What is it?' Jack spoke quietly, but there was some note in his voice that told me he knew something was badly wrong.

I turned to him. 'I think I'm going mad.'

He went on looking into my eyes. 'Tell me.'

But I couldn't. I forced a laugh – a silly, unconvincing sound – and said, 'Oh, it's nothing. The after-effects of the night's events, nothing more.'

He waited, clearly expecting me to elucidate. I wasn't going to. 'Gurdyman's obviously gone off somewhere, since he's not here,' I said, pleased at how close to normal I sounded, 'so I'll go up to bed and you can—'

But Jack shook his head. 'I'm not leaving you alone.'

'I don't think you ought to stay,' I said doubtfully. Although Gurdyman seemed to like him, having him take up residence in the house, even temporarily, was probably a step too far.

'I wasn't planning to.' Jack took my hand in the one not holding the torch and we went back up the steps leading out of the crypt. 'Is there anything you need for the night?'

'I already have it.' I indicated my leather satchel, which I always carry with me, and my shawl.

'Good. Come on, then.'

I thought we'd be going back to St Bene't's, but Jack turned the other way, towards the Great Bridge. We kept to the shadows and used the smaller, hidden-away alleys whenever we could, and I guessed he was still eager not to be seen by the night watch. Not that we saw any evidence of them; presumably all available men had been sent scurrying round in the aftermath of the latest murder.

As we drew near to the castle I saw that there were lights flaring, and I thought I caught the sound of raised voices in the distance. I guessed Sheriff Picot had been dragged from his bed, and wondered just how angry he was at having been disturbed. We passed the priory and took the turn on the right leading up to the castle. For a short while we had to walk out in the open, and anyone going to or from the castle would have seen us, but our luck held, and soon we turned into the narrow alley that wound round the base of the castle rise and led to the workmen's village.

I hoped and prayed that we weren't going to view any dead bodies tonight . . .

We moved through the deserted alleys and squares like shadows. Expecting to be terrified all over again, I realized suddenly that I wasn't; quite the contrary. I squeezed Jack's hand to catch his attention. When he turned to look at me, I said softly, 'I *like* this place,' and he grinned.

The little chapel loomed up before us, but it seemed we weren't going there. Passing it, Jack went on up a very narrow track, its surface no more than trodden mud, which we followed for perhaps twenty paces. We seemed to be in an alley of what had once been artisans' dwellings; small, one-roomed houses, at first attached to one another but then, as we went further from the deserted village, bigger properties set in their own small patches of land. One or two were clearly still in use.

We were approaching the end of the row and I saw open country beyond. The last house on the left was quite big, had a stout and well-made fence and looked to be in good repair, and I was just wondering what was the purpose of the fence, and what it could contain, when suddenly an unearthly noise fractured the deep silence.

It made me jump so badly that it took me a few moments to realize what it was, and by then it had virtually stopped. It had been made by a small flock of geese, and already Jack was among them, his calm, deep voice quieting them as he encouraged them back inside their pen.

He looked sheepishly at me. 'They make very good guards,' he said with a smile, 'and usually they don't make a sound when I come home.'

'When you—'

Of course.

It appeared I'd been right when I'd extended my imagination a little, and guessed that it was where he still lived.

'This was your parents' house,' I said.

'It was,' he agreed. 'It was where I was born, and now it's my home.' He pushed open the door. 'Please, come inside.'

With a quick look at the geese, still watching me warily as if just dying for an excuse to have a peck, I gathered up my skirts, went through the gate and closed it carefully behind me, then hurried up the path and into the house.

For a workman's house, it was indeed a good size, with a main room containing a hearth in which embers were glowing, shelves on which stood pots, platters and mugs, and a couple of offcuts of tree trunks to act as seating. The wall on the far side of the room was interrupted by an arched opening, beyond which I could just make out the shape of folded blankets, set on a low bed. As I've so often reflected, the secret of living in a restricted space – as the vast majority of us have no choice but to do – and not going mad with frustration is to keep it tidy and be vigilant over what you allow to come over the threshold. In my work as a healer I visit count-less homes, and I've seen the extremes: the dirty, crowded, desperate places where there is no comfort or solace, and the jewels of dwellings where someone – usually a woman – makes it her life's work to make a precious little haven out of next to nothing.

Jack's house definitely fell into the second category.

He'd been in the army, I recalled. No doubt that made a man tidy, even if he wasn't so by inclination. I was just wondering about that when

Jack said, with a degree of impatience, 'Are you going to go on standing in the doorway? I'd quite like to shut out the cold.'

He pointed me to one of the tree-trunk seats, and I sat down. He built up the fire, set water on to heat and very soon was handing me a hot drink. I tasted honey and chamomile, and smiled across the hearth at him. He grinned back. 'Not as good as yours, but I'm learning,' he said.

The good atmosphere that I had detected in the deserted village was here, too, in the cosy house. I realized that, for the first time in ages, I felt safe. A lot of that had to do with Jack's presence.

Which raised another question: were we both going to sleep here, and if so, where? Perhaps it was the result of everything I'd been through that night, but my heart was beating hard, my blood seemed to be racing through my body and I wanted more than anything to lie down beside Jack and feel his arms round me. I wanted to kiss him, hug him; I wanted us to be lovers.

The realization shocked me.

But I couldn't deny it. It was far too strong for that, and I don't believe in lying to myself.

I raised my eyes from the flames and discovered he was looking at me. I couldn't read his expression, for his face was half in shadow. The silence extended and the tension became unbearable.

My mouth was dry and I had to sip my drink before I dared try to speak. 'I'll be all right here alone if you have to go back into the town,' I said. It was cowardly, I know, for it might well make him think I didn't want to be alone with him, and if he thought that, then, courteous and considerate man that he was, he'd probably leave.

Which I wanted and didn't want, both at the same time, and so desperately that I was trembling . . .

After what seemed a very long time, he got up. He went through into the room beyond the arch, and I heard him moving about. Then he came back, a blanket in his hands.

'Go to bed, Lassair,' he said calmly. 'I'm not going into the town until morning. I'll sleep here, by the hearth.'

I stood up. For a moment we stood face to face. I very nearly reached out to him, and I think it was the same for him. Neither of us moved a muscle.

I went on into the further room, unslung my satchel, took off my boots and my headdress, lay down and pulled the bedclothes over me. 'Goodnight,' Jack's soft voice said from beside the hearth.

'Goodnight.'

Sleep came quickly. I wouldn't have expected it to do so, after all that had happened and given how I'd been feeling only a short while ago. But I must have been exhausted.

Just before I lost the power to think, something flashed into my mind. That strange moment in Gurdyman's crypt when the light went out came back to me, and once again I saw what I'd seen, or, perhaps, what I thought I'd seen.

It must surely have been the result of my over-stimulated imagination; I had, after all, just witnessed a brutal killing, and what more likely a moment was there to see things that weren't there?

And I *couldn't* have seen what I saw, for when Jack lit the torch, it was to reveal that the crypt was empty of any human inhabitants except the two of us.

Why, then, was I so very certain that, in that blink of an eye, I had seen Gurdyman, Hrype and a third, shadowy figure – whether male or female, I couldn't tell – standing there?

Nine

I woke from deep sleep to find soft morning light arrowing into the room through a long, narrow aperture set high up in the wall. I lay still, listening. Within the house, all was quiet. From outside, I heard the geese, cackling and quarrelling; perhaps they'd just been fed. There was also the splashing of water.

I had slept very well. I was sure I'd been dreaming; one or two very disturbing images still lurked somewhere near the surface of memory, but I forced myself to ignore them. I thought I'd woken once and called out, but perhaps that, too, was part of a dream. As was the feel of Jack's warm arms around me and his deep voice telling me softly that I was safe, and the gentle touch on the crown of my head that felt just like a kiss . . .

It was time to get up.

I folded the blankets and the soft, sleek pelt that at some point in the night had been put over me, leaving the bed as neat as I'd found it. I smoothed my hair, put on my coif and bent down for my boots, then went through into the main room. Jack had left a bowl of water beside the hearth. I dipped my fingers in, to find that it was warm.

Before I washed, I needed to visit the privy. I went outside, to see Jack, stripped to the waist, kneeling over a trough and washing his upper body. That explained the splashing sounds. I stopped, staring at him. I'd known he was strong – his chest felt hard and solid as a barrel – but now, seeing him unclad, I could see the perfect muscles and the powerful shoulders. I was used to seeing the nakedness of both sexes, for people who grow up in households like my home do not have the luxury of privacy, and in my healing work over the years I have been presented with every inch of the human body.

You'd have thought I could look at Jack Chevestrier's powerful form without my legs going weak.

I hurried across to the privy and was back inside the house before Jack had his head out of the trough.

By the time he came inside, fully dressed, his short-cropped hair wet and his face red from the cold, I was sitting primly beside the hearth, hands folded in my lap. 'Good morning,' I said. 'Thank you for the hot water.'

He nodded an acknowledgement. 'Did you sleep all right?'

'Yes.' No need to mention the dreams, good or bad.

He was moving around the room, checking on the small iron cauldron suspended over the fire, fetching wooden bowls and spoons, twitching items on the shelves into line. I realized suddenly that he was nervous. 'That smells good,' I said, too brightly, indicating whatever bubbled over the hearth.

'Porridge,' he said. 'Almost ready.'

We ate in silence. The porridge tasted as good as it smelt. He had stirred in some honey, which was a treat. All too soon we had finished, and he leapt up to wash the bowls. Then they were back in their usual place, the remains of the meal had been cleared away, and there was no longer any alternative but to talk to each other.

We both took the plunge together.

'I must go back and see what's happened to Gurdyman,' I began, just as Jack said, 'I really don't think you should go back to Gurdyman's house.'

We stopped. 'I *have* to see if he's all right,' I said firmly.

'Yes, of course,' he agreed. 'I only meant you shouldn't go there alone.'

'Why not?' I could feel my indignation rising. Was I going to allow Jack Chevestrier to tell me what to do?

He leaned forward, his eyes fixed on mine and full of anxiety. 'Lassair, we cannot ignore what's happening,' he said urgently. 'Victims are being picked off, to no logical pattern that we have yet determined, and the killer's hunger seems to be growing.' His words sent a chill through me. 'Until we know why he is selecting those he slays, we cannot possibly predict who may be next. All we do know is that there will be more deaths, and you,' he added brutally, 'are in as much danger as everyone else.' He paused, letting his words sink in. 'Please,' he went on gently, 'let me come with you.'

I was briefly at war within myself. The hard-headed, self-sufficient part of me wanted to walk out, head held high, ignoring Jack's fear for me and insisting I could manage alone. The sensible side of me was busy visualizing a strange silvery hand with cruel, vicious claws and a still corpse with a gap where a throat ought to be. Happily, the sensible side won.

I dropped my gaze. 'All right,' I muttered.

I know I ought to have been more grateful but I wasn't used to people wanting to look after me and it was hard to lower my guard and be gracious. Jack, though, didn't appear to take offence. He merely nodded, then stood up and reached for a sword that I now noticed stood just inside the door. Beside it was an axe whose edge, I could see from where I sat, was so sharply honed that it glinted pale silver.

Jack buckled on a heavy leather belt and slid the sword into its scabbard. Then he pushed a long knife under the belt, and picked up a smaller knife, which he stuck down the side of his boot. 'Are we expecting trouble?' I asked with a small smile.

But he didn't smile back. He just said, 'Yes.'

It was earlier than I'd thought, as became clear when we emerged from the total quiet of the deserted village and into the more frequented areas of town. There were signs of activity up at the castle, but the Great Bridge was empty of traffic, and when I looked down at the river and the quayside, the only signs of life were some spirals of smoke as people stoked up their fires to cook breakfast.

We didn't take any chances, though, for as Jack pointed out, there would certainly be watchmen patrolling. We kept to the back lanes, and soon found our way to the narrow passage leading through to the alley where Gurdyman's well-hidden house stands. We went inside and, once again, I hurried down to the crypt.

I lit a lamp and stood staring around. Everything looked just as it had done last night, and once more I was struck by how odd the crypt appeared without the normal clutter of Gurdyman's many activities, interests and projects. The chief reason it seemed odd was because Gurdyman wasn't there, but I tried not to think about that.

Jack had come down with me, and now stood beside me. 'What is it?' he asked quietly.

'Hmm?' I turned to look at him.

'Something has caught your attention.'

'Oh!' I hadn't realized that my preoccupation showed. 'Someone – Gurdyman, no doubt – has had a very good tidy down here. All his work stuff has been put away.' I was wandering round the crypt as I spoke, looking at the shelves, touching things. 'Quite a lot of the materials and implements he uses aren't actually here at all,' I went on. 'I wonder what he's done with them?'

Then a dreadful thought struck me. 'Oh, dear Lord – you don't think someone's stolen them? That someone' – I couldn't bring myself to suggest who – 'broke in, stole whatever it was he wanted, and – and . . .' I couldn't bring myself to say that, either.

'I'm quite sure that didn't happen,' Jack said with reassuring normality. 'Nothing has been disturbed and there are no signs of disarray – on the contrary, you just said how tidy everything looks. And,' he added softly, 'nobody's lying dead on the floor.'

I nodded, not trusting myself to speak. With one last look around the crypt, I led the way back up the steps. Jack waited in the inner court while I looked around, but, as in the crypt, there wasn't really anything to see, except that the same unusual order prevailed. Finally, I went up into my little attic room and, feeling suddenly drained of energy, sat down on the bed.

My eyes roamed round the small space. There wasn't very much in the room, and I could see almost at first glance that everything was just as I'd left it. I'm an orderly person by nature and even if somebody had climbed the ladder to tidy my room, they'd have found nothing to do. I stood up, glancing back towards the bed.

Then I did see something that was out of place.

Deliberately so; instantly I was sure of that.

The floorboard under which I hide my shining stone was infinitesimally out of alignment with the board next to it.

Heart thumping – *Oh, no, no, no!* – I threw myself down on my knees, two fingernails tearing as I scrabbled to raise the board. The leather bag was where I'd left it, and the stone was inside. I clutched it to my breast, fierce joy coursing through me. I'm not sure I'd realized until that moment just what it meant to me. I wasn't going to put it back in its hiding place, that was certain; wherever I went, it would come with me. I reached out to replace the floorboard and noticed that there was something else in the dark space.

It was a small object, pale green, with a strangely shaped gold-filled mark etched into it.

I picked it up and held it in my clenched hand. I felt its power, bucking like a living thing against my skin. I sent out a forceful thought to the person who had put it there; who had left it there for me to find, for I knew full well who he was. On the one hand, I was hugely relieved because I now knew where Gurdyman was; or, at least, who he was with, and that he was almost undoubtedly safe. On the other hand, I was angry because this person had not thought twice about coming up into my room – my own, private, precious space! – and reaching down into the secret hiding place where I keep my most treasured possession.

I waited, taking steady breaths, till I was calm. Then I went back down to Jack.

'I can't exactly tell you how I know,' I said, 'because it involves somebody else, and to explain might very well betray a confidence.' I wasn't quite sure what I meant, but somehow I knew better than to divulge what I'd just learned, even to Jack. 'Gurdyman's not here, but he's all right.'

'He's left you a message?' Jack demanded.

'Er – sort of.'

'Then we needn't spend any more time here. Come on!' He reached for my hand. I'd put the shining stone in its bag into my satchel back in my attic room, and now I swiftly buckled up the satchel straps and took Jack's hand.

I paused to lock the door. Gurdyman and I rarely bothered under normal circumstances, but what was happening now was far from normal. I hoped Gurdyman had a key, too. Would he have remembered to take it with him?

I couldn't think about that now. I said some silent words in my mind with the aim of keeping the house and its many secrets safe. Then I followed Jack away up the alley.

We went first to Mistress Judith's house, for I was concerned about Adela and feeling guilty that I'd left her on her own. As we approached, keeping out of sight as best we could, I saw that the door was open. Voices were coming from within, and then two sturdy young men appeared in the doorway, supporting Adela between them.

I hurried up to them. 'How is she?'

Adela herself answered. 'My head hurts like the very devil but I'll live, and there's no need to talk about me as if I'm not here,' she said with spirit. One of the young men caught my eye and grinned.

'We're her sister's grandsons,' the other one said, 'and we're taking her to our mother's.'

'Good,' I said, already rummaging in my satchel. Taking out a remedy in a twist of cloth, I gave it to Adela. 'This will help the headache. As much as will cover your thumbnail, in warm water, no more than three times a day.'

She took it and tucked it away in her bosom. Then, with an imperious command to the young men, she let them lead her off.

Jack and I melted back into the maze of alleys, taking a curving route to return to the marketplace some distance away. He stopped on the edge of the square and we leaned forward to peer out. I

131

had heard a mutter of voices as we approached and now I saw that all at once the square was thronging with people, and that most of them seemed possessed of the sort of anger that is a thin disguise for fear. There appeared to have been a spontaneous mass revolt against Sheriff Picot's order for people to stay indoors, and although a huge force of the sheriff's men were doing their best to push people out of the square and into the many alleys opening on to it, the people were fighting back. The townsfolk seemed only just to have discovered that if enough of them joined in the protest, there wasn't much the sheriff could do to make them obey the curfew. He simply didn't have enough men.

Sheriff Picot himself stood over on the far side of the square, up on a low wall. A gang of armed men was ranged around him in a protective circle and his nephew Gaspard stood beside him, frowning down at the crowd and managing to look both threatening and disdainful.

'He's arrested the storyteller!' a woman standing next to us said, eyes wide with horrified fascination. 'Sheriff Picot, that is. Gave him a beating, too, or his men did. Said he'd been encouraging rumours and making us all scared. As if we weren't scared enough anyway, what with all these murders and the sheriff's total failure to do anything to stop them!' she added recklessly.

Clearly, she hadn't recognized Jack.

I took hold of her arm. 'Be careful!' I muttered in her ear. 'I shouldn't think Sheriff Picot is a man who likes being criticized, and you never know who's listening.'

But she was brave, this woman; either that or foolhardy. 'I'll speak my mind if I want to,' she said crossly. 'And it's no more than the truth, and what everyone's saying.'

I felt Jack edge close. 'Don't worry, I won't tell,' he murmured. I sensed he was smiling.

Sheriff Picot's voice rang out over the crowd. '*Be quiet!*' he thundered. One of his men banged a cudgel against the ground. After a moment, the crowd fell silent.

'What are you going to do about all the killings?' someone shouted from over on our left. 'We're decent, honest folk, and we go in fear of being the next to die!'

'Why aren't you and your men protecting us?' another voice yelled from further back. Others joined in, demanding reassurance, wanting explanations. The man with the cudgel banged it again, several times, there was a brief scuffle behind where the sheriff stood, and somebody yelled in pain.

'*Silence!*' roared the sheriff. Slowly, the hubbub died away.

'I have already issued an order that you are all to remain in your homes unless you have permission to go out,' Sheriff Picot went on, 'in which case one of my men will escort you, and otherwise—'

'But we ain't *safe* in our homes!' a woman's shrill voice screeched. 'Mistress Judith only poked her nose outside and someone did for her, and that poor young priest was inside the *church*!' Her voice rose into an alarmingly piercing screech on the last word, and people standing close covered their ears.

Many others now joined in, all muttering and mumbling the same thing. They had a point. What was the purpose of restricting people to their houses when it now seemed that their homes, and even the church, could offer no sanctuary? Whoever this killer was, he was no respecter of tradition. Then a voice from the thickest part of the throng, in the middle of the square, rang out clear above the rest: 'It's the Night Wanderer, that's who's doing it! You can beat up and arrest all the storytellers you like, it won't alter the truth!'

There was a great roar from the crowd. There were shouts of, 'Yes!' 'Hear, hear!' and 'That's the truth, indeed it is!' People were nodding, turning to their neighbours in encouragement, and now the level of sound in the square from those massed voices rose to a frightened, angry crescendo.

Sheriff Picot yelled again and again for quiet, and finally got it. 'I'll have no more talk of the Night Wanderer, or there'll be trouble!' he bawled. 'You'll all do as you're told and go home, or else risk arrest!'

'You've not got the room in your cells for us all!' a man's deep voice shouted back.

Sheriff Picot spun round, looking for the source of the provocative remark. 'Oh, I'll find room, don't you worry about that!' he said coldly. 'And there'll be fines and floggings for those who incite disobedience, have no fear.'

We all knew Sheriff Picot. We all knew he meant what he said. He liked a good flogging and didn't need much excuse to order one.

The mood in the crowd had already altered. People were starting to drift away, and Jack pulled me back into the shadows of the alley. I was just wondering what we were going to do next – shouldn't he join his fellow lawmen in enforcing the sheriff's orders? – when he said, 'There's someone I need to find. He's one of the sheriff's men, but he's not like most of them. He's one of mine, and he has a good, loyal team.'

'Where will we find him?' I asked, already vastly relieved to learn that Jack and I weren't on our own.

'I'm not sure, but I have a few ideas,' Jack replied. He took my hand again and we hurried off, deeper and deeper into the maze of lanes, alleys and little streets around the market square.

Our search for Jack's man took us the remainder of the morning. We found him in a tavern on the quayside, close to Margery's whorehouse, where he and a small group of five other men were wolfing down a hasty dinner. The man – he was slim and elegant, with watchful dark eyes in a high-cheekboned face – rose smoothly to his feet when he saw Jack, chewing and hastily swallowing his mouthful.

'Sorry, master,' he said when he had emptied his mouth. 'Only I didn't reckon the men and me could have gone on much longer without victuals.'

'It's all right, Walter,' Jack said. 'All of you, finish your food.' He pulled up a bench and we joined the men at their board. 'This is Lassair. Lassair, this is Walter.' Walter and I exchanged glances and nodded at each other.

135

'She's the healer girl,' another of the men muttered to the others, not quite quietly enough. 'She tended my old mother when her heart was bad.'

I looked at the speaker. I remembered him: a lean, gingery man with a ready smile. I'd liked him when I was nursing his mother; liked the old woman, too, indomitable, bossy old soul that she was.

'How is she?' I asked.

'She's well, mistress, thank you,' the man replied. 'She'll see us all out, I'll wager, and nag me nigh into the ground in the process.' There were a few chuckles. It appeared that others of the company were acquainted with the man's mother.

Jack rapped gently on the table, and immediately had everyone's attention. 'Luke,' he said, addressing the sallow-faced, older man sitting at the end of the bench. The man got up, went to the door, peered outside and then came back. 'All clear, master.'

Jack leaned in closer to the circle of men. 'As you may know,' he began, 'Sheriff Picot has ordered me to cease my involvement in these murders, and he's put Gaspard in charge.'

'Man's an arrogant layabout,' one of the men muttered.

'Man's an arsehole,' said another.

'I'm not entirely sure what the sheriff intends me to do instead,' Jack went on, 'since he hasn't issued any orders and, in fact, has totally ignored me.' A brief spasm of anger crossed his face. 'Since I therefore have nothing else to do, I intend to pursue my own enquiries, and if anybody wishes to join in, they'd be very welcome. I must add,' he went on before anybody could speak, 'that such a course of action could result in a severe reprimand from the sheriff, even though I would of course make it perfectly clear that anyone who helped me was carrying out my orders, and had no knowledge of the fact that I had been removed from the investigation. If anyone prefers not to risk trouble, he may leave and there will be no repercussions. On that you have my word.'

He waited. Nobody moved. I saw a sort of joy fleetingly flare in his eyes, as if he had doubted the men's loyalty and trust in him and had fully expected them all to get up and leave.

He was a very modest man.

He cleared his throat. 'Very well,' he said after a moment. 'Let me share my thoughts with you, and we'll decide on a course of action and work out who does what.' He paused, took a breath and then said, 'It seems to me that the only hope we have of finding out the killer's identity, and of stopping him from further attacks, is to work out how he has been selecting his victims, and why they have to die. Of course,' he added, perhaps forestalling the question I could see in the expressions of at least one of the men, 'it may be that these are random slayings and the work of a madman, but I hope and pray that is not so. I don't believe it is' – he leaned forward, as if he couldn't contain his urge to share his conviction – 'for already common threads are emerging. Robert Powl, the first victim, brought goods of all kinds into the town, and something was stolen from the barn next to his house. Gerda, the second victim, was known to have numbered among her clients men who worked on the river, possibly for Robert Powl. Mistress Judith kept an apothecary shop, and almost certainly obtained supplies from Robert Powl's consignments; her shop, too, may have been robbed. The fourth victim, the young priest—' He broke off, hands spread. 'I have no idea what could connect him with the others.'

'We need to find out,' Walter said. 'We need to ask around, see where he lived, if his quarters have been searched and if anything's missing.'

'We should discover what sort of a person he was,' added the ginger-haired man, 'and what he did when he wasn't priesting.' There were a couple of quiet chuckles.

'Yes, good,' Jack said. 'Walter and Ginger, you get on with that. Gerald' – he turned to a fleshy, brawny man still quietly getting on with eating what remained on the table, on others' platters as well as his own – 'you're a good friend of Margery's girls.' Gerald grunted an assent. 'Lassair has spoken to them, but they hadn't much to offer in the way of helpful information. I'd like you to find out, if you can, who poor little Gerda saw regularly, whether she had any favourites, if anyone ever gave her presents, if she met anyone outside of her work.' How careful he was, I thought, not to disparage her; I wondered how many other senior lawmen – for it was becoming clear that he must be senior, both because the person Sheriff Picot had replaced him with was the sheriff's own nephew, and also because of these men's attitude to him – would have spoken of a dead prostitute with such kindness and respect.

Gerald grunted again. He looked at Jack, eyes raised, and Jack nodded. 'Yes, off you go,' he said. 'You too, Walter and Ginger. We meet here at sunset to report our findings.' I wondered if Gerald was slow-witted. I watched as he got up from the board, every movement careful and studied, and then flexed his huge arms. He had enormous fists and, if they weren't weapons enough, a knife in his belt and a heavy stick that he picked up from the floor under the board. If he found the man who had killed Gerda, I didn't think that man would last very long.

Three men remained. One, the sallow-faced Luke, was ordered to mingle with the lawmen under Picot's command; another was dispatched to seek out friends, neighbours and associates of Mistress Judith and ask a few careful questions. The last man was a boy, really, of about fifteen. He had an open, friendly face with an intelligent, alert look, a gap where a front tooth was missing, bright blue-green eyes and a shock of pale hair. He reminded me a little of my childhood friend Sibert, back home in Aelf Fen, and I liked him at once.

'Don't forget me, master!' he said cheerfully to Jack. 'What shall I do?'

Jack looked at him, assuming a frowning, critical look which I didn't think fooled the boy for an instant, if his broad grin was anything to go by. 'Ah, what's-your-name,' Jack murmured

– both the lad and I knew he was teasing – 'yes, now I remember, Henry. You, my lad, are coming with me.'

Henry, looking as if his prayers had just been answered, leapt to his feet. Jack looked enquiringly at me, and I too stood up. 'We three,' Jack said solemnly, 'are going to make our way to Mistress Judith's storeroom, where we shall do what Lassair and I were hoping to do last night, before the young priest died, which was to search through all the shelves and, by thinking very hard and putting our heads together, try to work out which of the items that ought to be there are missing.'

Ten

Wherever Sheriff Picot's patrols were that afternoon, they weren't in the little passage behind Mistress Judith's garden. Jack and I climbed over the wall in exactly the same place as we had done the night before, and I noticed Henry looking on, wide-eyed in wonder at the sight of his senior officer doing something that was, in the normal course of events, very definitely against the law.

With old Adela being cared for by relatives we knew the house would be empty. With any luck, we would be able to take our time.

We sprinted across the knot garden and slipped inside the house. Jack closed the door behind us, pausing for a few moments to listen, but all remained quiet. If anybody had heard a noise that shouldn't be there, he or she had the good sense to shut themselves inside their own house and ignore it.

In the clear light of a sunny afternoon, the scullery and its workbench were far more readily visible than they had been by the flickering light of a candle flame. The same applied to the storeroom, and the illumination improved when Henry pushed the door right open and wedged it in place.

I stood quite still and took a long, slow look at the shelves. As before, I had the strong impression that the contents of the upper shelves had been disturbed, and the more I stared, the more it looked just as if someone had removed something, then hastily rearranged the various glass and pottery vessels to disguise the fact. Something occurred to me. I stood up on tiptoe, but it didn't make me tall enough. I turned to voice my request, but Henry, who had been watching me closely, had anticipated my need and was already handing me a small three-legged stool. I nodded my thanks, climbed up and looked right along the top two shelves.

I'd been silently praying that Mistress Judith's housekeeping routine hadn't extended to a weekly clean of the shelves that were up high and out of her reach, and my prayer was answered: it hadn't. On the topmost shelves there was a clear pattern in the dust that showed where vessels had been stored until very recently. Those that now remained no longer stood where once they had.

'Something *has* been taken,' I said softly. I looked round, expecting Jack and Henry to be exploring the rest of the storeroom, and jumped when I discovered they were right behind me.

'Can you tell what's missing?' Henry whispered.

I made a rueful face. 'Well, it's much harder looking for something that's not there than something that is,' I said, 'but I do have an advantage in that I know pretty much what an apothecary usually keeps on her shelves.' Already I was picturing my aunt Edild's store, visualizing the contents.

Jack gave a sort of groan. I guessed he'd realized what we were going to have to do. Henry wasn't far behind, and, with the eagerness of youth, he said excitedly, 'You'll need writing materials. I saw quill, parchment and ink horn back there' – he pointed to the scullery – 'so shall I fetch them?'

'Yes, please.'

Quite soon, I had made myself comfortable in Mistress Judith's prettily carved chair, quill in hand. With my eyes closed, once more I brought Edild's storeroom to mind. I wrote down everything she keeps on her shelves. I worked as swiftly as I could, but still I sensed Jack's impatience. I ignored it.

When I was done, I said, 'I'm ready. You can start.'

So Jack and Henry began working their way along the shelves, picking up bottles, pots and jars, finding labels where there were labels to find and reading them out for me to note down. Where there was nothing to say what a vessel contained, they would open it, bring it to me and I would have a look, or, more usually, a sniff. The task was slow and laborious, and we only had the faintest, most optimistic hope that it would lead anywhere.

We stopped for a short break. Bending over my piece of parchment and concentrating so intently was making my head ache, and it was good to stand up, stretch and take some good deep breaths. I glanced at Henry, who was standing in the scullery, gazing out through the little window on to the knot garden.

'I was surprised to discover that he can read,' I murmured to Jack.

Jack too looked at the lad. 'He was raised by the monks,' he replied. 'They discovered he was bright and hauled him out of the monastery

143

farmyard, where he'd been shovelling muck, then taught him to read and write instead.'

'Why isn't he still a monk?'

Henry had heard our voices, and turned to look at us. He was smiling, and clearly not at all offended that we had been discussing him. 'I ran away,' he said, the smile widening. 'The monks were too ready with the beatings and, besides, I didn't like the idea of celibacy. Know what I mean, miss?' He gave me a cheeky wink. From a fully-grown man it might have been offensive. From Henry, it was delightful.

'How right you were,' I murmured. 'Just think of all those poor girls who would have been left bereft and pining if you were still scribbling away in a cold scriptorium.'

Henry opened his mouth to reply, but whatever pertinent and probably rude remark he was about to make never came, for Jack, perhaps detecting rather too much frivolity in his team, ordered us back to work.

It was evening before I found what we were looking for. I found what the missing item was, at least, although I had no idea why anyone would go to such lengths to steal it; if indeed it had been stolen, and was not simply an item that Mistress Judith elected not to keep.

I was fairly certain she would have included it among her stores, however, for I had come across it on Gurdyman's higgledy-piggledy shelves and Edild kept no more than a very small amount, maintaining that in general its toxicity outweighed its usefulness. Quite a lot of substances, I'd found, were common to healers and to . . . well, whatever Gurdyman was. Wizard, magician; I never quite know.

Gurdyman was very wary of this stuff and Edild kept it high on her top shelf, out of reach of curious hands. Both my mentors had warned me of its perils.

As we prepared to leave Mistress Judith's house – Henry was on watch at the end of the garden, crouched on top of the wall and checking to make sure the alleyway was clear – I said to Jack, 'I would wager that it was a consignment of the same stuff that was stolen from Robert Powl's secret store. I was wondering if it would be an idea to go and check through his parchments, but then I realized that if it's suddenly so precious and sensitive that he had to hide it away, he's not likely to have kept any record of having had it in his possession.'

'Yes, the same thing occurred to me,' Jack said. We were outside now, and he was carefully securing the door. He sighed. 'We'll just have to hope that Walter or one of his men has discovered a link with one of the other victims.'

We were the last to arrive back at the tavern down on the quayside. Walter, Ginger, Fat Gerald, Luke and the man whose name I didn't know were tucking into a generous bowl of stew, hunks of bread in their hands, mugs of ale close by. They all rose when Jack, Henry and I came in.

'Don't stop,' Jack said. 'Is there any more?'

There was, and the tavern-keeper quickly brought three more bowls and some extra bread, followed by three more mugs of ale. I was ravenously hungry, and the food and the ale were both excellent. The tavern-keeper – who seemed to be an old friend of the lawmen – tactfully melted away once he had ascertained we had all we needed.

When everyone, even Fat Gerald, had at last had enough, Jack asked each man for his report, beginning with Luke; Jack's first concern, it seemed, was to see what progress Gaspard Picot was making.

'He's made a score of arrests and he's promising a couple of floggings in the morning,' Luke said lugubriously, 'although the word is that, since he's named no names, it's just piss and wind. Excuse me, miss.' He turned to me, touching his forelock. 'Fact is, he's come up with nothing better than this notion of keeping all the townsfolk inside their houses and hoping that'll stop the killer. Naturally, people aren't taking kindly to being prevented from carrying on with their everyday lives, and Sheriff up at the castle is now drowning in hundreds of requests from people demanding special leave, and a sheriff's escort, to go about their legitimate business.' There were several quiet chuckles at the idea of Sheriff Picot's discomfiture.

'But Gaspard hasn't been questioning the victims' families and acquaintances?' Jack asked.

'Not that I've heard,' Luke replied.

Jack turned to the others. 'What about those of you who have been doing just that?'

Walter was the first to respond. 'Ginger and I have been finding out about the young priest,' he said, 'and neither of us saw any of Gaspard's men, or heard anything to suggest they'd been sniffing around.'

Jack nodded. 'Gerald? Matty?' So that was the last man's name. 'Any evidence of Gaspard's interest in either Gerda's or Mistress Judith's friends?' Both men shook their heads.

Jack absorbed that in silence for a moment. I wondered what he was thinking. Then, turning back to Walter, he said, 'What did you find out about the priest?'

'He was an outsider, new to the town, studious, quiet, kept himself to himself,' Walter said. 'Liked his books better than his fellow men, according to his master at St Bene't's. I was allowed to have a quick look at his cell in the priests' lodging house, and you'd have thought nobody lived there. Narrow little bed, sparse amount of blankets, big wooden cross on the otherwise bare wall, and that was about it.' He jerked his head in Ginger's direction. 'Ginger has something to add, though.'

'Go on, Ginger,' Jack commanded.

'I managed to catch one of the other young clerics milling around the church,' Ginger said, 'and I got him away from his fellows in the hope that it'd encourage him to open up. It turns out that our priest – his name was Osmund – had got into trouble more than once because he was late for offices or stayed out after lock-up. He'd taken his punishments without complaint – and they were pretty tough – but, according to my source, even the threat of harsh discipline didn't seem to stop Osmund's unexplained absences.'

'Did your informant have any idea where he went?'

'He did,' Ginger said with a grin. 'He has an insatiable interest in his fellow man – most

147

fortuitous, as far as we're concerned – and one evening he followed Osmund.' He paused, looking round to ensure he had everyone's attention. 'He went down to the river.'

We all thought about that for a while. Then Jack said, 'Matty, what did you discover?'

Matty closed his eyes as if it helped him remember, then said quickly, 'Mistress Judith had been bothered because she'd had several orders for one particular substance, although nobody could tell me what it was, and she was having difficulty finding a reliable source. She did know Robert Powl, and he frequently brought consignments into the town for her, but, again, nobody knew if it was him who was transporting the stuff she had a problem finding.' He opened his eyes again. 'If you see what I mean.'

'We do,' Jack assured him. He looked around at the group of intent faces. 'Well, thank you all. We have a picture, of a sort, although I could wish for more detail.' He fell silent again, frowning. Finally he said, 'This is what I think: a certain group of people in the town have all at once discovered a need for some substance that is rare and possibly hard to come by. It appears to be something that is obtained from an apothecary. Mistress Judith – a good businesswoman – decided to fulfil that need, and no doubt make a worthwhile profit, and she found out where to obtain it. She put in an order, and asked Robert Powl to bring the consignment on one of his boats.'

He stopped, his frown deepening. Then he said slowly, 'Now there are two possibilities: either someone else wants all the supplies of this substance for himself for some reason, and is prepared to kill to obtain them, or else someone disapproves of the activities of those who are using the substance, and is therefore killing both them and everyone connected with its acquisition.'

'What about Gerda?' Fat Gerald said, his deep, slow voice thrumming in the quiet room.

'Yes, Gerda,' Jack said. He met Gerald's anxious eyes. 'I don't know.'

Walter had been studying Jack closely. 'You haven't yet told us what you found out, master,' he said.

Jack grimaced. 'I haven't, and now I will.' He glanced at me, then back at Walter. 'We already knew that something had been stolen from Robert Powl's barn, and it now looks as if Mistress Judith's storeroom also has an item missing.' He hesitated. 'We can't know for sure, but it looks as if the missing substance is cinnabar.'

'Cinnabar?' Ginger echoed. 'What's that?'

Jack turned to me. 'Lassair?'

'It's a mineral which looks like reddish, dusty rock,' I said. 'I believe it's mined in Egypt.'

'And brought all the way here?' Fat Gerald sounded incredulous.

'Yes,' I said.

He frowned. 'Why?'

'It's used to make quicksilver and it has certain applications in healing, although it's poisonous and you have to know what you're doing.'

'So why is someone stealing it?' Ginger asked. 'The victims aren't being poisoned, they're dying because their throats are ripped out.'

I shrugged. 'I don't know.'

149

I could have added, *but I'm just beginning to have an idea*. That idea, however, was so dim and cloudy in my mind that I didn't.

We now knew, or believed we knew, what was at the root of the thefts, and in all likelihood of the murders, too. But why it should be, and what the killer was hoping to achieve by those brutal slayings, as yet we had absolutely no idea.

Full night had come on while we had been talking. Looking up and noticing this, swiftly Jack dispersed the men. He warned them to be careful, for the night watch would by now be out in force and he didn't want any of them to be picked up and punished for being out after curfew. Studying his expression as he watched them leave, however, I didn't think he was seriously worried; they were a canny bunch.

We gave them a little while to get well away, then we too slipped out of the tavern and into the darkness, heading off along the quay towards the Great Bridge, and the castle and the deserted village beyond. But before we had even got as far as the bridge, we heard the unmistakable sounds of a patrol. There were at least ten, maybe a dozen men, and they were crossing the bridge from the castle side. They were armed, booted – their marching feet rang out in unison as they went over the bridge – and with dismay we realized they were coming our way. Even as we drew back into the deep shadow of a warehouse, we saw the leading pair wheel off to their left and down on to the quay.

Jack took my hand and said very softly right into my ear, 'Back away from the water. Be *very* quiet.'

He didn't really need to tell me.

We crept down the narrow gap between the warehouse and its neighbour, edging steadily away from the light of the patrols' flaring torches, bright as midday in the darkness. Presently I felt grass beneath my feet. We were out in the open, behind the buildings that line the quay, on the edge of the patch of pasture and woodland between town and river.

For a moment I thought we were safe. But then the lights told me otherwise: the men of the patrol were being thorough for once, investigating down between the quayside buildings to the open space beyond.

Jack grabbed my hand again and we ran. My satchel banged against my hip bone, and somehow it spurred me on.

We came to a stand of alder, and used the welcome shelter to pause and catch our breath. But it wasn't much of a hiding place, and if the patrol ventured out across the fields they would very soon think to check among the trees.

Then I had an idea. Leaning close to Jack, I said, 'We could hide by the sacred well.'

He looked at me, his expression quite cross. 'There's nowhere to hide there!' he hissed. He was right, for, although the well is quite a special spot to me, it really is pretty much just a well; a hole in the ground with a slatted wooden cover and a small construction built over it like a little roof. It's a rarely frequented spot, and only a few of the townsfolk bother much with it nowadays.

'I know someone who lives just the other side of it,' I whispered. 'He's a friend of Gurdyman's and I've visited him once or twice. We could hide in his outhouse, and if the worst comes to the worst and the patrol follow us there, I'm sure he'll take us in and swear we've been there all along.'

Swiftly Jack thought about it. Then he nodded, muttered, 'I hope you're right,' and we were off again.

We passed the sacred well, with its lone oak tree spreading out sheltering, protective branches. I wished there was time to stop, for it's a healthy, restorative place and always seems to make you feel better, even on a brief visit. I gave a dip of the head in its direction, and muttered some words under my breath. Then we were past, hurrying on.

Very soon, the lonely little dwelling of Gurdyman's friend Morgan loomed up ahead. Like Gurdyman, Morgan is a magician; a strange old man who lives mostly in a world of his own, but who is kind and gentle. I'd always rather liked him. It was a small house, low to the ground, and gave the impression that it was doing its best to look inconspicuous. Beyond the house there was a smaller building constructed on the same lines, where Morgan stored his reserve supplies. Neither house nor store showed a light, but then it was late now, and more than likely that Morgan and his young assistant – a spotty, stuttering youth with nervous yellow eyes who goes by the name of Cat – had retired for the night.

I was planning to go round the house and creep into the store. 'We'll hide in there,' I said, pointing. 'He'll never know.'

But as we drew level with the house, we saw that the door was partly open. There was a dark shape lying across the threshold, with something dumped down on top of it . . .

I thought I heard a high, eerie humming in the air. I smelt a familiar metallic smell.

With a muttered exclamation, Jack stepped over whatever lay in the doorway and pushed open the further door, into the living quarters. Soft light spilled out from the hearth. It looked as if the fire hadn't long been made up.

Two earthenware mugs stood beside the hearth, steam rising from their fragrant contents.

With huge reluctance, I looked down.

Morgan lay at my feet. Cat was splayed across his body, as if perhaps he had tried to protect him. Both were dead, their throats torn out.

The humming increased its intensity. It seemed that the air was stiff with chill.

I couldn't move. I stood sick with horror, trembling.

Then Jack took hold of my arm. 'Come inside the house,' he said firmly. He pulled me with him. 'We must check to see if anything is missing, and we must be quick.'

I had forgotten about the patrol. I looked up and saw their lights, still along the quayside. I nodded. 'Very well.' My mouth was almost too dry for speech.

Morgan kept many of his supplies inside the house, and hastily, frantically, my eyes raked along the neatly ordered shelves and worktops. Something on the broad stained workbench caught my eye: an experiment, I guessed, that Morgan had been working on. I was puzzled. Why on earth would he be doing *that*?

There was a sound from outside.

Someone – something – was out there but it wasn't the patrol. I'd only just seen the lights of their torches, back on the quayside, and they couldn't possibly have got here so quickly.

The high humming had risen to a pitch that hurt the ears. It was now accompanied by a sort of low, vibrating, drumming sound, as if the air was disturbed by huge blows struck by some unnatural, unknown means. Then, horribly, through those sounds there threaded a weird, inhuman laugh.

And instantly I remembered what old Adela had said about what Mistress Judith had done when she peered outside her house: *she laughed.*

Oh, oh, supposing it wasn't Mistress Judith who had laughed? Supposing it was the Night Wanderer? And now he was *right outside*, his evil magic affecting the very air, his terrible laughter filtering inside like a poisonous miasma?

Then, from within my satchel, I felt an answering thrumming. My fingers suddenly strong and capable, I undid the straps and reached inside. Loosened the strings that hold the soft leather bag closed, I thrust my hand within.

The shining stone was hot to my touch, and, as if it felt the vast sense of threat and was fighting back, it too was throbbing. In the blink of an eye it showed me an image – a line of symbols, swirling and twisting, out of which a word formed which seemed to say *animal*, or perhaps *anima*. There was no time to decide, for the symbols vanished. I felt the waves of power coming off the stone and into my head came the wordless, furious, urgent message: we had to get out.

It was my turn to grab Jack. I did so, my fingers closing on his upper arm like a vice. Not caring who or what heard me, I yelled, 'We must go! *Now!*'

Perhaps the shining stone was working on him, too. Perhaps it was simply that he trusted me; or, more likely, recognized desperation when he heard it. Together we leapt over Morgan and Cat – I sent them a swift message asking their forgiveness for abandoning them, and I thought I heard Morgan's gentle spirit murmur back, *Hurry! Save yourselves!* – and I made a silent promise to return when I could and see them safely into the ground in a way they would have wished.

Jack and I ran. Over the humpy, hillocky grass at first, tripping and stumbling, holding tightly to each other's hands, my free hand always on the stone, feeding from it, heartened and strengthened by it. And oh, we needed all the help it could give: something awful seemed to press down on us, and I felt that at any moment that clawed hand with its long, sharp, cruel and bloody talons would reach out for us, wind itself around my neck, take out my throat.

Aghast with dread, I sobbed as I ran.

Then grass gave way to smoother ground, and our pace became more even. Ahead were the houses that lined the road leading up to the Great Bridge from the south-east: somehow, by pure luck, we had stumbled upon the old, half-forgotten track leading from the road out to the sacred well.

There was purity and deep, ancient goodness in the very stones of that track. Had it called out to us as we fled from evil? Had the shining stone guided us? I had no idea and, as we reached the first of the houses and both saw and heard the blessed signs of human presence, I didn't care.

My hand was still clutched around the stone. It had gone still and quiet: I sensed it was telling me we were safe.

Safe, anyway, from the terror that stalked out in the fields.

Jack edged forward between two of the houses and peered out into the road. 'All clear,' he whispered. Light from a small high window fell on his face as he turned to me. He was as pale as I felt.

Treading softly, we emerged on to the road. Keeping as much as possible to the shadow of the houses, we hurried along to the Great Bridge. Looking over the parapet, we could see the lights of the patrol, at the far end of the quay. I was just thinking that they hadn't got very far when I realized that time had become confused. Only a very short time had passed since we first saw the men of the night watch.

We reached the far side of the bridge and soon, with great relief, plunged off down the alley that wound round the castle rise and led to the deserted village. It seemed to embrace us; as I'd remarked to Jack, it was a *good* place.

His house, at the far end of the lane, was like a haven. He closed and barred the door, poked up the fire, fed it with small and then larger pieces of wood, and put water on to heat. He went through into the far room and came back with a thick, warm blanket, which he wrapped round me. I hadn't realized that I was shivering so much that my teeth were rattling.

He made the drinks – hot, sweetened with honey, infinitely comforting – and we stood side by side, close to the hearth, revelling in its warmth. Then he said, 'Tomorrow at first light, I shall take you back to Aelf Fen.'

I swallowed too fast, scalding my throat. 'I'm not going.'

He looked at me, his green eyes steady. 'I believe you must.'

'I can't!' I snapped. 'I have work to do here, I have people I need to treat, I must make sure Adela is all right, I need to ensure that Morgan and Cat are buried according to their own rites, and I must look after Gurdyman's house. Or had you forgotten he's missing?'

The last bit was uncalled-for, but I was very distressed, although I hadn't worked out precisely why, and it is so often the human instinct to hit out under such circumstances.

Jack went on looking at me. 'It's not safe here,' he said.

'No, I *know* that!' I cried. 'People are scared, they're in danger, there's widespread panic looming because of the Night Wanderer, and I can help! I'm a *healer*, Jack, and it's what I do, look after people when they need it!'

He cast down his mug and took hold of me, his big hands hard on my arms. 'You're not only a healer, you're a wizard's pupil!' he yelled back. He shook me, and my teeth rattled all over again. 'In case you've forgotten, you and I just discovered the bodies of another wizard and his pupil, recently dead, bloody, and missing their throats!'

A horrible image floated before my eyes, and

I had no choice but to see it. I wanted to weep with pity, with dread, with fear. 'I don't want to leave you,' I said in a tiny voice, but I think he was so agitated that he didn't hear.

'You have to leave!' he shouted, shaking me again. 'You, more than anybody, are in danger!'

'I—'

'Don't you understand?' he yelled. 'I will *not* have you risk your life! I can't bear it!'

I stared up at him, at the naked fear in his bright eyes. The fear wasn't for himself, and suddenly I understood quite a lot of things.

I didn't know what to do. 'I can't—' I began.

He gave a sound of violent impatience, then he wrapped one strong arm around me, pulling me tightly to him. He took my jaw in his hand, turning my face up to his, and then he kissed me, long and hard, full on the mouth.

If I say it was a shock or even a surprise, I'd be lying. My passion rising as fast as his, I kissed him back. He broke off to nuzzle into my neck, under my hair, touching the skin with tender lips, then he kissed me again, his body hard against mine leaving me in no doubt of how much he wanted me. Oh, I wanted him, too, and I melded myself to him, arms round him as powerfully as his around me.

As suddenly as he had begun, he stopped.

Stepped away from me, confusion and a sort of shame in his face, hands stretched palm forward towards me as if warding me off.

'I'm sorry, sorry,' he muttered, turning away. 'I have brought you here for sanctuary, and I have violated your trust, contaminated my duty.'

I was amazed. 'No you haven't!' I said, almost laughing. 'I was kissing you back, wasn't I? I—'

But he wasn't listening. He had picked up the blanket that had fallen to the floor and was wrapping me up in it, covering my head and overshadowing my face, almost as if he was desperate to hide me from his passionate, desiring eyes. Before I could protest, he took hold of me by the shoulders, turned me round, away from him, and pushed me into the far room. 'Go to bed, Lassair,' he muttered. Then he hurried out again. I watched in amazement as he slid a bench across the opening; was he trying to keep me in, or himself out? I smiled, but only very briefly. It wasn't really funny.

I sank down on to the bed. I realized all at once that I was totally exhausted. I took off my boots and my coif and loosened my hair, already tumbled and tangled by Jack's fierce caresses. I lay down and drew up the covers.

I needed comfort. I needed him, but I knew I wasn't going to have that need answered.

I noticed that he had put my satchel in the room. I opened it and took out the shining stone, taking it out of its bag and holding it tightly, close to my heart. 'I'm sad,' I whispered to it. 'I need a friend.'

Strongly into my mind came the reply: *You have a friend.*

Was it referring to itself, I wondered, or to Jack? *And he's just out there.*

Now I really did smile. I'm sure it was only my overwrought imagination – I'd been through quite a lot, after all – but, even if it was, the remark was perfect. I turned on my side, the stone still clutched in my hands, and let myself relax into sleep.

Eleven

Rollo stood huddled in his cloak up in the bows of the small ship that was taking him across the Channel to England. Already he could see the distinctive line of high white cliffs ahead, over to the north-east. The captain said he expected to reach harbour in the late afternoon. Rollo hoped he was right. Being at sea again, even for the relatively short crossing from Dieppe to Hastings, had brought back vivid memories of *Gullinbursti*, and Rollo wasn't ready to entertain them.

He had used the time in Rouen profitably. He was too travel-worn now to mix in the circles frequented by the elite of society, and didn't have the funds to rectify that condition. So he had spent his last available coins in the taverns and the inns, loosening tongues with wine and ale and asking carefully artless questions about life under Duke Robert's rule.

In the eyes of the common man and woman, Robert Curthose had traditionally been viewed as a bit of a joke: a silly, muddle-headed boy who needed the help of older and wiser men to keep him on the path of good sense and prudence. Now, though, the joke had worn thin. Robert was weak; his barons warred among themselves with no admonishment from him; indeed, frequently he contrived some financial gain from the incessant wrangling and had been known to confiscate disputed castles and lands and then charge his vassals for their redemption.

Many, if not most, of Duke Robert's people lamented the good old days of his powerful father. Robert, soft and careless, preferred indolence to action, and all that the vigorous, able Conqueror had achieved was falling into decay and confusion. And it wasn't only the barons for whom life was difficult and the future uncertain, for the general lawlessness meant that marauding bands of brigands roamed the villages and the countryside, plundering the peasantry who had no strong system of law to defend them.

The talk in the taverns suggested that the person who Robert seemed to be expecting to come to his aid was his brother William. Which, from the point of view of Rollo and his master the king, was all to the good. Even more encouraging, perhaps, was that a duke who was not very popular, and regarded as weak and ineffectual by his people, might be the very man to be tempted by a grand, romantic, heroic, chivalric gesture such as setting off on crusade, should the call come.

And Rollo was quite sure it would.

The captain was as good as his word, and the ship docked an hour or so before sunset. Rollo was one of the first down the gangplank, and he waited while the crew brought his horse ashore. Then, with a nod of farewell, he mounted up and set off up the road to London, twenty miles or so beyond which lay Windsor.

He wasn't certain where the king was residing and he might equally well be in Gloucester, Winchester, or any of a dozen other places as at Windsor. But Windsor was nearest, and if Rollo's luck was out and the king wasn't there, then at least somebody would be able to tell him where to go.

For, although Rollo's first duty was to seek out his king and paymaster and make his long, detailed report, there was something else he had to do. As the sometimes endless-seeming journey had finally stumbled towards its conclusion, this other task had steadily grown in importance in his mind, taking over his thoughts, so that it was with a strange and untypical reluctance that he contemplated his forthcoming meeting with King William. And it was this task – second in the order of its achievement but first in Rollo's mind and heart – that made him pray as he rode that he would find the king at Windsor.

Because after he had seen the king, and the king had thought up and asked every last question concerning his spy's mission, Rollo was going to ride as swiftly as he could to the fens.

I woke to an empty house. It was very early, and the light was faint, misty and soft. As soon as I was conscious, all the events of the previous night came rushing into my mind. Fear swept through me, and I had a sudden, bitter sense of disappointment. Surely Jack had promised to keep me safe? Where was he, then? Had he set out on some important errand, leaving me alone in this empty, unpopulated place?

I must have made a sound – of distress, no doubt – because the door flew open and I saw Jack outside. He was wrapped in a heavy cloak and he had a sword in his hand. A hefty, knobbly ended staff stood against the door frame. He looked pale with cold. Feeling very guilty, I realized that, far from deserting me and leaving me to face unknown dangers alone, he'd been on guard outside.

He stared at me for a moment. Then he looked away. 'There's hot food ready.' He indicated the blackened iron pot suspended over the hearth. 'But eat quickly. We need to be on our way.'

He turned away and the door closed behind him.

Oh.

It looked, I thought as I helped myself to porridge, as if his way of dealing with what had happened late last night was to pretend it hadn't. Very well. I was prepared to accept that for now – we did, after all, have more important things on our minds – but I wasn't going to for ever.

I ate quickly, then rinsed out the pot and bowl, tidied the bed, kicked ashes on the embers of the fire, slung my satchel over my shoulder and wrapped myself up in my shawl. I went out to join Jack, saying no more than, 'I'm ready.'

He nodded. He closed and fastened the door, then led the way through the deserted village and out on to the road. There was nobody about. The track to the fens branched off on this side of the river, but we didn't take it. Instead, as we crossed the bridge, Jack said, 'We have to see Walter. I must tell him of the deaths of the magician and his pupil.'

While I was desperately eager to get away and off into the relative safety of the open countryside, all the same I was glad that those two brutalized bodies weren't just going to be left till somebody else stumbled across them. I didn't know what orders Jack would give Walter. The important thing was for the sheriff and his officers to be told, as soon as possible, that the Night Wanderer had now killed six people.

I waited outside the tavern while Jack went in. He was very quick and, shortly afterwards, we were returning across the Great Bridge and setting out on the track to the fens. It was still too early for anyone to be about, and I was all but certain nobody saw us leaving. We had gone perhaps half a mile when he turned off the track along a path running between well-tended fields, largely pasture. There was a long, low building ahead, set in two wings around a central courtyard, and several horses had put their heads out of their stalls to have a look at the newcomers.

The horse at the near end was a grey with a smooth, silky mane and intelligent dark eyes. I smiled involuntarily, for I remembered Jack's gelding Pegasus.

Jack went through the door into the room at the end of the stalls and I heard the mutter of brief conversation. Then he emerged again with saddle and bridle in his arms, and shortly after he led Pegasus out and off up the path, and I fell into step behind.

Jack stopped when we reached the road. 'You ride first,' he said, busy with the girths and not meeting my eyes, 'because I feel—'

Annoyance flared into anger, and, before giving myself time to think, I burst out, 'Oh, for heaven's sake, Jack, we can share the horse! It was just a kiss, and I enjoyed it as much as you evidently did, and I don't think for one single moment that you were abusing my trust, or assaulting me, or taking advantage of my weakness after such a fright, and I *really* wish you'd stop treating me as if you've got to maintain a distance of several feet at all times and totally avoid looking at me!'

My voice had risen to a shout, and I listened with fast-growing embarrassment to the dying echo of my words. I could feel the hot blood rise in my face.

Jack stared at me. Then his lips began to twitch, and his mouth spread in a broad smile. 'Actually,' he said mildly, 'all I was going to say was that I feel the need for some hard exercise, so I'd rather walk for a few miles.'

'Oh.'

My face felt red-hot. Without another word, I stuck my foot in the stirrup, hauled myself up on to Pegasus's back and touched my heels to his sides. Eagerly he set off, and I urged him to a brisk trot.

If Jack felt like hard exercise, he could damned well have it.

I thought that Jack would remain with me at Aelf Fen. I imagined us together in the deep rural peace of my little village, with the time to talk, to walk by the fen edge at the end of the day when work is done, to open up our diffident hearts and begin to reveal to each other how we felt.

But it was just a lovely daydream. As soon as we had reached my aunt Edild's little house, and he had seen me over the threshold and handed me, as it were, into her keeping, he gave me a long, hard look and said, 'Be on your guard, for it may be that your whereabouts can be guessed.' Then he nodded a curt farewell to Edild – who was seated by the hearth and picking over a large basket of fungi, watching us closely – and without a single word or gesture in my direction, turned and hurried back down the path.

I ran out after him. I called out, 'Jack! *Jack!*', and the hot words rushed up, fighting to be spoken. *You're leaving me here? When will you come back? Do you want me to return to you? How will I know when it's safe? How will I be sure* you *are safe?*

I said nothing. I watched him swing up into the saddle, mutter a word to Pegasus, jerk at the reins to turn the horse's handsome head, and then ride away.

I went back inside and closed the door. Edild looked at me, her face expressionless. Something in her eyes – a hint of compassion, perhaps – suggested, however, that she hadn't missed one nuance of the little scene that had just been enacted on her doorstep.

All she said was, 'Since you're here, Lassair, I would very much like some help with these mushrooms.'

The day seemed endless. In the early evening I went along to my parents' house, where my mother was busy preparing food and my father just in the act of removing his wet boots after a hard day out on the fen. They greeted me with pleased surprise. 'We weren't expecting you back so soon,' said my mother, shoving me out of the way as she reached for a string of onions.

'I'm not staying,' I replied quickly. Wasn't I? I only wished I knew.

'Oh,' my father said. Then, recovering, he added, 'Well, we'll just have to make the most of you while you are here. Stay and eat with us.'

I accepted; I'd been sure they'd suggest it, and Edild wasn't expecting me back till bedtime. I slipped into the habits of home as if I'd never been away, anticipating my mother's needs as she cooked food and set out bowls and mugs, murmuring responses to her flow of comments about the rest of the family, all the time looking out for the small, bright-eyed shade of my Granny Cordeilla, hovering in the corner where her little cot used to stand. She's been dead these two years, but she's still watching over us. Sometimes I hear her voice. I treasure those moments.

My younger brother Squeak came bursting in, arriving as usual just as the food was being put on the board, and accompanied by the youngest child of the family, little Leir. Not so little now, I thought, for at six years old, he was leaving plumpness behind and growing straight and tall.

It seems always to be the way of family members returning to the fold that after one or two cursory enquiries as to what you've been doing, everyone rapidly loses interest and reverts to talking about their own concerns. Thus it is with my kin, too, and, after a few moments of hot resentment that nobody seemed very interested in my life in the city, I sat back and let my sore soul be bathed by the comfortable familiarity of home.

I didn't, of course, say a word about the Night Wanderer.

When we had finished the food and talk was giving way to yawns, I stood up and announced I'd better be going back to Edild's house. As he always does, my father got up to escort me. Sometimes I protest that there is no need, although this is always to spare him if he's looking tired, for those all too short walks through the night-quiet village are pretty much the only moments that I get my beloved father to myself, and they are very, very precious.

Tonight I didn't even think of trying to deter him.

We walked quite slowly, arm in arm. He said quietly, 'Is everything all right, child?'

'Yes!' I said, far too quickly.

Apart from my anxieties about Jack and my deep fear at the presence of a killer on the loose in Cambridge, there was something else that stood between my father and me. Although he had no idea what it was, I knew that he sensed it. I was very afraid that he felt I had distanced myself from him, and it broke my heart.

I had found out something about his past. I knew that his father was not who he believed him to be: the quiet, unassuming man who had been married to my Granny Cordeilla and fathered her other children. My paternal grandfather was an Icelander known as the Silver Dragon, and his real name was Thorfinn.

When last I had seen my grandfather, I had yelled at him that it was neither right nor fair not to reveal the truth to my father. I longed to tell him myself, but it wasn't my secret. I loved my father profoundly, no matter whose son he was, but I hated having to hide from him something so vital.

I squeezed his hand, leaning close against him. 'I love you, Father,' I whispered.

He chuckled. 'I know that, child,' he said. 'What's brought this on?'

I hesitated. 'Oh – just that I wouldn't want you to feel that I don't think about you, and miss you, when I'm away,' I said eventually. 'I – I worry sometimes that perhaps you think I'm growing away from you' – I fought back the tears that threatened – 'and I want you to know that could never be true.'

It was his turn for a thoughtful pause. Then he said, 'Lassair, you're a young woman now, hard-working, learning a good occupation, and it's true that at times recently I've sensed a withdrawal in you.'

'I don't—' I began hotly.

But he hushed me. 'It's only natural, my dear heart, for you to make your own way in the world, and I would never stand in your way.' He paused. 'Just as long as you remember to come back now and again,' he finished.

I nodded, unable for a moment to speak. So he *had* sensed something. I very nearly blurted it out, there and then, never mind whose secret it was.

But then, loud and clear inside my head, I heard Granny Cordeilla say, *Not yet, child.*

I held my peace. *Not yet*, she'd said. Oh, but that was encouraging: it sounded as if the time might be near when the pain of keeping quiet would be over. *Very well*, I said to her. *But make it soon!*

My father and I walked on. Just as we reached the end of the path up to Edild's house, I stopped, reached up to kiss him and said, 'I'll always come back.'

I stood in the doorway and watched him stride away. While I was happy that we'd spoken words of such care and love to each other, all the same I was still cross with my grandfather, and with everyone and everything to do with the secret I had unwittingly discovered and had to keep.

And unfortunately one of the people involved in that suppression of the truth was sitting by the hearth beside my aunt.

'What are *you* doing here?' I said rudely to Hrype. Edild frowned at me, but I didn't feel like apologizing. 'I'm very tired,' I went on, 'it's been a long day, and I want to go to bed.'

That was even ruder, since I could hardly hope to roll out my bed and slide into it with Hrype sitting by the hearth. Now Edild did speak: eyes sparkling her anger, she said, 'Hrype is here at my invitation, Lassair, and you will show courtesy to my guest.'

I very nearly yelled at her. I almost shouted, *He's not a* guest, *he's your lover, and don't pretend otherwise when you're fully aware I know!*

170

But I have too much respect for her. I bowed my head, stomped through to the little storeroom and muttered, 'I'll finish sorting those mushrooms. Let me know when he's gone.'

I closed the door behind me, leaning against it and broiling with anger. Too much had happened; I just wanted to close my eyes and try to shut it all out.

After a while, I heard a soft tap. 'It's me,' said Hrype's voice. 'I want to talk to you.'

'Well, *I* don't want to talk to *you*.'

There was a short silence. Then he pushed the door open and came into the storeroom. He shut it again, and we stood looking at each other.

'Where's Gurdyman?' I demanded in a hiss.

He raised his eyebrows in surprise. 'Gurdyman? I have no idea.'

'He's not at his house,' I said, still keeping my voice low. 'He disappeared two days ago.'

Hrype looked at me. 'And why should you imagine I know where he is?'

'I *know* you were there in his house because I found the message you left for me.' I took the rune stone out from the purse at my belt and held it out to him.

Briefly he glanced at it, in the palm of my hand with my fingers curved around it. There was a sort of lurch in the air: I knew, without understanding how I knew, that he burned to touch it, to take it from me.

He managed to control himself. He raised his eyes to mine and gave a shrug. 'It's just a stone,' he said dismissively.

He was so convincing that I very nearly believed

171

him. Was I wrong? Was it just a stray piece of green stone with a strange gold mark that had lain there beneath the floorboard in the attic room for many, many years?

But I caught him looking back at the rune stone. Just for the blink of an eye, the naked desire was clear in his face.

'Take it.' I gave it to him. 'If you persist in pretending you don't recognize it, then have it anyway. It's sufficiently like your own jade rune stones to act as a replacement if you ever lose one.'

His hand closed on the stone. 'Thank you,' he said very softly.

And I wondered why I was being so hard on him. He had left the rune stone for me to find, and we both knew it. For reasons of his own, he was now denying it, but it had been a kindly gesture. Following that awful night when Jack and I witnessed the murder of the young priest and then I discovered Gurdyman had gone, subsequently finding Hrype's stone was the only thing that comforted me, making me believe, as it did, that Gurdyman hadn't been spirited away by some brutal, vicious murderer but was safe with Hrype.

'Thank *you*,' I replied. I managed a smile. I indicated the rune stone. 'It achieved its purpose.'

He turned away. 'You can go to bed now,' he said as he went back into the main room. 'I'm leaving.'

I gave him and my aunt a few private moments to say goodnight, then, when I heard the door close after him, went in to Edild. With barely a word to each other, we made our preparations for the night and settled down.

As I lay in the darkness, watching the last embers of the fire, I thought back over my exchange with Hrype. I had very much wanted to tell him that I *saw* him down in the crypt, with Gurdyman and that shadowy third figure, in that strange flash of vision. But something had held me back.

Hrype was keeping secrets from me; that was perfectly obvious. He *did* know where Gurdyman was, and I was sure of it. He'd probably taken him away to whatever safe refuge he now inhabited, possibly with that third person, who was perhaps a friend to one or the other of them. So why had he chosen not to tell me? Surely he knew I was trustworthy; he must be aware of how fond I was of Gurdyman; how close to him.

There was a reason, and it was staring me in the face. I didn't want to acknowledge it, but I realized I must: Hrype didn't tell me where Gurdyman was in hiding not because he didn't trust me but because he didn't trust Jack.

I turned on my side, away from the swiftly dying light. I was unhappy and anxious about far too many things, and the best thing, it seemed, was to try to sleep and hope the outlook would appear rosier in the morning.

Twelve

The house was isolated. It stood on a small area of ground that was very nearly an island; joined to the shore by a mere neck of land some two or three paces wide – in places less – and perhaps twenty long. At times of even modest high water, the patch of ground became a true island. Then it was only reachable by boat. Not that its sole habitual inhabitant would use a boat – nor even possessed one – for solitude was the desired state.

The house was a simple dwelling, with walls of wattle and daub and a roof of reed thatch. It had one main room for eating and sleeping, and, separate from it but linked by a covered way, a second, larger workroom out of which led a tidily arranged store whose shelves and hiding places were crammed tight with a variety of materials. A wooden workbench stretched the length of the room, its surface scarred with scratches, pale rings where wet or hot vessels had been carelessly put down, and rather a lot of dark and sinister burns. It had been wise to set the workroom away from the house, for quite often the fierce and uncontrollable demons of fire raged there.

Outside there was a privy. No pump, well or trough, for the house stood so close to the water that there was no need. Trees grew profusely, in a thick canopy comprised of alder, willow and one or two oaks, beneath which grew the all but impenetrable carr of bushes and smaller trees. The marsh fern, rare in its ability to flourish beneath the thick carr, was now turning from bright green to rusty brown as the advance of autumn forced its life force to retreat into itself.

The dense vegetation stood as a frowning, over-shadowing barrier. Accordingly, the fen water appeared almost black.

Hrype approached the narrow causeway just as the first pale streaks of light appeared beneath the skirts of cloud on the eastern horizon. He had left Aelf Fen in the middle of the night, slipping out of his bed without disturbing Froya or Sibert, with whom he shared the house, and he had been walking for several hours. He paused, feeling the usual strange reluctance to put his feet on to the narrow, perilous path. *Do not be foolish*, he upbraided himself. *There is no danger here, only wonder.* In addition it was, he reflected, as safe a sanctuary as he could think of.

He strode up the causeway. The stump of his feet must have sent vibrations deep through the earth and into the water, and some night creature, swirling and thrashing in protest, briefly broke the surface with a loud splash. Hrype jumped, then smiled at this demonstration of nervousness. It was indeed a strange place . . .

A faint light showed along the crack between the top of the door and its frame. Hrype tapped softly, and, when a voice within instantly answered, pushed the door open and went in.

'You were expecting me,' he said to the rotund

figure sitting huddled in a brilliantly coloured shawl beside the hearth.

'Indeed I was,' agreed Gurdyman. 'Here, warm yourself.' He handed Hrype a pewter mug filled with hot spiced ale. Hrype accepted it gratefully and drank deeply.

'Aaah,' he said after a moment, settling beside Gurdyman, 'he still brews a tasty drop.'

Gurdyman smiled but did not speak.

Hrype looked around. 'Where is he?'

Gurdyman jerked his head in the direction of the low door at the back of the room and the passage to the workroom beyond. 'Out there working. Where else?'

Hrype nodded. He let his eyes roam around the room. It was pin-neat and clean, with bedding rolled up and stowed in a corner, a scrubbed board on which stood one or two bowls, a third pewter mug and some rush lamps, a jar of tallow and a bunch of spills tied up with string set ready beside them. A woven basket full of precisely cut firewood stood beside the hearth. The earth floor was strewn with rushes, clean-smelling and obviously quite fresh.

Above the door leading to the workroom had been pinned a piece of parchment. On it was a drawing, and, narrowing his eyes, Hrype stared at it. It depicted a winged figure, a sword in the right hand, one side clad in knee-length tunic and hose, the other in a flowing skirt. The figure had two heads, crowned with a single crown. The feet in their mismatched shoes stood upon the back of a winged dragon with claw-like feet; the dragon, too, had two heads.

Gurdyman had noticed the direction of his glance. He studied Hrype without speaking. 'He still devotes himself to the same perplexing study?' Hrype asked.

'*Perplexing* does not begin to describe it,' Gurdyman said with a sigh. 'He is wearing himself out. He breaks the bright flame of his intellect against it like a wave on a rock, over and over again, yet makes no impression.'

'He will yield before the rock does,' Hrype said very softly.

Gurdyman nodded. 'Yes, indeed. That is what I, too, fear.'

There was quite a long silence.

Gurdyman stirred. 'But I have not asked you if she is safe!' he exclaimed.

'Of course she is,' Hrype replied with a smile. 'As you very well knew, since I'd have told you the moment I arrived had it been otherwise.'

'The Norman lawman escorted her to the village?'

'Yes.' Hrype paused. 'His feelings for her go deep, although I sense that, as yet, she is not sure of hers for him.'

Gurdyman thought about that. 'He does not remain at Aelf Fen?'

'No. The present emergency' – Hrype smiled wryly at the understatement – 'has no doubt summoned him back to Cambridge.'

'Have there been more deaths?' Gurdyman's voice was barely above a whisper.

'I don't know,' Hrype admitted. 'I fear there will have been, but I did not wish to display my interest by asking Lassair.'

'Quite right,' Gurdyman said. Then, hesitantly, 'Did she ask about me?'

'Naturally she did,' Hrype replied. 'She is very fond of you.'

'But you didn't tell her where I am?'

'No. I disclaimed all knowledge of your whereabouts, as you and I agreed.' He turned to look at Gurdyman. 'She knows, though, of my involvement.'

'Hardly surprising, since you insisted on leaving one of your precious rune stones exactly where she'd be sure to find it,' Gurdyman said somewhat caustically.

Hrype made a sound of impatience. 'As I just said, she's very fond of you. Did you really want her to worry herself to desperation in case you'd been spirited away by the Night Wanderer and left throatless in some hidden alleyway? She *had* to know you were safe, and leaving her my token was all I could think of to reassure her.'

His voice had risen. It was rare for him to show his feelings. Gurdyman smiled. 'You have more heart than you pretend,' he murmured. 'In truth, Hrype, one might even imagine you cared for the girl.'

Hrype made no reply but a wordless 'Hrumph!'

Gurdyman reached for the jug of ale and refilled their mugs. 'I would guess,' he said presently, 'that she imagines your refusal to divulge my hiding place is because you, and perhaps I, do not trust Jack Chevestrier.'

'Do you trust him?' Hrype demanded.

'I do. As Lassair would realize, if she turned her mind back. I told her quite recently that he was decent and honest; hardly words I would have employed to describe a man I did not trust.' He lapsed into a thoughtful silence. 'She may well work it out for herself, in which case she will understand that, although it is not Jack, there is indeed someone that I' – he glanced at Hrype – 'or, rather, *we* do not trust.'

'She's capable of that realization, I suppose,' Hrype said grudgingly.

Gurdyman studied him, eyes narrowed. 'Despite what I just said, you do persist in acting as if she is a splinter beneath your skin,' he remarked.

Hrype chose to ignore that. 'You still believe that you are correct in your suspicions?' he asked.

'The man is very obviously up to something,' Gurdyman replied, 'and I am informed that he has a newly full purse. Fuller, even, than normal, and the word is that he plans a costly extension to his already commodious dwelling.'

'Mere gossip?' Hrype suggested.

'He also has a fine new horse.'

Hrype put down his mug on one of the hearth stones, the sudden sound ringing out in the quiet. 'It is slim evidence on which to link a man's name with such terrible crimes,' he muttered.

'Yes,' Gurdyman agreed, sighing. 'We are not, I fear, either at a resolution or an end to these horrors.'

With a groan and a wince, he got himself laboriously to his feet and, crossing to the far corner of the room, took out two bedrolls. 'Let us sleep for what remains of the night,' he said, handing one to Hrype. 'In the morning, we will extract Mercure from his workroom and make him talk to us.'

179

Hrype snorted. 'If luck and the gods are on our side.'

The two men lay down. The fire bathed them in warmth and soft light, and quite soon both were asleep.

I woke in the morning in my accustomed place beside my aunt's hearth. Edild was already up and I could hear her in the little back room where, from the sound of it, she was busy washing pots and potion bottles.

I thought about the day – days – ahead. I would have to help her in the healing work, and, although I didn't mind, and in fact usually enjoyed the variety and the challenge very much, just now I knew my heart wasn't going to be in it. Jack had brought me to Aelf Fen for my own good, because he was sure I wasn't safe in Cambridge with a killer on the loose; moreover, a killer who lately seemed to have targeted people engaged in the same sort of activities as those I was engaged upon with Gurdyman. He, indeed, had already fled, and so I couldn't argue with the fact that it made total sense for me to have done too.

But I didn't want to be safe in Aelf Fen. I wanted to be in Cambridge, with Jack.

The morning progressed as countless others have done in my village, and as no doubt countless more will do in years to come. Edild and I saw a steady stream of patients requiring our help, the majority of whom were showing early signs of the usual phlegmy noses, sore throats and aching, inflamed joints and chesty coughs that always crop up in the fens when the weather loses its summer heat and the damp creeps out of the marshes to wind into bones and soft tissue. I threw myself into the work. If I couldn't be where I wanted to be, I thought, at least I could let others benefit by my presence. Once or twice I caught Edild's eyes on me, assessing, judging and, today, with the faintest hint of admiration. Or so I told myself.

Luck had ridden with Rollo, for, just as he had hoped and prayed, King William was in residence in his castle at Windsor. He was to depart imminently for Gloucester: had Rollo delayed by even a day or two, he would have had to follow his king westwards before he was free to go where his heart commanded.

He had sent word in to the king that he was there in the little settlement that huddled around the great castle and humbly begged audience. He knew he would have to wait, for nobody wrote directly to a king – certainly, no one of Rollo's lowly status – and his carefully worded, blandsounding missive would have to work its way up past many other pairs of eyes and many astute brains before it reached the king's. But in fact a message came back very quickly, summoning Rollo to the king's presence that morning.

Now Rollo stood in a corner of the dirty and crowded lodgings which were all he could afford, shaving and washing and, as best he could, banging from his garments the dust, dirt and assorted vermin of long travel. It was ironic, he mused, to have to go through the frustrating

181

channels of bureaucracy in order to gain the king's ear, since, when he finally did get to speak to William, the king would undoubtedly demand in a bark why he hadn't got there sooner.

Rollo was in no doubt that the king would be more interested in what Rollo had to say than anything else he would hear that day; perhaps that whole week. He had journeyed too far, and at too high a personal cost, to have the time or the patience for false modesty.

His preparations finished, he ran a hand over his hair (still slightly damp) and his jaw (not bad for a shave with a blunt razor and cold water). He looked down at himself. At least, he observed with a grim smile, his boots shone from the buffing he'd given them. Then, filled with a nervous excitement to be at last at the very end of his long mission, he set out for the castle.

The king's father had built it and it stood high on its hill above a bend in the River Thames. The Conqueror knew very well how to seek out and utilize a good defensive position, and, in addition, the site was close to a little village that had once been part of a royal Saxon hunting ground. The sport, they said, was still first rate. Not that sport had been on the Conqueror's mind when he built the castle, for he was newly come to his kingdom in England and his prime concern was to defend what he had grabbed. Windsor Castle was one of nine, built in a ring around London and all within a day's march of the capital. It had been constructed as a motte and bailey, with three wards surrounding a central mound. At the top of the well-protected timber keep, provision had been included for the king's private apartments.

Rollo approached the outer defensive wall, a soaring structure of timber palings sharpened to points at their tips. Guards had seen him coming and were already moving out of the guard house to block the narrow, gated entrance. Rollo produced his summons, the king's seal prominently displayed, and with a jerk of the head the officer in charge let him through. He sensed someone fall into step behind him as he crossed the inner ward. The gate guards were going to keep an eye on him until they handed responsibility to the next men in the chain.

Rollo glanced around. There were sounds of labour – the clear ring of a hammer on metal; the loud, shouted command of an overseer – and he saw that parts of the wooden structures were being replaced by stone. He began to climb the motte, was admitted through another palisade that ringed its base a little way up – here the guard tailing him was quietly replaced by another – and then he was inside the big square central tower.

William's apartments, Rollo thought as he was ushered through a studded wooden door into the king's private chambers, typified the man. While they had clearly been designed for practicality and the basic needs of a man engaged in a brutal process of conquest, that man's son had other ideas. The second William might be as ruthless as his formidable father on campaign, contenting himself with simplicity in the interests of speed and efficiency, but in his own quarters, it soon became evident, he liked a little luxury. He also,

Rollo couldn't help but notice, liked the company of a band of young men, dressed in the height of fashion and smelling strongly of something vaguely flowery. Five of these were lounging in the anteroom to the king's own chamber, and one muttered a remark which provoked gales of lusty laughter. *He lacks the presence of a queen consort*, Rollo thought, responding to the further jibes of the youths with a coolly polite bow.

Then abruptly the inner door was flung open and William stood there. His long robe was open at the throat, displaying a fresh white undershirt and quite a lot of gingery-fair chest hair, and his face was ruddy, as if he had recently been scrubbing it. 'Come in, then!' he said impatiently. Rollo hastened to obey and William slammed the heavy door in the avid faces of the courtiers. He muttered something that sounded like 'Parasites!'

Rollo waited in the middle of the large room. A wooden-framed bed stood in the corner and several chests of clothing were placed around the walls. A small altar had been set up in a recess. There was thick dust on both the altar and the brass crucifix set upon it.

'Sit,' William said, waving a hand at a leather-seated chair beside the hearth. Rollo sat, and William pulled up his own chair close beside him. 'So,' he went on, 'will there be an appeal from the east?'

Rollo hadn't expected any courteous civilities: *How was your journey?*, *Good to see you safely returned* and *Are you well rested?* were not phrases a king used to his spy; or, anyway, this king didn't. He was far too impatient. Knowing his master as he believed he did, Rollo had come prepared. Now, he launched into a swift and efficient distillation of all that he had learned in the Holy Land and in Constantinople, concluding with his own opinion: that Alexius Comnenus would have no choice but to ask the west for help, and that the request would not be long in coming.

What he believed would happen if the kings and the lords of north-west Europe answered the appeal, Rollo didn't say. He had had a vision: a dreadful, haunting image of long, straggling lines of ordinary people, tired, hungry, diseased, far from home, dying. Far from the well-drilled, expensively accoutred and ultimately victorious army that others might predict, Rollo believed he had received a clear warning that the truth would be very different.

But since he wasn't going to be among the rabble and nor was his king and master, there was no need to mention that fact.

When at last he had finished speaking, William sat for a long time in silence, his elbow on the beautifully carved arm of his chair and his chin in his hand. 'Robert will go,' he muttered, more to himself than to Rollo. 'He won't be able to resist. He'll want to go in style, too, with a hundred matched horses, richly coloured silks and the loud bray of trumpets to announce his coming.' He tapped the fingers of his other hand on the chair. Short, stubby fingers, Rollo observed, with tufts of hair on the backs, and not made more elegant at all by the costly rings that adorned them. If anything, the opposite was true.

Quite unexpectedly, Rollo felt a sudden stab of compassion for his tubby, determined, capable and clever king.

'Enough!' William barked suddenly. Rollo jumped guiltily back into the present moment. It surely wasn't done to feel pity for a king, and it was always dangerous to daydream in his presence. But then he realized that William's exclamation must refer to whatever thoughts were going through his own head, not Rollo's.

'Pour wine for us,' William commanded, pointing to the beautiful glass jug and the two fine goblets set on a board beside the bed. Rollo leapt up, poured the rich red wine, and returned to his seat.

'You have done well, Rollo Guiscard,' the king said, raising his glass in Rollo's direction.

'Thank you, my lord king.'

William went on staring at him, the eyes with their bright flecks intent. 'You have earned your reward, and you shall have it.' He reached down to the small wooden chest, bound with iron, beside his chair, turned the key in the lock and threw back the lid. Inside were many leather bags of varying sizes, and the king extracted one, handing it to Rollo.

It took all his strength not to pull open the drawstrings and look inside.

William sat back and sipped his wine, a broad smile on his face. 'You trust your king to pay you well, then?' he said.

Rollo bowed. It was, he sensed, a moment for honesty. 'Indeed I do, my lord.'

'You do my bidding precisely to the letter,' said

186

the king, 'and you are utterly reliable. Both qualities, believe me, are rare and to be valued.'

Rollo bowed again. He wasn't sure if he should speak; he opted for silence. It was certainly not, he thought with a private smile, the moment to mention his visit to Normandy . . .

'What shall you do now?' William asked.

Deciding it was mere politeness, perhaps a way of easing towards a conclusion to the meeting, Rollo chose levity. 'I shall find a bathhouse, a barber and a purveyor of fine woollen garments, my lord.'

The king laughed. He rose to his feet, and instantly Rollo did the same. 'Enjoy them!' he exclaimed. 'You have earned some pleasure.'

Bowing deeply, Rollo edged towards the door. Just as he was about to open it, King William said, 'Do not venture too far, Rollo Guiscard.'

Thirteen

I spent two more days at Aelf Fen.

They were uneasy days. Apart from the fact that I longed to be back in Cambridge – despite the reassurances from Hrype, I was still anxious about Gurdyman and, most pressingly, very worried about Jack – I couldn't help feeling uneasy. I tried to reassure myself: I was in my own home village, where I knew every inhabitant, every house, every hiding place and winding track through the waters.

But I couldn't convince myself. Even though I couldn't see them, I was still utterly certain somebody was watching me.

I'd had an identical sensation not many weeks back, when Jack and I were in the fenlands together, and I wondered if the same eyes were on me now. Was Jack also absent from the town – not with me, but on some private errand of his own – and was Gaspard Picot spying on me because he thought I'd lead him to Jack?

I was horribly afraid it was so. Rather than go on suffering in doubt, however, I decided to try to find out.

In the late afternoon of the second day I slipped out of Edild's house, the shining stone in my satchel, and took a path leading to the fen edge. I followed it down to one of my favourite places, opposite which is the little island where many of my forebears, including my Granny Cordeilla, lie buried. I wasn't planning to cross over to the island this time, for the day had turned cold and I didn't welcome the idea of getting wet to the waist. Instead, I sat down cross-legged, face to the island, and got out the stone. I laid it in my lap, on the fabric of my gown stretched between my knees, and, my hands placed lightly on either side, stared down into it.

I felt the instant when it became aware of me and responded. Felt and saw it: there was a very faint sort of thrumming in the rapidly warming stone in my hands and a flash of brilliant green from its dark depths. Very softly I said, 'Greetings.'

Straight away an image appeared: I saw eyes, shaded under a hood, staring at me out of the shadows. It might have been because the fear of someone watching me was uppermost in my mind; the stone could simply have been reflecting my own concerns back at me. I'd all but convinced myself that was so when I saw something else.

Fear raced through me. For now there was a second watcher, and if the motives of the first were unclear, there was no doubt at all that this one had nothing but malice – evil – in mind.

I quelled my fear as best I could and strove for the sort of neutral state of mind that is best for staring into the shining stone. As my anxiety subsided, I realized that my first panicky impressions were right. One set of eyes looked at me with love: *It's Jack*, I thought with a surge of joy, *and he's come back secretly to make sure I am safe.* I felt a warm happiness spread through me, and the stone too felt suddenly hotter.

But then I saw the other eyes, and I cried aloud.

They were hostile: whatever Gaspard Picot wanted with me, he didn't mean me any good. His face was in shadow and I could barely make out any details. He was deliberately keeping well hidden. He had no way of knowing I had suspected he was near, nor, of course, that I had a powerful ally in the shining stone. Well, forewarned was forearmed, and I would—

But then all thoughts of Gaspard Picot were driven out of my head.

The images came swiftly, one after another, flash, flash, flash. I saw again those terrible corpses, their throats torn out: Robert Powl; poor, pretty little Gerda; Mistress Judith; the young priest I'd seen die with my own eyes; Morgan and Cat.

The vision-sight seemed to linger on Morgan. Something strange was happening, and it felt as if my mind was unable to interpret what I saw. Morgan was dressed in his usual dark robe, high-fitting at the neck until the killer had torn it away to get at his throat. He was Morgan, his sad old face showing still the shocked expression of brutal death. But then he wasn't quite Morgan: he was subtly altered. The slash in his robe was now extending, right down to the waist and beyond, and I saw . . .

'*No!*' I shut my eyes tightly. I didn't want to see what the shining stone seemed to want to show me. Morgan's body had been decently clad when I saw him in death, and I didn't want to see what lay beneath his garments. Death robs men and women of so much, and I surely owed it to Morgan not to look.

The shining stone went cold.

Just like that, in an instant.

It was icy in my hands, and, wincing, hastily I wrapped it in its sheep's wool and replaced it in the leather pouch, putting it in my satchel and fastening the strap.

Shaken, I stood up and hurried back to the village and the safety – or so I fervently hoped – of Edild's house.

I said nothing to my aunt about what had happened. As we sat beside the hearth with our bowls of savoury gruel that evening, however, I think she was aware something was amiss. Well, I'd have been surprised if she hadn't been, for she is an astute and sensitive woman and knows me well.

I cleared away and washed our supper crocks and was just stacking our bowls in their accustomed place ready for the morning when we heard running footsteps on the path outside. A moment later, there came a frantic banging on the door and my elder brother Haward's voice cried out, 'Edild! Lassair! You must come at once, Squeak and Leir have been attacked!'

My aunt and I grabbed our satchels and she flung open the door. Haward looked awful: wide-eyed with shock, hair on end, face flushed and sweaty from exertion. 'Come *on*!' he yelled.

We gathered up our skirts and flew down the path behind him.

As we ran, I tried to go over in my mind what sort of injury my brothers might have sustained. Squeak, fourteen years old, worked with my father with the eels; out in all weathers, often up to his neck in water, vulnerable to all the unseen obstacles that lay half-buried in the dark mud. And eels have teeth . . . But no, I told myself, the eels were largely dormant now, retreating down into the black fen depths to see out the winter before spring, and the longer, lighter days, called them up again.

And what hurt could have come to Leir? He was still a little boy, for all he yearned to work beside Squeak and my father at a man's job. But Leir was Squeak's shadow: everybody knew that, and the village smiled indulgently at the sight of the small figure trotting along behind the boy on the cusp of manhood, trying in vain to make his short legs match his elder brother's long strides.

My mind and my heart full of my brothers, I realized how much I loved them. Fear for them put new life in me and, outpacing even Haward, I was the first to reach my parents' house.

The door opened as I approached, and my father looked out. 'Do not worry,' he said calmly, 'neither of them is going to die.'

I threw my arms round him in a brief, tight hug. Then he released me and gently pushed me inside. Haward and Edild came in behind me, and Edild and I knelt down beside the grouped figures by the hearth.

My mother held Leir in her arms, cradling him to her broad comfortable bosom as if he was a baby again. He, too, had set aside all aspirations to be older than his years. His thumb had crept into his mouth, and he was twiddling a stray strand of my mother's long fair hair between the fingers of his free hand. His eyes, wide and intensely blue, were red-rimmed from weeping and his nose was running.

Squeak lay flat on his back. The lacings of his tunic were open, revealing a long cut all the way from the top of his shoulder to his breast, where it stopped just above his heart. It was pouring blood. Edild gave a short exclamation, reaching in her satchel for a pad of clean linen, which she folded and pressed hard against the wound. It would need stitching, I thought. That was going to hurt.

Save for Edild's quiet words of command to me, and my occasional replies, there was silence in the room. My aunt and I had performed these tasks so often together: the wash with hot water and lavender, the careful checking of the cut for dirt, grit, and other minute objects whose presence would interfere with healing and perhaps set off infection, and then the closing of the wound. Edild's needle was very sharp and her hands were deft and swift, but nevertheless Squeak had to bite his lips raw to stop himself crying out, and the poor boy was only partially successful.

Eventually, though, it was done. Edild washed the blood off her hands and packed away her equipment, while I put a fresh pad on my brother's chest and bandaged it carefully in place. 'Will it leave a scar?' Squeak asked hopefully, with a flash of his old spirit.

'Oh, dear Lord, yes!' I assured him. 'You're marked for life, little brother. The girls will flock from miles around to see.'

He smiled in satisfaction.

But not for long, for, now that his injury had

been treated and the immediate emergency was past, it was time for the questions. My father fixed Squeak with a steady look and said, 'Now, son, what happened?'

I could see what an ordeal it was going to be for Squeak to relate his story. He looked, if anything, even more fearful than when Edild had hovered over him with needle and stitching gut. But he pulled himself together, brave boy that he was.

'You'd left me to watch that little tributary at the far end of the main stream,' he reminded our father, 'in case there were any signs that the eels that live there were still active. I didn't spot anything, and after a bit Leir came to find me and said it was time to go home, so we set off. It was getting dark, and we had quite a long way to go, so we were jogging along and chatting and laughing and then suddenly—' Abruptly he stopped, and his already ashen face grew paler.

'What happened?' my father prompted gently. For all that he spoke quietly, I could see the furious tension building up in his big, strong body. Somebody had attacked his child. In my father's philosophy, that could have only one response.

Squeak swallowed. I saw the developing Adam's apple bob in his thin throat. 'Someone came out of the shadowy gulley beside the stream,' he whispered. 'He – it jumped out at us.' He shuddered. 'It was *huge*.'

'Go on,' my father said tonelessly.

'It was dressed in a dark cloak, or something, with a deep hood that was drawn right forward, and all I could make out was dark, deep, staring eyes.' He shuddered again. 'It had something in its hand, something that glinted sort of silvery. It was sharp-pronged, like a gleeve.'

I pictured the eel-catcher's tool: the trident-shaped gleeve with its deadly, sharpened points.

There was a pop as Leir took his thumb out of his mouth. 'It wasn't a gleeve,' he piped up.

'I didn't say it *was* a gleeve, I just said it had pointy ends *like* a gleeve,' Squeak snapped, with the abrupt, furious anger of someone who had just been very badly scared and was trying to hide it. Leir's bottom lip wobbled and tears came into his eyes. My mother, anxiety all over her face, silently wrapped her arms more tightly around him. He put his thumb back in his mouth and leaned against her.

Squeak muttered, 'It was a weapon of some sort, anyway.'

Leir, apparently restored a little by his mother's big, warm presence, removed his thumb again and, aware of our eyes on him and looking slightly ashamed, hid it behind him. 'It wasn't a weapon at all,' he said in a quiet, firm tone that carried far more weight than a screech or a yell. 'I know because I had a good look while it was – while it was doing what it did to Squeak.' He hesitated, then, finding his courage, said, 'It was actually part of its arm. Like a claw.'

It felt as if a cold hand had clutched my heart.

'He – it – the figure spoke,' Squeak said. He stared up at his father, as if drawing strength from the steady gaze.

'Go on, son,' my father said calmly.

'It said – it demanded—'

'It wanted to know where the girl was,' Leir interrupted, 'and when we said we didn't know what it was after and who did it mean because there were lots of girls, it sort of *spat* and said it was hunting for the girl who works for the magician, and that's you, isn't it, Lassair?' He looked at me, and I had to force myself to meet his innocent gaze. 'You work for that man with the funny name when you're in Cambridge, don't you?'

'Yes,' I whispered.

My father asked the question I didn't dare voice. 'Did you tell him where she was?'

'We said we had no idea what he was talking about, then I wriggled out of his grasp and we fled,' Squeak said, pride in his voice. 'Did we tell him, indeed! Of *course* we didn't!' he added scornfully. Then he, too, looked at me. 'She's our sister.'

I felt like weeping.

I don't think any of us slept very well that night. We left Haward, his wife Zarina and their little boy bedded down in my parents' house, where Zarina said she felt safer. My father wanted Edild and me to stay too, but Edild said she must get back and I went with her. I'd half-expected Hrype to be there; it would have been just like him to have picked up out of the air that something bad had happened and turn up at Edild's house to protect her. But he didn't.

Edild barred the door with a bolt of wood and we both went to bed with big sticks beside us.

In the long hours of the night I thought over all that had happened, and I quickly concluded that

196

remaining at Aelf Fen would do more harm than good. The Night Wanderer seemed to know I was there; or, at least, I guessed he did. Anyway he clearly knew I was somewhere in the vicinity. My presence in the village was only going to bring peril to my family. Squeak had already been injured, and both he and Leir had been scared out of their wits.

I kept seeing the heart-turning sight of my smallest brother, trying to be brave as he cast his mind back to abject terror. No six-year-old should have to deal with that. Life was tough enough without sinister ghouls looming up out of the darkness with weapons for hands.

I would have to fight against my united family, however, if I insisted on returning to Cambridge. I had an idea about that, but it wasn't much of a one, and even thinking about it made me uneasy. I resolved to sleep on it – if indeed I could sleep – and look at the problem again in the morning.

The morning, however, brought problems of its own. Edild and I went back immediately we'd eaten to check on Squeak, and to our dismay there were signs of infection in the wound.

I tried not to think where else that savage claw-hand had been, and what filth it bore on its talons.

Edild bathed the cut thoroughly, pouring undiluted lavender oil into it, and then she covered it all along its length with a thick paste of chamomile and marsh mallow. Both of these are reliable vulneraries that we use to counter inflammation and promote healthy healing. I was distressed to observe that Squeak was feverish, muttering in his sleep. I realized now, when he could no longer mask his true feelings with a display of bravado, just how frightened he had been and I was filled with protective fury. Someone had hurt my brother and I wanted to kill them.

Edild did not seem too concerned about Squeak, however; when I asked her once too often if he was going to be all right, she turned on me and snapped, '*Yes*, Lassair, as far as what skills I have and my long experience tell me, and if you want a better answer, go and ask your shining stone.'

I didn't pester her any more after that.

But I had now made up my mind what to do and how to do it. Early the next day, when my family and most of the village would be busy setting off for work, either out on the marshes or up in the fields, or else deeply involved in their own homes, I would take my chance. I would tell Edild I was going to fetch more mushrooms, and slip out of the house with my satchel and my shawl. Then I would set off as fast as I could for Cambridge, and pray that I'd reach the town by nightfall. I knew full well that Cambridge was no sanctuary: far from it, for it was in the vicinity of the town that all the murders had been committed. But I reasoned that it had the big advantage over Aelf Fen of being full of people, many of them well-armed lawmen and one of those lawmen Jack Chevestrier.

The Night Wanderer was coming to Aelf Fen, and it appeared that he was looking for me. For everyone's sake, including mine, it made sense for me not to be there when he arrived.

Fourteen

I woke some time in the night, worrying about the finer details of my plan, none of which I had considered in the bright and optimistic light of day. Foremost among them was concern for my family, who when I disappeared without trace might very well imagine that the fearsome, malign figure who had tried to make Squeak and Leir tell him – it – where I was had succeeded in finding me and had spirited me away to some terrible fate. And that concern, in the misery of the sleepless pre-dawn darkness, led directly to another: what if I did as I had resolved to do and walked straight into the arms of the Night Wanderer?

I will not do that, I vowed with silent vehemence. The Night Wanderer believed I was hiding out in the fens. The best thing to do would be return to Cambridge, because that was the one place he wouldn't look for me.

So said my logic.

I returned to the huge and worrying problem of my beloved father and the rest of my family imagining me dead in a monster's clutches, and how I could convince them I wasn't. In the end I came up with an answer, of sorts, although it wasn't all that more satisfactory than my reasons for persuading myself I was safer running back to Cambridge than staying in the village. Recognizing that it was the best I was going to do, I forced myself to relax and eventually fell into a deep sleep.

Edild had to shake me awake. Horrified that I'd slept right on past the time when I should have been making my escape, I shot out of bed and, dizzy from the sudden movement, would have fallen had she not grabbed my arm.

'Steady,' she said. 'No need to hurry so. It is not late.'

I took some steadying breaths and set about my simple morning routine, trying to impose on myself an air of calm. It wasn't easy, when a voice was yelling in my head, *Hurry up! Hurry up!*

I wandered through into the little storeroom and said, trying to sound nonchalant, 'We worked through all those mushrooms yesterday, so I'll go and fetch more. There's a good patch up near the old oak tree.'

'Yes, do,' Edild replied. 'All the time this mild weather encourages them to grow, we should take advantage of it.'

Shortly afterwards, feeling very guilty about having deceived my aunt, I left the house. I put the mushroom basket down behind the privy. There was no point in burdening myself with it, and Edild would need it.

I flew up the low rise behind Edild's house and emerged on the higher ground. There were quite a few people about, making their way to wherever their day's work summoned them, and one or two nodded a greeting. I walked along for a few paces behind a trio of raucous lads heading for the large area of strips on the upland, then quietly stepped off the path and under the spreading branches of the ancient oak tree that stands behind the village like a lone sentinel, dwarfing the few other trees nearby.

It was as good a place as any from which to observe my friend Sibert's house, and I only hoped I wasn't too late.

After only a short time, I saw him come out. He called something to someone still inside – his mother, Froya, no doubt – and then he set off up towards the higher ground. Almost as if he knew I was there, he strode right up to the oak tree.

I called out softly as he drew level. 'Sibert! May I speak to you?'

He stopped dead. 'Lassair?'

I emerged from behind the tree's massive trunk. 'Yes. Good morning.'

'I heard you were back,' he said, smiling. 'I was going to come and see you, but I heard about your brother getting hurt and thought maybe you wouldn't want visitors.'

'It's always nice to see you,' I said truthfully. Once I'd believed myself in love with Sibert, but I'd been quite young. Since then we had shared a lot together, and I look upon him as a true friend.

'Where are you going?' he asked. 'I'm heading that way.' He indicated. 'Shall we walk together?'

'No,' I said. Too dismissively; his face fell. 'Sorry, but I'm not staying in the village.' Very quickly I explained about how whoever had attacked Squeak was looking for me and how, fearing that my continued presence would bring more danger to my kin, I was heading back to Cambridge.

Sibert looked at me for a long moment. 'I understand your reasoning,' he said eventually,

201

'but, honestly, Lassair, it's a bit daft to leave a village full of family and friends who'd all protect you and scurry off on your own, isn't it?'

He was absolutely right, but I didn't want to acknowledge it. 'I'll be quite safe,' I said hurriedly, 'because the Night – the person looking for me thinks I'm in the village.' Sibert's mouth opened to interrupt but I didn't let him. 'And once I get to Cambridge,' I went on, raising my voice to drown his, 'I'll be safer than anywhere else, because I'll go straight to Jack Chevestrier.'

Sibert's expression changed. Something left it – something quite vulnerable – and his features stiffened into formality. He turned away. 'You must do as you see fit,' he said distantly.

'Will you do something for me?' I asked timidly.

He spun round to me again. 'What?' He sounded cagey.

'My family will worry about me and—'

'You mean you haven't told them of this hare-brained scheme you've come up with?'

'Of course not, they'd stop me.'

Slowly he nodded. 'Indeed they would. I imagine,' he went on, 'you want me to wait till later, when you're well away from here, and then, just when they all start to panic because you're nowhere to be found, calmly explain where you've gone, and why, and that I knew all about it yet didn't try to stop you.'

When he put it like that, I could readily see his objections. '*Please*, Sibert!' I said in a sort of suppressed shout. 'I *have* to go, but it'll make everything so much more horrible if they think I'm – er, if they start imagining the worst!'

He looked at me, and I wasn't sure I could read his expression. 'Can't I come with you?' he asked. 'I could look after you till you get to the town.'

'No,' I said firmly. I reached out and took his hand. 'Don't think I'm not grateful for the offer, but I'm quicker on my own.' I was also quieter and a lot less noticeable, having taught myself long ago to move through the landscape of my native fens soundlessly and all but invisibly. Once off the main tracks – I had planned in my head the route I would follow – it would take a better man than the Night Wanderer to find me.

Or so I hoped.

Sibert went on holding my hand. 'I'll tell them. Good luck.' Then he leaned forward to put a kiss on my cheek, dropped my hand and strode away.

I watched him till he was just one more figure among many. It was only then that I remembered I'd meant to ask if he had any news of Hrype; if, indeed, Hrype was in the village.

Too late now.

My journey went more smoothly than I'd dared hope. Almost as if invisible hands guided me, I seemed to know instinctively which paths to take, which short cuts would work, and even, at times, where a hidden causeway just under the surface of the water would take me safely across an inlet and cut off a good couple of miles.

The last one was a skill I'd used before. It was good to know it hadn't deserted me.

My luck held even after I'd emerged from the fens and was heading off down the road into Cambridge. A very fat woman driving a rather insubstantial little cart was going my way and she offered me a lift. I accepted gratefully, although I felt sorry for the poor horse having to pull the extra burden, and as we trotted briskly along, the fat woman told me she was on her way to town to stay with her daughter, who had just given birth to her first child, taking a cartload of good fresh milk, cream and cheese, a newly baked loaf, some apples just off the tree and a side of bacon. She clearly believed you only got wholesome food in the countryside.

'Your daughter will be glad of your support,' I said when I could get a word in edgeways.

'Aye, that she will,' the fat woman agreed. We were close to the town now and an aggressive glint came into her kindly eyes. Reaching down beneath the narrow little bench on which we sat, she brandished a huge club with several nails sticking out of the thick end. 'And just let this here Night Wanderer come anywhere near my new grandson, and he'll regret it!'

He does not fear you or your club, I thought, although I didn't know where the thought came from; I didn't believe it originated with me.

A deep shudder of fear ran through me. *You didn't have to come back here*, I told myself bluntly. *You have come running back to this town full of dread, and must face the consequences.*

Hurriedly changing the subject – just then I couldn't bear to think about what I'd done, how foolhardy and reckless I'd been – I asked the fat woman what the new baby was to be called.

* * *

204

I went first to Gurdyman's house. It looked just the same and at first I didn't think anybody had been there; certainly, there was nobody at home now. I emerged from the crypt and walked slowly along the passage. Just as I went out into the little inner court, warm with the afternoon sun, something prompted me to look into the shining stone. I sat down in Gurdyman's chair, took the stone out and gazed into it.

But it seemed only to want to show me things I already knew about, mostly concerning the journey I'd just made. I saw myself under the oak tree looking at Sibert's retreating form, and then I was out on the fens, making my sure-footed way over small hillocks sticking up out of the dark water. I was wondering whether this was the stone's way of boosting my self-confidence when all at once I felt a wave of love. Then, fleetingly, I was standing at a greater distance from the image of myself in the stone than I had been, as if I had been transported into the mind of someone else looking at me. That person, whoever he was – I was almost sure it wasn't a woman – loved me. There could be no doubt of that.

As suddenly as I'd flown to that other view-point, looking back at myself, I was returned to me watching me. It's hard to explain how I knew – the shining stone is full of mysteries, and this, it seems, is one of them. I wrapped the stone and put it away. I knew why it had wanted me to look into it; it wanted to reassure me that I'd been right to believe I'd be in no danger on my journey, because someone had been guarding me. Perhaps, I mused, sitting there in the warmth and letting my mind drift, this was another instance of the stone wanting to boost my confidence in my own abilities; to reinforce, yet again, the old message that my human mentors also kept repeating: listen to your instincts, and the more you act upon them, the more reliable they will become.

My instincts were telling me the identity of the loving eyes that had watched over my journey, and I was full of happiness to think I would soon be with him.

Sooner than I thought: I heard the door to the alleyway creak open, footsteps came hurriedly along the passage and Jack stood there, drawn sword in his right hand and knife in his left.

He looked at me in amazement. '*You!*' He lowered his weapons, putting the sword in its scabbard and the knife through his belt.

'Er – yes,' I agreed. Why was he so surprised? He'd been tailing me all the way from Aelf Fen, so wouldn't he know I was in Gurdyman's house?

The shock in his face was rapidly replaced by a smile. 'I'm very glad to see you, Lassair, but what are you doing here?'

'Well, I just thought I'd check to see if Gurdyman had come back,' I said tentatively.

He shook his head. 'I didn't mean here in this house. I meant here in Cambridge.'

My confusion increased. For the second time that day I explained about the assault on Squeak, my certainty that the Night Wanderer was the assailant, and my fears for my family. 'But I was right, wasn't I?' I could hear the pleading in my voice. 'There was no danger on the journey, as

I was sure there wouldn't be if I was careful and took those little-travelled tracks.'

Now it was Jack who was confused. 'Is that what you did? It was a wise precaution, but I still think it was rash.'

Is that what you did? I heard the words again inside my head. He had no idea what route I'd taken from Aelf Fen to the town; had had no idea I was even here, until he'd walked in on me just now.

'What are you doing here?' I asked, far too brusquely; he could not have guessed why I was upset.

'I've been checking on this house ever since you left,' he replied. 'When you came in just now you left the door ajar – anyone could have followed you in – and I came to see who had broken in.' Then, his expression changing, 'Lassair, what's wrong? Why are you angry?'

I shook my head. It was so stupid. But then, he was owed an explanation. 'I thought you were following me,' I admitted. 'I imagined you'd decided to watch over me and make sure I came to no harm.' *Because that's what the stone just told me*, I could have added.

Or, at least, I'd thought it had . . .

He came swiftly over to me, crouching down beside Gurdyman's chair. 'Of course I would have done, had I known you were making the journey,' he said with quiet force. 'But I wouldn't have hidden from you. I'd have wanted to enjoy the walk with you, not spend it watching from the shadows.'

It was so exactly the way I, too, would say

he'd have acted that I knew he was telling the truth. 'Thank you,' I muttered.

He stood up. 'Although I wish you were miles away, I really am pleased to see you,' he said, 'because there are many things I want to discuss with you.' *Oh*, I thought, disappointment flowing through me. *Not because of the pleasure of my company then, or because you really, really want to kiss me again.* 'We'll go back to my house,' he was saying, already walking off along the passage, 'and I'll prepare food for us. You must be ravenous.'

We took our usual roundabout route back to the deserted village. I was eager to see what the mood in the town was, whether fear and mistrust had increased, what people were thinking and feeling, but we saw barely a soul. *The town is dying*, I thought. It was dramatic, but I was very afraid it was true.

Walking along behind Jack, I wondered who, if not him, had been my loving benefactor that day. Almost straight away I had the answer: Sibert. My dear friend, worried for me, anxious that I was going into danger and unable to persuade me otherwise, had risked the wrath of the overseer and followed me all the way across the fens till I was picked up by the fat woman in the cart. How lucky I was in my friends, I reflected. I just hoped he hadn't got into too much trouble for missing a day's work.

The geese set up their usual alarm as Jack and I approached his house, and Jack quickly hushed them. They still, it seemed, took exception to my presence. We went into the house and he kicked up the fire. He put a stout bar across the door. Then he melted lard in a skillet and fried bacon and onions, throwing in roughly cut slices of bread to soak up the fats, and the simple food was some of the most delicious I'd ever tasted. The little room had quickly become warm and cosy, and, with food in my belly, I was starting to feel drowsy.

But when we had finished and were sitting side by side by the hearth, mugs of light ale in our hands, he said, 'I need to tell you what's been happening while you were away. I've been doing a lot of thinking and I want to share my tentative conclusions with you, only you won't follow them unless you know all that I know.'

'Very well,' I said. I gave myself an imaginary nudge in the ribs. *Wake up and listen!*

'I'm still being kept well away from Gaspard Picot's investigation,' Jack said matter-of-factly, 'and he's now threatened the men he suspects of keeping me informed with dismissal and worse if they persist.'

'So you've been working alone?'

Jack smiled. 'Not entirely. Walter and his lads are just being a lot more careful.'

While it was heartening to think that the men's loyalty to Jack outweighed their fear of retribution, nevertheless I felt anxious for them. 'I hope so,' I muttered.

There was a short pause. Then Jack said very quietly, 'Lassair, many of us in this town heartily dislike the fact that our sheriff is a corrupt and self-serving man. Now that his nephew holds almost as much power – and he, if anything, is even worse – there's a growing movement for change. I don't have to cajole and bribe Walter and the others to work with me.'

I thought about it. 'But you have charisma,' I said slowly. 'You're someone people are willing to put their faith in, and that carries a heavy responsibility.'

He didn't answer. I turned to look at him, and saw the awed expression on his face. *He doesn't realize*, I thought.

'If that is really so,' he said eventually, 'I shall have to make quite sure I don't let them down.' He topped up our mugs, then, in a different tone, said, 'Now, this is what I've been thinking. There are two crimes being carried out: the murders and the thefts.' He was talking quickly now, the words tumbling out, and I listened intently. 'The murder victims are Robert Powl, Gerda, Mistress Judith, the young priest, Morgan and Cat. Each was killed in the same way, and surely by the same hand.'

Not a hand, a claw, I thought. I saw again that horrible wound on my brother Squeak's shoulder and chest, and sent out a quick prayer that he was truly on the mend.

'Now, the thefts,' Jack continued. 'Something was taken from the locked stone vault in the barn beside Robert Powl's house; something that we have to conclude was very precious, either in monetary terms or in some other way, first, because he went to the expense of making a secure place in which to lock it up, and second, because whoever stole it went to great lengths to get at it.'

'The thief knew it was there,' I put in.

'Yes, good,' Jack said. 'Knew, or perhaps, well aware of Robert Powl's habits, guessed.'

'His warehouse was searched,' I said. 'Everything had been turned upside-down.'

'Yes,' Jack said again, 'and we concluded that something had been taken, although we couldn't say what. Mistress Judith's storeroom had also been searched, and you concluded from a consideration of what ought to have been there that some cinnabar was missing.'

'I only thought it was something she'd probably have,' I protested. 'I don't think we should see too much significance in its not being there.'

'Very well,' Jack conceded. 'So, of our six victims, two we know to have been robbed, or at least to have had their premises searched.' He paused, a thoughtful frown on his face. 'We come again to poor little Gerda,' he said. 'I went back to Margery's the day before yesterday to talk to the girls again, specifically to ask if Gerda's room had been searched and if anything was missing, but I think we can discount robbery in her case. For one thing, she didn't own much more than the clothes she stood up in, a change of personal linen and a little silver chain with a pendant, and, although it was missing when she was found, nobody thought it was worth very much, if anything. One of the girls – Madselin – said it looked old and was worn very thin. For another thing, she didn't have a room of her own but simply a bed in a dormitory with the others, and, since the dormitory is very rarely empty, it would have been almost impossible for anyone to go in and search it without someone noticing. And, again, why would anyone bother when Gerda didn't have anything to steal?'

Poor Gerda. It didn't seem to have been much of a life, yet the women I'd spoken to all said she was a happy, cheerful little thing, affectionate and kind, her sweet nature unaffected by the life that circumstances had forced her to lead. She hadn't been local, and what family she had seemed to have abandoned her.

I said suddenly, 'What was the pendant?'

'Hmm?'

'What was it? A cross? A medallion?'

'I don't know,' Jack admitted. 'Margery didn't say. Do you think it's important?'

Yes I do, I wanted to say, *because the question just popped out of my mouth without my having thought about it, as if someone – some*thing *– else wanted to know the answer.*

But I didn't know Jack well enough to tell him about the strange forces that increasingly seemed to be lined up on my side; forces which, I strongly suspected, originated from the shining stone.

'I think it would be interesting to find out,' I said carefully.

'Then we will,' Jack said. 'We should also discover if the dwellings of our other three victims were also searched, and if anything was taken. We must visit Morgan's house, and also the young priest's room.'

'But I thought your friend Walter already checked the priest's cell? He said it was as if nobody lived there, and there was just a bed and a cross on the wall.'

'Yes, quite right,' Jack agreed. 'Do you recall what else he and Ginger found out?'

'Yes.' I concentrated, bringing the details to

212

mind. 'His name was Osmund, he wasn't local, he hadn't been in the town long, and he was hard-working and kept himself to himself. He was frequently late for the offices but being quite harshly punished for it didn't make him improve. He was known to go down to the river, and I can't remember if anybody found out what for or why, although it seems to be a question begging for an answer.'

'It was Ginger who found out about the connection with the river,' Jack said, 'and he too thought it ought to be followed up. He spoke again to his young cleric, who admitted that he hadn't followed Osmund very far, only to where the path goes down towards the river, but he was able to say which direction Osmund took. Ginger and I went out last night to see what we could discover, but we didn't see anything out of the ordinary. Osmund can't have gone far, because his friend said he was back in time for the evening office and for once he wasn't late, so his purpose in going to the river remains unclear.'

'Was the place he went near to Robert Powl's house?'

'No, not very.'

'Or Margery's establishment?' Young clerics were, I was sure, visited with the same temptations as other men.

Jack grinned. 'No.'

'Maybe he went to meet someone. Or perhaps he finds the smooth flow of the water soothing.' I clenched my fists in exasperation. '*I* don't know!'

'It's flimsy, I agree,' Jack said. 'Which is why

Ginger and I also made a surreptitious visit to the priests' house and had a good look round Osmund's cell.'

'Oh, well done! And what did you discover?'

'Not much,' Jack admitted, 'for it was as sparse and tidy as Walter said. But we found this.' He reached inside the purse at his belt and held up a big iron key.

'That looks very like a door key!' I exclaimed. 'Do we conclude, then, that he had another room somewhere?'

'It appears that he did, but so far I have no idea where it is.'

But from somewhere deep in my mind a memory surfaced, and I thought perhaps I knew. I saw a dark passage between two big buildings, and at the end a low door. 'Robert Powl's warehouse,' I said.

Jack frowned. 'But we looked there. It wasn't locked, if you remember.'

I shook my head. 'I don't mean the main building. There was an alleyway going along between Robert Powl's warehouse and the next one, with a door at the far end. I thought the door must be the way into the neighbouring building, since access to Robert Powl's was through the open area facing the quayside, and why would you need another entrance?'

'Unless it was to a separate part of the warehouse,' Jack said slowly.

'One that had to be kept locked,' I added eagerly, 'and whose key was found in the possession of a secretive and reclusive young priest who's just been murdered.'

Fifteen

Jack stood. He looked down at me expectantly.

'What?' I demanded.

'We should get going!' he said, in a tone that suggested it should have been obvious.

I had a feeling I knew the answer to the next question, but I asked it anyway. 'And just where are we going?'

He had put out a hand and was hauling me to my feet. 'It's not that late and the quayside may well still be quite busy, so we'll leave seeing if you're right about this' – he held up the key – ''till last. First, we'll head out across the fields and see what we can discover in Morgan's house.'

There were still signs of activity up at the castle, so Jack led us out of the deserted workmens' village via a different path; one that passed a row of one-room wattle-and-daub dwellings quietly sinking back into the earth, their poor-quality thatch in tatters and many of the roof supports missing. Good timber isn't that easy to come by in the fens, and people in need are always ready to help themselves.

We went round the eastern side of the priory, emerging on to the road just before the Great Bridge. We waited in the shadows while a patrol came across, presumably heading back to the castle. The guards' muttering voices sounded unnaturally subdued: this was a town under the influence of evil, and people – even well-armed guards marching in a phalanx of a dozen – were jumping at their own shadows.

When the guards had gone, Jack and I sprinted across the bridge and past the quay, running on down the road until we could branch off across the fields. Now, at last, we were out of the danger of being spotted by Sheriff Picot's patrols, and we ought to have felt a release of anxiety. But we were hurrying towards another, far worse peril, for ahead of us was the sacred well, and close beside it the house where the two latest victims of the Night Wanderer had been slain.

I wished, as my frightened thoughts circled round and round in my head, that I could say the last victims, but I was almost sure there would be more . . .

Presently Morgan's house materialized before us. It was a clear night, with enough moon to give good light, and a soft mist was rising up out of the grass, so that the low, humpy shape of the little dwelling seemed almost to be floating. The door still stood open, but no bodies now lay across the threshold.

Impulsively I said in a furious whisper, 'They might have shut the door!'

Jack didn't answer, save by a brief, companionable hand on my shoulder.

We went into the house. It was cold, dark and it felt *very* empty. Only now that Morgan's gentle spirit was no longer there did I realize how much it had permeated and warmed the house he had lived in for so long. The hearth still held blackened fragments of wood; the last relics of the final fire. The comings and goings of the law officers who had attended Morgan's and Cat's deaths had trampled ash and embers all over the floor, so I fetched a broom and swept up.

Jack lit a lamp and, wandering round the four walls, said, 'Did it look much the same before?'

There was no need to say before what.

I looked up from my sweeping. 'Yes, as far as I recall. Morgan and Cat were tidy, and they really didn't use the house for much other than eating and sleeping, and Morgan didn't sleep a lot.' He'd had that in common with Gurdyman: two aged magicians, ancient in years and steeped in wisdom and long experience, who, perhaps sensing that the time remaining to them was all too short, elected not to waste it in sleep.

Amid my deep sorrow at the way Morgan's life had ended I felt a sudden pang of longing for Gurdyman. Missing him, worrying about him, I realized I loved the old man.

'I don't think there's anything helpful for us here,' Jack said eventually. He put some crocks straight on a board set back against the rear wall, tied up a roll of bedding that was spreading across the floor, then turned to me. 'You've done a good job.' He smiled.

I felt embarrassed that he should comment on my sentimental act. 'I – er, I just thought it wasn't right to leave it all disturbed and dirty,' I said.

Jack looked steadily at me. 'No need to explain,' he said softly. 'Haven't I just been doing the same?'

I ducked my head down, replaced the broom

in its corner and led the way out of the house, across the narrow yard and into Morgan's workroom. We stepped inside and Jack lit more candles from the lamp's flame. The room burst into light, and we stood and stared.

I felt instantly at home. Not because I'd been here before – I don't think I'd done more than poke my head round the door to call out a greeting – but because it was so incredibly familiar: so like Gurdyman's crypt. The space was quite different, for Gurdyman worked in a stone-walled cellar deep beneath the ground, its roof held up by stout pillars, and Morgan's workroom was really a rural barn. But the contents looked to be interchangeable: a long, scarred wooden bench; a stand of irregularly spaced shelves on which a jumble of bottles, jars, pots, bowls and cups jostled for position; a shady corner storage space with an array of mysteriously coloured liquids in glass bottles. And, of course, the peculiar assortment of experimental equipment that people like Morgan and Gurdyman use in their work: retorts, alembics, gourds and pelicans, and on the floor in a corner the peculiar little furnace called an athanor that is used when a steady heat has to be maintained for long periods.

Turning slowly, my eyes going all round the room, I was now facing the door by which we'd just entered. Above it hung a heavy golden chain, the bright metal of its links catching the bright light of the candle flames. It was the Aurea Catena; the symbol of the passage of knowledge, always and only by word of mouth, from master to pupil; from adept to adept. And that knowledge must never, ever, be written down, for it is secret.

Gurdyman had a similar length of chain. I was his pupil, his adept, just as poor Cat had been Morgan's. I could have wept for all of us.

Jack seemed to pick up my sorrow. 'Will you check to see if anything has been taken?' he asked. 'I'm sorry to ask,' he added quickly. 'I can tell this is hard for you.'

Surreptitiously I dried my eyes. 'They were different, and people regarded them with suspicion, but Morgan was kind and gentle, and Cat was so shy and awkward, and he'd found a safe haven with Morgan and was happy, as far as you could tell,' I said. 'For two such harmless souls to be killed as they were is just . . . just so *wrong*.'

Jack came over and put his arms round me, and I was grateful for his solidity and warmth. 'I know,' he said softly. 'And all we can do to try to put things right is find out who killed them and bring him to justice.' He paused. 'It's not really enough, is it?'

I shook my head. For a moment I buried my face against his chest and then, drawing strength from him, stood up and moved away. 'Come on,' I said decisively. 'Hold up the lamp, and I'll start on the shelves.'

I looked at every item. There was no cinnabar. Also, the small hidden space which Jack located at the base of one wall, just above the floor, had been emptied. What had Morgan kept in there? Had it been the same precious stuff that Robert Powl had secreted away in his stone vault?

I slumped down on a bench. Oh, how I needed

Gurdyman just then. As I tore my mind apart trying to think what possible use anyone could have for a lot of cinnabar, what a magician would store in a secret hiding place and was so precious that a thief would kill for it, and what connected the two, my head began to ache and my vision blurred.

Jack, watching me closely, said suddenly, 'We must go.'

I jerked my head up and looked at him. 'Why?' Terror clutching at my heart, I whispered, 'Is someone coming?'

I'd been so preoccupied with trying to work out an impossible puzzle that I hadn't been paying enough attention to my surroundings. Even now, was a soft-footed, cloaked figure with holes for eyes in a dead-white face creeping up on us? Would we—

But, 'No,' said Jack with a rueful smile. 'We're safe, but it's time you stopped torturing yourself. You've gone quite pale.'

I stood up, stumbled, and he took my hand. We left the workroom – in truth, I didn't need to stay any longer, for I had found out all I was going to from Morgan's special place – and, checking that both its door and the door to the house were firmly closed, we set out across the misty fields and back to the town.

We managed to negotiate the quayside path without anyone seeing us. At one point we were startled by a sudden eruption of drunken shouting from one of the taverns further along the track, and we slipped quickly into the deep shadow of

one of the tall warehouses. But whatever disturbance had broken out was soon quashed, and
silence fell down again.

We reached the narrow passage between Robert
Powl's building and its neighbour. Jack took the
key out of his pouch. We had brought Morgan's
lamp with us – I was sure he wouldn't mind –
and now, as we reached the far end of the tunnel-
like entrance, Jack relit it, shading with his hand
all but the smallest ray of light. It was enough
to allow him to put the key in the keyhole. To
the surprise of neither of us, it fitted and turned
the lock.

We stepped inside, and Jack closed and fastened
the door. Then he held up the lamp.

If, as we believed, the young priest Osmund
had rented this place from Robert Powl for some
private purpose of his own that had to be kept
secret from his fellow clerics, it was now pretty
clear – to me, anyway – what that purpose was.
Here were the same items we had just been
contemplating in Morgan's workroom. Here was
the athanor, with some substance in a blackened
copper pot sitting on top of it. There was the
store of powders, liquids, pastes and everything
in between; there was the brightly coloured array
of metal samples.

Osmund, it seemed, had also been an artist. Rolls
of parchment were scattered all over the long
wooden bench, covered with the most neat and
even handwriting and illustrated with beautiful
little images, brilliantly coloured: I saw a glowing
patch of lapis, a quick flash of gold. And on the
wall behind the workbench there were a couple

of larger paintings, perhaps two hands' lengths by three. One depicted the head and shoulders of a man, with a younger woman standing beside and just behind him; both leaned out towards the viewer, their faces intent and serious, and each had a forefinger to their lips in the universal *hush!* gesture implying secrecy. The other painting was strange: it too depicted a man and a woman, but they were somehow fused together, the right side of him joined to the left side of her, he dressed in tunic and hose, she in a long flowing robe. Beneath their feet was a two-headed dragon and on their joined heads was a crown.

I didn't speak. I wasn't sure I *could* have done. I stepped forward, looking down at the bench. A small purse sat at one end, the sort that is made of a circle of leather with a cord threaded around the circumference, so that the cord can be drawn up to enclose whatever is inside. I untied the cord and opened the circle of leather out, spreading it flat.

The lamp light caught a brilliant glint of green: Osmund the shy, secretive young priest had somehow managed to get hold of a small purseful of emeralds.

I picked one up. Held it to the flame. The brilliance increased, sending out a flash that made me blink with sudden, momentary blindness.

'Are they real?' Jack breathed from right beside me.

I was peering closely at the stone in my hand. I put it down and picked up another. Then another, till I had examined all seven. Then I said, 'I believe they are.'

'How can you tell?'

I'd seen fake stones; Gurdyman had instructed me in how to tell them from the real thing, as in our work there was no virtue whatsoever in anything unless it truly was what it purported to be. 'They have inclusions,' I said. 'Marks, flaws, cracks, tiny patches of cloudiness. It's impossible to fake those, and so you have to be suspicious of a perfect stone.'

Jack sank down on to the three-legged stool beside the workbench. 'Do you think these are what were stolen from Robert Powl's stone vault?'

'I don't know,' I said. 'Not these very ones, I'd have thought, though, since it would be a bit foolish to steal from the man from whom you rented your premises and then bring the booty right there under his roof and next to his own warehouse. But these are worth a great deal of money.' I picked them up again, one by one, stunned by their beauty. 'If you had gone to the trouble of constructing a secure vault, I should imagine these are exactly the sort of things you'd want to put in it.'

Reluctantly I put the emeralds back in the purse and drew up the strings. With their radiant light hidden once more, the room seemed suddenly dull. I moved over to look at whatever had been going on in the copper pot on top of the little furnace. It held a dark mix that was slightly sticky in texture – I wasn't silly enough to touch it with my finger but poked it with a glass rod lying on the bench – and, when I bent over to sniff it, it smelt somehow exotic.

I spun round, my eyes searching along the

223

shelves. At the far end of one I found a quantity of cinnabar.

I said softly, 'Nobody knew he rented this room. Whoever has been doing the stealing and the – the killing' – it was even more awful to think about it here – 'it doesn't look as if they found out about this place. They didn't uncover *that* secret.'

I stared down at the emeralds. I was just beginning to work out what had been going on here. Again, and even more intensely, I missed Gurdyman; I needed him, needed his wisdom, his ability to put awesome and potentially terrifying things in proportion. I didn't think I could manage this – what I knew, the task that somehow I was going to have to do – without him.

I straightened the copper pot on top of the athanor and wiped my hands on my skirt. I turned to face Jack. 'There are some things I have to tell you,' I said, 'but I don't think I'd better do so here.' *It doesn't feel safe*, I could have added. This was the place where Osmund had worked so hard, pushed on deeper and deeper into mystery, disobeying his superiors and enduring harsh punishment because the force that was driving him on would not relent.

Whatever Osmund had released was still there. I could sense it, and the hairs on my head felt as if they were crawling with alien life. And that wasn't the only danger: someone had known what he was doing and, to stop him, they had struck him down in his own church, with no regard for the sanctity of either the place or for the precious spark of Osmund's life.

No; Jack and I were better far away from here.

I put my silent pleading for understanding into my eyes, and Jack picked it up. 'Very well,' he said coolly. He looked both apprehensive and just a little resentful. 'We'll lock up here and go back to the house.'

He reached out to pick up the emeralds, no doubt thinking that they'd be safer in his keeping than left here, where anybody breaking in would see them. But I cried, '*No!* Leave them!'

He looked questioningly at me – something else I'd have to explain – but did as I asked.

He locked the door again and tucked the key away. Then he strode off up the little passage and I hastened to follow.

I wished that the walk back to the deserted village, and Jack's house, was twice or three times longer than it was. I knew I had to talk to him. However it had come about, he and I were working together now, and it would be neither right nor fair to keep back things that were at the heart of what was happening.

Had the secrets been mine, I believe I would not have hesitated to share them with Jack. I knew by then that I could trust him; that he was a good man. Moreover, had he been in possession of all the information he ought to have been, his clever, agile, lawman's mind would undoubtedly have begun instantly to see links and hints that I'd missed. He knew so much more about the town, its inhabitants and how the place operated than I did, and, who knew, he might have been able to go straight to the murderer – the

Night Wanderer – and apprehend him that very night.

But they weren't my secrets.

I hadn't actually been sworn not to divulge what I was only just beginning to glimpse behind the veil. I knew, thought, as I knew my own name, that these deep matters were not for sharing. My problem, then, was that, knowing it was my absolute duty to help Jack discover what was really happening here and bring it to an end, I was bound by another, equally profound honour, not to reveal any more than was strictly necessary.

If only we were walking back to Aelf Fen, and I had most of the night to decide what to say . . .

We didn't pass a soul on the way home. We heard shouts and a brief clash of metal in the distance – perhaps one of the patrols was encouraging some unruly citizens back to their beds – but the town seemed otherwise deserted, and a deep silence hung over the village. Not even a rat stirred in the ditches.

It was a relief to get inside and watch Jack bar the door. Even as he turned to poke life into the fire, feeding it with small kindling and then larger logs, I was framing my opening words. He put water on to heat and sat down. I crouched beside him.

Then, without giving myself any time for second thoughts, I said, 'You remember Lord Gilbert?'

Jack looked surprised, as well he might. 'The lord of your manor. Yes, of course. Fat and rather lazy, with a clever wife.'

I smiled briefly. That pretty much summed up Lord Gilbert. 'I can, of course, only be here in Cambridge with his permission, and he's given it because he believes what I'm learning with Gurdyman will make me a more useful inhabitant of Aelf Fen. Isolated villages like ours need a good healer, and, while my aunt Edild is an excellent teacher, Lord Gilbert has been convinced that Gurdyman's breadth of knowledge is wider, and he likes the idea of his village healer having wisdom above the usual run.' I paused, thinking very hard. 'Gurdyman is a well-travelled man,' I went on, carefully weighing my words, 'and, in his youth, he travelled in a land called Al-Andalus, which I think is in Moorish Spain, where he encountered the wise Arabs who were the inheritors of all the wisdom of the Greeks and the Persians, and so he knows all manner of things that nobody else does, at least, nobody in England.' Gurdyman had told me this with such conviction that I believed him. 'One of his main interests is medicine, and he's taught me enough already that I can see how incredibly advanced Arab doctors are in their knowledge compared to us in the Christian north, and—' *Careful*, I warned myself. 'Anyway, I'm just telling you this so you'll realize that Lord Gilbert's not being misled, and I really am learning a great deal of the healer's art from Gurdyman.' I paused, feeling rather as if I was about to dive into deep water. 'But—'

'But that's not all he's teaching you,' Jack said quietly.

I felt myself blush. 'What do you mean?' I

hadn't meant to sound so accusatory, but I was on the defensive.

Jack sighed. He stoked the fire, checked on the water, then said, 'Lassair, your Gurdyman is a very private person, discreet, subtle and quite clever enough to perceive that if the inhabitants of this town knew what he really was they'd flush him out like a rat from a sewer and drive him far away.'

'*He's not!*' Stupidly I denied the accusation before Jack had made it. 'He's *good*, and no threat to anybody! He's quite harmless, and – and—'

Harmless? Even I baulked at that.

Into the abrupt silence Jack said calmly, 'He may well be good but he certainly isn't harmless. The fact that he doesn't do harm isn't because he can't but because he doesn't choose to, which emphasizes his goodness.'

Jack waited for me to comment, but I couldn't speak.

'Now I have been quietly studying Gurdyman,' he went on after a while. 'Not that it's easy, for he is a recluse and extremely careful who he chooses for friends. But I keep my eyes and ears open and I've spent a lot of time with you—' I must have made some faint sound of protest, for he said swiftly, 'Oh, don't worry, you have been very discreet and barely said a word about him, but you can't help what you are, and you reveal all the time that someone other than your village aunt has been teaching you.'

'Edild is a fine woman!' I protested. 'She's—'

But Jack held up a hand. 'I *know*, Lassair. I'm

228

not demeaning her, I'm merely stating that your mind has been opened and developed far beyond the range of anything she, or anybody else come to that, could do.' Reluctantly I turned to look at him. 'Gurdyman is extraordinary,' he said gently. 'You cannot know how much I envy you, being his adept.'

I felt as if my heart had stopped. Then it gave a powerful, almost painful lurch. I whispered, 'You know, don't you?'

He gave me a very sweet smile. 'Of course I know.'

It was as if a careful, secure construct that I'd built around myself had come tumbling down. I'd imagined, in my fond arrogance, that the land into which Gurdyman was leading me – that fascinating, wonderful, dangerous, mysterious, magical and frequently terrifying land – was like a foreign country which, when I left it and returned to the everyday world and the doltish, blinkered people who inhabited it, left no sign on me to show I'd ever been away. I'd thought myself so special, hugging my growing store of arcane knowledge and, yes, my increasing array of skills, believing everyone I encountered thought I was a simple village girl who was learning to be a healer.

But not everyone had been fooled.

'Do – do they all know?' I whispered. I could hardly bear to ask.

'No!' Jack replied instantly. 'Oh, no. You're that healer girl. Renowned as trustworthy and hard-working, I might add, and your reputation grows.'

'But that's all?' He nodded. 'You swear it is so?' I pressed urgently.

'I swear,' he said solemnly. Then: 'I wouldn't lie to you about this, Lassair. You have learned well from Gurdyman that the other studies you undertake with him are not to be advertised; that to speak of them is potentially dangerous, for both of you.' He looked straight into my eyes. 'I will never do anything to put you at risk.'

Perhaps it was just the emotion of the moment that had made him speak with such quiet, powerful intensity.

He, too, must have felt the awkwardness. He got up, tested the water again and then set about mixing drinks for us. He took longer than usual about it, and I guessed he was giving us both time to recover.

When once more we were seated side by side beside the hearth, he said, in very much his normal voice, 'So, we now suspect that Morgan too was robbed, probably of cinnabar and maybe also of his hidden stash of emeralds. We know too that although the thief or the killer – perhaps both, and perhaps they are one and the same – must have been desperate to find Osmund's secret workroom, they didn't succeed, for the emeralds are still there.' He glanced briefly at me. 'I am guessing that you have a fair idea what these people – Osmund, Morgan and Cat, maybe your own beloved Gurdyman – have been up to. I'm surmising that it's an experiment of some kind, and that it is somehow extremely important. Perhaps it holds out the promise of vast wealth; perhaps its riches are spiritual. Robert Powl, I

230

suggest, was shipping certain very special ingredients into the town, and somehow he came to understand that what he carried – in all innocence, probably – was a great deal more valuable than he had imagined. Perhaps he sold some of these substances before he realized; Mistress Judith seems to have had them in her store.' He paused, frowning. 'Our thief, then, is motivated simply by greed. Our killer, for some reason of his own, doesn't want the experiments to continue. Or, as I just said, maybe thief and killer are the same, united in a single evil man – or woman – who operates under the Night Wanderer disguise.'

I put down my mug and dropped my face into my hands. All at once I was exhausted. I'd come all the way from Aelf Fen that day, discovered Gurdyman was still worryingly missing, been surprised and jumped almost out of my skin when Jack burst in on me, thought I was safely indoors for the night at his house only to be dragged out again to revisit the scene of gentle Morgan's and innocent, pitiable Cat's deaths and then creep along in the shadows to investigate poor Osmund's pathetic hidden workroom.

Now, back once more in the warmth and security of Jack's house, I'd been brought face to face with the fact that he knew far more about me than I'd thought he did, and then, on top of that, he seemed to be asking me to conduct a full analysis of the Night Wanderer's crimes. It was too much; far, far too much.

And through it all I kept seeing Morgan's and Cat's bodies, the young apprentice thrown across his master as if he'd given himself in a futile

231

attempt to save the beloved old man's life. Jack knew that Gurdyman was engaged in the same work as Morgan – how many others knew too? Did it mean what I was so very afraid it meant, that Gurdyman was also in danger? Already dead? Hrype had told me he was safe, but that had been days ago, and, besides, I didn't think Hrype was above lying if he felt it was for the right reasons.

I didn't know how I would even begin to cope with it if Gurdyman suffered – had already suffered – the fate of the Night Wanderer's other victims.

I held my emotions at bay for as long as I could, but anxiety, fatigue and grief were overcoming me and I had nothing left with which to fight. A sob broke out of me, and very soon I was crying in earnest.

Jack's arms went round me, and he made an inarticulate sound of dismay and sympathy. 'There's no reason to believe he's been harmed,' he said gently. *How did he know?* I wondered wildly. 'Every other victim has been left in plain sight, almost as if the killer wants them to be quickly found, so why should he suddenly change his habits?'

It made sense but I was too far gone to appreciate it. 'We can't know for sure!' I wept.

Jack's arms tightened, and all at once I was pressed to his chest. I could hear the fast drumming of his heart. 'You would know, Lassair,' he whispered. I felt the touch of a kiss on the top of my head.

It's funny how the body works. I'd been weary beyond measure, sick at heart and full of sorrow, but abruptly I was filled with something totally different.

I turned in his arms, raised my head and, putting my face up to his, kissed him. He tried to hold back – he muttered something but I didn't listen – then, with a sort of sigh, he gave up the struggle.

I was no expert in love. Something happened that night between Jack Chevestrier and me, though, which I knew even then I would never forget, all the days of however long my life would be. I think I already knew he loved me, and there was something in his total absorption in me, his very evident wish for my joy, his care, his skill and the extraordinary, shared moment of ecstasy that we experienced, that informed me quietly how deep that love might go.

It sounded a very small note of warning.

I didn't listen to that, either. I was far too wrapped up in him: in his beautiful, solid, strong and muscular body, in the vast relief of the warmth, comfort and safety I felt emanating out of him to enfold me.

Eventually we lay quietly, side by side in his bed. I was still in his arms – I was hugging him too, and I couldn't let go of him – and my head was pillowed on his chest. He didn't speak, and neither did I.

There were no words to say.

Sixteen

I woke alone. It was early – I could tell by the light – and the house was cold. Dragging a blanket off the bed, I wrapped myself in it and went into the main room. Jack wasn't there, and the fire was out. Just for a second I thought, *He's gone. He regrets what happened last night and can't face me. I won't see him again.*

Only for a second. This was Jack. He wasn't that sort of man.

Hastily I washed and dressed, then set about building the fire. I put water on to boil and looked through Jack's supplies till I found oats for porridge. Then I tidied the bed, leaving everything neat. I packed my own belongings back in my satchel. You wouldn't have thought anyone but Jack had ever been there.

The food had been ready for only a short while when he came in. He looked at me – it was only a brief glance, but I read a great deal in it – then, the smile remaining on his face, said, 'I thought you'd still be asleep. I'm sorry I wasn't here when you woke – oh, good, is that porridge?'

He sat down beside me, reaching for the bowl I was holding out. His manner was so natural, so unstrained, that it was as if we'd shared a house and a bed for years.

'I was worried and it woke me,' he said between mouthfuls. 'As soon as dawn broke, I went out to see Walter and the lads down in the tavern.' He glanced at my bowl. 'You've nearly finished, and so have I – as soon as we're done, we need to go back there. Ginger's suffered a very bad beating.'

'*What!*' I leapt up. 'Why didn't you say so straight away?' I demanded, already gathering up my shawl and reaching for my satchel. 'While we've been calmly eating, I could have been tending that poor man!'

Jack too was on his feet. 'It hasn't taken very long to consume a bowl of porridge,' he said calmly. 'We'll be better able to help Ginger, and tackle whatever else this day throws at us, with food in our bellies.'

He was right.

As we hurried off through the deserted village and out on to the road, he told me briefly what had happened, and why he had been worried. 'When Ginger and I did our second search of Osmund's cell—'

'When you found the key,' I put in.

'When we found the key, yes. I had the sense that someone was watching us, but we both had a good look round and didn't spot anyone. I forgot about it, which I shouldn't have done, and then I remembered it early this morning. I couldn't suppress the thought that something was wrong, and that was why I went down to the tavern on the quay. Ginger was dumped on the doorstep only a short time before I got there.'

'Do you think someone saw you coming out of Osmund's cell with the key, and beat him up to make him reveal what it opened?'

'They might have seen Ginger and me but they wouldn't have seen the key,' Jack said. 'It was I who found it, and it was well concealed. He'd fixed it to the back of a small stone relief of the Madonna and Child that hung over the bed. I slipped it inside my tunic and didn't tell Ginger about it.'

My mind leapt to understand. 'So whoever beat up Ginger knew the key was there.'

Jack gave me a smile. 'That's what I think, too.'

'And Ginger knew nothing about the key, so of course he wouldn't know what it was for. Oh, *no*!' The full horror of that struck me like a blow. 'He couldn't tell them what they wanted to know, so there was no way to stop the pain!'

I grabbed Jack's hand and broke into a run.

Ginger lay on a low narrow cot in a little room at the back of the tavern, stripped to the waist. His face was bloody, he had two black eyes and, I thought at first glance, probably a broken nose. There were bruises all over the ribs on his left side. He was bleeding from cuts to both forearms and also from a deeper gash across his abdomen.

Walter crouched beside him, and the other men hovered anxiously in the doorway.

Walter looked up as we hurried into the foetid little room. 'I'm right glad to see you,' he said, eyes on mine. 'I was going to send for his old mother, but the other lads said why add to his pains?' One of the men gave a small laugh.

I knelt beside Ginger. He was unconscious. I felt all around his head, looking for the swelling that is often such an ominous warning sign. There were a couple of lumps, one on the left side of the crown, one just under the hairline above his right eye. Neither was very large, but I would watch them carefully. He was lucky – if anything about receiving such a violent beating could be called lucky – in that neither blow had landed on the temples. Edild told me that the area of skull there is the weakest part.

I ran my hands down to Ginger's face. Swellings and cuts on the eyebrows, the nose definitely broken, the jaw, as far as I could tell, intact, although heavily bruised. I felt his shoulders, arms, ribs. Broken ribs, probably – the bruising was extensive – but, as with his nose, there wasn't much to be done about that. The cuts on the forearms were fairly superficial, but his left wrist was broken, as was his little finger.

'Is there any damage to his lower body?' I asked.

'Doesn't look like it,' Walter replied.

I checked anyway. I suspected someone had kneed poor Ginger in the testicles, which had probably hurt more than all the other injuries put together. Otherwise, below the waist he seemed undamaged.

I sat back, thinking what I needed. 'Heat some water, please,' I said, to nobody in particular.

'Already being done,' someone said.

'I need splints and cloth for bandages,' I went on. 'Straight lengths of wood,' I elaborated, 'the length of a forearm.' I reached for my satchel, mentally going through the contents. Everything else I needed, I had.

Ginger remained unconscious while I treated him, which was just as well since it took quite a lot

237

of effort to straighten the bones in his wrist, and in the end Jack had to help me.

I hadn't been aware of time passing, but the sun was shining halfway up the sky by the time I had finished. Somebody brought me a drink – it was a pretty, plump-faced young woman, and, from her cheerful banter with Walter's men, I guessed she worked in the tavern.

'Will he be all right?' she asked, jerking her head towards Ginger. He was snoring now.

'I hope so,' I said. 'It's difficult to say, though, with blows to the head, and we won't really know till he wakes up.'

She nodded. 'We won't mention anything to his old mother yet, then,' she murmured. 'Shame to make her worry till we know if it's necessary,' she added wisely.

'I'll sit with him,' I said, returning the empty mug to her.

'You all right on your own?'

'Yes, thanks.'

I realized then that the men had all gone. I had a vague memory of Jack bending down and saying something about having to go and check on something, but I couldn't remember the details. I made myself comfortable and waited for Ginger to open his eyes.

I didn't have long to wait.

He looked up at me, eyes bloodshot between the grossly swollen lids. 'Fuck, my balls hurt like buggery,' he muttered. Then he closed his eyes again.

The second time he opened them, he looked at

238

me with recognition and said, aghast, 'Did I just say what I think I did?'

'Yes, but don't worry.' I put a hand to his forehead to check if he was hot. 'I've heard far worse.' Reassured that, as yet, he showed no sign of fever, I reached in my satchel for a palliative. I would make it strong.

'They came on me like shadows,' Ginger muttered. 'I'm quick on my feet, but I didn't stand a chance. One behind me, two in front, and a little runt of a fellow who didn't do much. Caught me like a rat in a gulley.'

'Did they want to know if you'd found anything in Osmund's room?' I suppose I should have left it to Jack to ask, but I was too impatient.

'Yes. I didn't tell them anything, miss,' Ginger said with sudden urgency.

'You couldn't when you didn't *know* anything.' I held the cup of pain-killing medicine to his lips, and he sipped it. 'I'm so sorry, Ginger.'

He tried to smile. 'Not your fault. Nobody's fault, really, except those bastards that beat me.'

Four of them. I was puzzled, and very anxious. If Ginger was right, then the Night Wanderer had accomplices. That was worrying, because for some reason I had it fixed in my head that he worked alone. If Ginger was wrong, it could mean either that he'd exaggerated to make it less shameful to have been overcome, or that his memory was faulty. And that, really, was the worst possibility, because it could suggest he had sustained much more damage than I thought. I really didn't want that to be the explanation. I had discovered that I really liked Ginger.

The long day eventually passed. Jack, Walter and the others filtered back in ones and twos, till they were all gathered again in the room in the tavern. Food was served and for a while everyone was too busy eating to talk. When we'd finished, Jack said to me, 'Do you need to stay with Ginger?'

'No,' I said, 'he's as good as I can make him. He'll heal, with luck, although we should keep an eye on him over the next day or so.'

'And look for what?'

'Dizziness, vomiting, confusion.'

'Better not take him out on the piss, then,' Fat Gerald said, 'since that's how he usually ends up.'

'I resent that!' came Ginger's voice from the little room beyond. It was good to know he was up to retaliating.

'I'll watch him,' Walter said quietly. He must, I reflected, know Jack very well, since he had detected before I had that Jack wanted to take me off somewhere.

Jack looked at me. 'Come on, then.'

Gurdyman resumed his pacing. The little house on the island at the end of the causeway was very quiet. Darkness had fallen, and it had acted like a blanket and deadened even the usual small sounds from the wide fen that stretched out on three sides of the island.

'You are wearing a path in the reeds on the floor,' said a quiet voice ironically.

Gurdyman stopped. 'I am sorry,' he said. He

sat down by the hearth, emitting a deep sigh that seemed to express frustration, anxiety and irritation. 'But, *oh*, how I tire of these four walls.'

Hrype reached out to turn his boots, slowly drying in the heat from the fire. He had arrived as the sun set, and the water had in places been lapping up over the causeway. 'You are safe here.'

'Safe but bored,' came the swift reply. 'I am not used to being away from my own house.'

'From your own workroom,' Hrype corrected.

Gurdyman gave a short laugh. 'True.'

Hrype glanced at him. 'You have not asked Mercure if you might work with him? You'd have to assist him in whatever project he is pursuing rather than carry on with your own work, of course, but would at least take your mind off the tedium of having to be here when you long to be elsewhere.'

'I haven't asked and I shan't,' Gurdyman said. 'Mercure works alone. He always has, and no doubt he always will.'

'Do you know what absorbs him so?' Hrype asked. 'He does appear here in the house from time to time, I take it?'

'Oh, indeed, quite frequently. He is the most kindly and hospitable of hosts, when he remembers he has a guest. I am free to eat and drink what I like; to make free with his books; to borrow anything of his. For a recluse, he is surprisingly well-equipped here.'

'No doubt the pedlars include him on their rounds,' Hrype remarked. 'Several come to Aelf Fen, and here on the southern edge of the fens we are closer to the town than they are out there.'

There was a short silence. Then, '*They*,' Gurdyman said softly.

'Hm?'

'You refer to the inhabitants of Aelf Fen as *they*, yet it is your home too, so surely it should have been *we*.'

'I make no place my home,' Hrype said roughly. Gurdyman let that pass.

After a while he said, 'I don't believe anybody ever comes right out here to Mercure's island. Your pedlars, I would guess, announce their presence at the landward end of the causeway, and Mercure trots along to purchase what he needs.'

Hrype shrugged. He was clearly indifferent to Mercure's domestic arrangements. But Gurdyman was still thinking, and eventually he said, 'I don't think Mercure sees anyone. We are probably the first people he has spoken to for a long time.'

Now Hrype looked up. 'What *is* he working on? What is it that so absorbs him that he is content to act as if the rest of humanity doesn't exist?'

Gurdyman muttered something that might have been *lucky man*. But he was smiling; in his heart, he knew he could not have lived contentedly in isolation like Mercure's. Then, aloud, he said, 'The same thing. Like others who have set their feet on that path, he seeks a way to refine the human soul; to rid it of its many imperfections and render it pure.'

'The work is gravely misunderstood,' Hrype commented. 'The few who even suspect its existence believe it is all about turning base metals into gold.'

'The smoke screen is deliberate,' Gurdyman

said. 'The real goal is only for the most devout of initiates, and ever they disguise the work behind symbols and careful, convoluted codes designed to mislead.'

The yearning was clear in his voice. Looking at him with sympathy, Hrype said, 'You *will* be back in your crypt. There have been no more killings, and it is to be hoped that the murderer has now slain all those he deems deserving of death, or perhaps, aware that the forces of law and order are hunting him, he has decided to go to ground.'

Gurdyman shot him a swift look. 'You have a higher opinion of those forces than they warrant. Sheriff Picot is not a man to inspire fear in the criminal mind, and his nephew thinks only of his own advancement and enrichment. Furthermore, the one man capable of ferreting out who is responsible for the atrocities has been banned from doing so. Or perhaps that is not still the case?' He looked hopefully at Hrype.

'It is,' Hrype replied. 'Jack Chevestrier is not involved.' He paused. 'Not officially.'

Gurdyman's face brightened. '*Aaah*,' he said with a smile.

Hrype was silent for a while. Then he said, 'She is back in Cambridge.'

Gurdyman's smile vanished. 'But I thought she had gone to Aelf Fen?'

'She crept out of the village and returned to the town. She sought out Sibert and told him to inform her parents that evening, and the fool of a boy didn't try to stop her and simply did as she asked. She didn't want her family to think she'd disappeared and start worrying.'

'But she is with Jack?' Gurdyman demanded. 'She's safe with him?'

'She's with him, yes. Safe? I imagine so. As safe as anybody else in Cambridge.'

'Sibert is not a fool,' Gurdyman said after a short silence. 'It might have seemed wiser to you had he informed Lassair's kin straight away that she had gone, but he is not you, and he put loyalty to a friend above wisdom.'

'He thinks a great deal too highly of her,' Hrype said coldly. 'She's not for him. He could do far better.'

Hrype was staring into the hearth, watching the flames lick along a length of well-seasoned oak. Gurdyman studied him for some time. Then he said, his tone mild and quite without reproof, 'You are surely wrong, my friend, when you say she is as safe as anybody else. Few people, indeed, know of her connection to me, but I fear that knowledge may have reached the attention of the very eyes from which it should at all costs have been kept.'

'The Night Wanderer?'

'Yes. It – he – knew about Morgan and poor Cat. They lived a quiet, self-contained life, and their true work was known to very few, yet that was no safeguard.'

'You surely do not compare Morgan and Cat with yourself and the girl!' Hrype protested. 'She cleans for you, keeps house for you, and you share with her some of your vast store of medical and healing knowledge, but that's all.' He stared at Gurdyman, eyes blazing. 'She is no Soror Mystica!' he spat.

Gurdyman met his eyes calmly. 'Oh, Hrype,' he said sadly.

But Hrype ignored the gentle interruption. His mounting anger overcoming him, he hissed, 'You have no need of any such assistance! You have always been alone, all the long years I have known you, an entity contained within yourself.'

'I cannot—' Gurdyman began, but Hrype over-rode him.

'Mercure works alone,' he cried, thumping a fist against the floor for emphasis, his normally pale face flushed with fury. 'He has no need of any girl apprentice. Morgan, I admit, was the exception among the three of you, for he had Cat, but at least he had good sense and chose for his adept someone of his own sex!'

Gurdyman studied him. Hrype, eventually finding the steady gaze uncomfortable, looked away. 'The pairing is normally a male and a female,' Gurdyman said mildly, 'for both animus and anima should be present. Whilst it is true that the usual arrangement is for the master to be male and the pupil female, it is not always so.'

Slowly Hrype turned his head to meet the steady blue eyes. 'What are you telling me?' he said, his voice very soft. There was a note of apprehension in it; fear, almost.

'Morgan lived a reclusive life,' Gurdyman said, 'and saw few people other than Cat and one or two like-minded souls, myself and Mercure included, although Mercure rarely ventures far away from the safety of his sanctuary here. It was always, therefore, quite easy for Morgan to

245

present himself to the small portion of the world who ever saw him as he wished to be seen, not as he truly was.' He looked expectantly at Hrype, like a teacher encouraging a promising pupil to come up with the right answer.

After a moment, a sudden explosive curse emerged from Hrype's tight lips. Then he said, 'Great gods, are you telling me what I think you are?'

And Gurdyman nodded.

The silence lasted for some time. Then, reaching out a hand and briefly touching Hrype's shoulder, Gurdyman said, 'Hrype, my friend, I believe you are allowing your misogynistic sentiments to get the better of your good sense and your intelligence.' Hrype began an angry reply, but Gurdyman did not let him speak. 'You do not like or trust women. This is not worthy of you.'

'They give me little reason for affection or trust.'

One woman does, Gurdyman thought.

Presently he said, 'If I may be allowed to say so, you live a wrong life, Hrype. Your heart is given to a woman whom you cannot love openly, and you live with one you do not much like but with whom you remain through a sense of loyalty. Have you never considered that both you and Froya, and probably Sibert, not to mention Edild, would all be happier if you confessed the truth?'

'I cannot,' Hrype said baldly. 'Froya was my brother's wife, and I lay with her when my brother was sick and dying.'[3]

3 See *Mist over the Water*.

'You bedded her once, at a time when both of you were in dire need of comfort.' Gurdyman spoke softly. 'When you told me, my instinct was pity for the pair of you, not accusation.'

'You do not live in a small isolated village in which gossip is the sole entertainment,' Hrype flashed back. 'And if you believe the Aelf Fen villagers would treat such a revelation with compassion and generosity, it merely demonstrates how little you know of human nature.'

'So let them gossip, let them point the finger of blame, let them amuse themselves saying how wicked you are,' Gurdyman replied. 'It will not last. And, perhaps, the worthier among them will balance their righteous indignation with the thought that you have remained true to your brother ever since by caring for his widow and her son.'

'My son.' The two words were barely audible.

Gurdyman sighed. 'So I have long suspected,' he said. Then, briskly, he went on, 'Face the disapproval of your village, Hrype. Tell the truth, hold your head high, and weather the storm.'

'I cannot.'

'You must, my friend.' Now Gurdyman spoke urgently. 'You are living a lie, and poisoning your very soul.'

Hrype went as white as if a knife point had pierced his heart. He stared at Gurdyman for a long moment. Then, muttering an incoherent sound, he gathered up his boots and flung himself out of the house.

Seventeen

'Where are we going?' I asked Jack as we set off. It was almost fully dark and, save for lights in a few of the taverns along the quayside, there were no signs of life.

'I've been thinking,' Jack replied. 'As I told you this morning, I'm almost sure someone was watching Ginger and me when we went back for a second search of Osmund's cell but, with all the drama over poor Ginger and his beating, I didn't pursue it.' He frowned. 'To be honest, I forgot, which I shouldn't have done, because I think it was important. Anyway, I've come up with a theory, which I think we ought to test.'

'Right,' I said, panting a little in the effort to keep up with him. 'So what is this theory?'

'We know that Ginger didn't tell his assailants anything because he didn't know about the key,' Jack began. 'But the men – or, rather, their master – must have suspected there's another room somewhere belonging to Osmund, where he works in secret, and that's what they were trying to find out about.'

'Why—' I said.

But Jack was in full spate. 'It would have been very evident that there was nothing of value in Osmund's cell, and wherever he did his work it wasn't there in the priests' house that he shared with other young clerics, under a very strict

248

regime. Ginger and I were spotted going back for a second search, and the man behind the attack on Ginger surmised we'd found something; or, at least, our actions proved there was something there to be found.'

'But—'

'Ginger, even suffering the agony of a severe beating, went on insisting he had nothing to tell them,' Jack went on relentlessly, 'so what I'm pinning my hopes on is that they'll conclude we really didn't come across anything relevant, and so whatever there is to find is still there.' He looked at me. 'Did I make that clear?'

I grinned. 'Yes.'

'Good. The only trouble is that, even if we replaced the key in some more obvious place for them to find, there's no real possibility that they would guess what door it opened. You did,' he glanced at me again, almost shyly this time, and the expression in his eyes moved me profoundly, 'but they are not you.'

It took a moment or two before I thought I could speak without giving myself away. 'We could leave them a more informative clue, I suppose,' I said tentatively, 'but why would we want to reveal – *oh!*' Suddenly I understood.

'Quite!' said Jack with a smile. 'They thought Ginger and I discovered something when we went back to search Osmund's cell again. But Ginger said otherwise, because he didn't know about the key. If they believed him – and we have to hope they did – then their next action may well be to go to Osmund's cell themselves, in the hope of finding what we missed. And we—'

'We are on our way to make quite sure they do just that,' I finished for him. 'What have you in mind? And where should we hide it?'

We were hurrying now, out on the open road crossing the Great Bridge, and he waited until we were safely over and had dived off into the network of alleys and passages surrounding the centre of the town. Then he leaned down and whispered the details of his plan into my ear.

The house where Osmund had lodged with his fellow priests was near St Bene't's. It was composed of four long, low buildings set around a courtyard, and the lack of either visible activity or lights in the windows suggested that the young priests kept early hours. I followed Jack as he ran soft-footed along the covered cloisters, then slipped into the deep shadow of a narrow passage between one building and the next. We waited for a while, but there was no sign to say that anyone had seen or heard us.

We emerged again and Jack led the way to the door to Osmund's cell. It opened, and we went inside. Jack shut the door and checked that the shutter was securely fastened over the one small window, and then he struck a light, putting it to a cheap candle that stood on the floor beside the bed.

Very meagre accommodation, and it smelt of dirty feet and musty damp.

Jack and I stood close together in the middle of the cell. Then Jack reached inside the pouch at his belt and took out a small circular wooden token. He held it out to me, and I saw that it had

250

a shape like the letter P carved into the surface, and inside the loop of the P there was a stylized image of a stubby little boat with a billowing square sail.

'This will suggest Robert Powl to anyone who should find it,' I whispered. The same device was on the real sails of his life-sized boats. 'But will that link be enough to lead them to the little room at the end of the passage?'

Jack nodded. 'I believe so. Not them, necessarily, but the man for whom they work will know. He's already searched Robert Powl's house, barn and warehouse, and it should be fairly easy for him to find out what other property Powl owns.'

Fairly easy. I thought about that. I also thought that the tentative idea I'd come up with concerning who was behind the crimes might be right.

We inspected every inch of the little room, searching for a hiding place. It wasn't easy, for while it had to be somewhere others could find, they shouldn't do so with an ease that would raise their suspicious as to why it hadn't been discovered before.

Jack found a suitable place. He had been working right round the door frame, gently feeling the gap between wood and wall, when he came to a spot where the straw and muck daub gave to the touch. He beckoned me over.

Holding the area of daub carefully away from the door frame, he said, 'Put the token in here; your hands are smaller than mine. There's a space behind here – *careful*!' I had been too eager, and the loose flap of daub threatened to crack off. I spat on my finger and rubbed it along the joint

251

of the flap, merging the dirt to disguise it. Then I reached up to put the token into the dark little space. 'Push it well in,' Jack added, 'we want it to be adequately hard to find.'

I did as he said.

My questing fingers found a little shelf along the top of one of the wood beams going horizontally across the wall, hidden away behind the daub. I couldn't see it but I could feel it, and was able to rest the token on it.

Then my fingers brushed against something else; something that was already there. It was soft to the touch – cloth, I guessed – but the softness covered something small and hard. A little bag with something inside?

Very carefully I pulled it out, and I was just about to remark on it when there came the sound of footsteps, slowly pacing along the cloisters. Quickly I shoved the object inside my satchel, just as Jack grabbed my free hand.

He opened the door a crack and looked out. Walking slowly along the cloister on the opposite side of the quadrangle was an elderly priest, bent over, mumbling to himself, and happily oblivious to anything but his own stumbling progress. He opened one of the row of doors and went in. Jack and I took our chance and ran.

We didn't run far. We emerged from the priests' lodgings and jumped the low wall into St Bene't's churchyard, from which we could watch the quadrangle through a gap between two of the rows of cells.

'What if they don't come tonight?' I hissed after quite a long time.

'Then we'll watch again tomorrow,' he hissed back.

I was almost sure we were wasting our time. But, round about the middle of the night, when the moon was riding high and the clouds had melted away – it had grown very cold – two men materialized out of the shadows and ran light-footed across the churchyard and into the quadrangle. One was thick-set and brawny, and wore a dark hood pulled up over his head, concealing his face. The other was small, slight and light on his feet; he moved like a dancer. Jack and I moved out of our hiding place so that we got a better view of the door to Osmund's cell, and watched as the smaller man went inside. A light flickered briefly, then disappeared as the door was closed. The big one stood guard, arms folded across his impressive chest.

The small man was in the cell for a long time. At one point he put his head out and whispered something to his companion, spreading his hands in a gesture of helplessness. The big man cuffed him quite hard across the head, and the little man went back into the cell.

He emerged again quite soon after that. He held up a small object, and both he and the big man ran off. It looked as if Jack's ruse had worked.

We gave them enough time to get well away, then left the churchyard. 'I hope,' I said as we strode along, 'we're not now going to the room at the end of the passage to watch for them there, too?'

Jack grinned. 'It's tempting, but I don't think so. Those two will have to report back to their master, since the token alone doesn't tell them anything. I shouldn't think we need keep a watch on Osmund's workroom till tomorrow night. And,' he added after a pause, 'it won't just be you and me doing it.'

Something about the way he said it made me very anxious.

We crossed the Great Bridge and turned off the road towards the deserted village. I was already tense with nervous excitement. There wasn't much left of the night, and I was beyond tired, but very soon Jack and I would be in bed together. At that thought, my exhaustion vanished.

We reached the house and went inside. I turned hungrily to him, and, as if he couldn't wait any longer either, he took me in his arms and kissed me, long and hard.

But then, gently, he disengaged himself and pushed me away.

'I have to go out again,' he said, his voice low and full of regret. 'Dearest Lassair, don't look at me like that!'

'I don't want you to go,' I muttered. It was quite an understatement.

'There's no need to be afraid,' he said quickly. 'The geese will set up a noise to wake the dead if anyone comes near, the door is stout and nobody knows you are here.'

'I am not,' I said pointedly, '*afraid*.'

He smiled delightedly. 'Ah. I see.' Then, quickly, he went on, 'Luke – you remember Luke? The one I sent to find out what was happening with the official investigation into the killings?' I nodded. 'I had a message that he wanted to see me, and it has to be tonight. I think something's happened, and if it's what I hope it is, then it will affect how we plan for tomorrow night.'

'But what—'

He didn't let me finish. He kissed me again, groaned softly then turned, picked up his sword and ran.

The former workmen's village was not totally deserted. In the ruins of a small lean-to a little way down the path from Jack's house, at the far end of the row, someone had made a rudimentary camp. Some old and half-rotten bundles of straw had been used to shore up the missing wall, and a length of fabric impregnated with animal fat was spread over the gaping hole in the roof. A bedroll stood on end in one corner, a stone jar of water, a small cup and half a loaf of bread beside it.

In the darkness, Rollo stood in the doorless entrance, watching the house at the end of the row.

He saw the powerfully built man in the leather jerkin leave and run off down the track. He was carrying a sword. There was no sign of Lassair. She must still be in the house.

Rollo didn't know what to do.

He had now been observing her for four days. After his meeting with the king at Windsor, he had made good speed up into the fens. He had never anticipated simply jumping out in front of

255

her, to announce he was back and expect her instantly to drop whatever she was doing and rejoice at being with him again. He was only too aware of how long he'd been away; of the many months that had elapsed without his having sent her any loving, encouraging message. For all she knew, he had thought gloomily as he covered the miles, he could be dead.

He felt increasingly guilty. He *could* have sent word. His net of spies was spread wide, and it would not have been that hard to send a message from the shores of the Mediterranean to the fens. It wouldn't even have taken all that long. He knew, because he had done it. Well, the message hadn't been destined for Aelf Fen but for Winchester, although the distance would not have been very different.

He admitted honestly to himself that he hadn't wanted to contact her. He had thought about her often – he remembered one or two moments when he'd been sure she was in danger, and his corresponding feelings of anguished helplessness – but, in truth, the appeal of his mission was greater than any idea of hurrying back before its completion to seek her out.

He was good at what he did – it did not seem immodest to admit it within the privacy of his own thoughts – and he enjoyed it. The work was often perilous, exhausting and lonely, the missions long and sometimes with scant chance of success. But he *did* succeed; no wonder he enjoyed it.

Arriving in the fens, he had gone first to Cambridge, finding his way through the maze of alleyways to the house of the old magician. There had been nobody there. The town had been in a ferment, and it hadn't taken him long to understand why. Deciding that Lassair and Gurdyman must have fled to seek sanctuary well away from the violence, he then set off for her village. He went on foot, as she must have done; if he intended to disguise his presence until he had found out whether or not she would truly welcome him back, it would be that much more difficult if he had his horse with him. He found stables outside the town, leaving his horse there for a well-deserved rest.

He knew roughly where her village was and it proved quite easy to find. He chose a vantage point in a stand of hazel and alder close to a lone oak tree that stood on the higher ground above the village, and settled down to watch.

He spent a reasonably comfortable night under the trees. He was used to sleeping under the stars, and the weather was mild. The following day, he saw her. She seemed to be living in a small house set a little apart from the rest of the village, and he surmised that it belonged to her healer aunt. He almost went down to her and declared himself, but something held him back.

Then, early the next morning, concealed by the alder and hazel trees of his vantage point, he heard her.

She was standing under the oak tree, and she was talking to a slim young man with fair hair bleached almost white by the sun. She was smiling at him, talking easily, but he sensed a deep, underlying tension in her. The young man asked her something, but she shook her head and he heard her say she wasn't staying in the village. Then she lowered her voice and spoke urgently to him; Rollo had the impression she was telling him something of grave significance.

The young man didn't seem to like what she was saying. He made some sort of a protest, then, in a louder voice, Lassair said, *I'll be quite safe because the person looking for me thinks I'm in the village, and once I get to Cambridge, I'll be safer than anywhere else, because I'll go straight to Jack Chevestrier.*

There had been more – she appeared to be asking the young man to do something for her, and with obvious reluctance he agreed – and Rollo heard him offer to go back to the town with her, only to have her kindly but very firmly turn him down.

Rollo had observed and noted the latter part of the exchange only with some automatic part of his well-trained mind. The majority of his attention had turned inwards, because when she said what she did about being safe with this Jack Chevestrier, he was watching the young man's face. He, too, must have picked up what Rollo did, for his expression changed. He had been looking at her with a faint, fond smile, his feelings for her clear to read, and then the softness was abruptly wiped away.

He hears it too, Rollo thought as dismay overcame him. *He hears that note of excited tension in her voice as she speaks of a man she can't wait to get back to. A man she loves, even if she doesn't know it?*

He prayed that it wasn't so.

He had almost turned and walked away. He had been away too long, she had given up on him returning and, in her busy life in the town, had met and allowed herself to be attracted to somebody else. It was only to be expected, he told himself. She was young, she'd have been lonely, she was beautiful – in his eyes she was – and also intelligent, capable, brave and, as far as he was concerned, exceptionally good at her job.

And I will not let her go without a fight.

Thinking was over. So was imagining he was going to step back and let this other man – this Jack Chevestrier, whoever he might be – have her all to himself.

Allowing Lassair a short while to get ahead of him, Rollo set out behind her on the road that curved round the south of the fens on its way to Cambridge. She seemed to be in danger; somebody, it appeared, had come to Aelf Fen to hunt her down. Well, that person might not be as easily fooled as she seemed to believe; if they had realized what she was up to and were even now shadowing her footsteps, planning some sort of assault, then she wouldn't have to face them alone. Rollo would be there.

He tailed her all the way back to the town.

He watched as she went into Gurdyman's house. He didn't think the old man was there, for although he listened intently, standing close to the partly open door, he didn't hear voices.

Then he heard the heavy thump of booted footsteps coming along the alley and slipped into a gap between two houses to hide and watch.

He saw a big, strongly built man with light-brown close-cropped hair and very clear green eyes in an intelligent face come hurrying round the corner. He was dressed in a simple wool tunic over hose tucked into good boots, and he wore a sleeveless jerkin of thick, scarred leather. He was armed; Rollo saw a sword in a scabbard and at least one knife stuck through the broad belt.

Now that, Rollo thought, *is a lawman, if ever I saw one.*

Could he be Jack Chevestrier?

He waited. He heard voices inside the house – Lassair's and the big man's – and presently they emerged. With some difficulty, Rollo trailed them as they took a very convoluted route through the hidden areas of the town, over a wide bridge across the river and down a narrow track leading around the base of the castle and emerging in what seemed once to have been a village; perhaps for the workers who built the castle. Rollo had seen similar places before.

The quiet was suddenly ripped apart by a violent cackling of geese. The big man quieted them, and he and Lassair went inside the house at the end of the track.

Stunned, Rollo stood for some moments, trying to absorb and make sense of what he had just seen.

She is in danger, he thought. He already knew something of what was happening in the town, and now the mention of this Jack person as someone with whom Lassair would be safe made more sense. Was that why she was with him?

Because the peril from the killer at large was a particular threat to her?

'I could protect her,' he murmured aloud. Should he go and tell her he was there, right outside, and that she had no need of any other man's strong sword arm?

He almost did just that.

But then he heard her voice again inside his head.

I'll be safer than anywhere else, because I'll go straight to Jack Chevestrier.

He stayed where he was.

Presently, thinking Lassair and the man had settled down for the night, Rollo made his way back into the town. The streets were virtually deserted, and he had to dodge a couple of patrols that were enthusiastically and brutally enforcing the curfew. Going back over the bridge – he had some idea of making camp in one of the other empty houses in the village by the castle – he heard raised voices and, looking down, saw lights in several of the taverns along the quay. He went into the one that seemed the most crowded, ordered ale and food and sat listening.

In the time it took to eat his meal and drink a couple of mugs of very good ale, he had found out what he needed to know. He discovered that the rumours he had picked up before, when he had briefly visited the town, concerned a vicious killer known as the Night Wanderer, who some said was a dark figure who came up from hell, out of the old legends, and whose weapon was his own arm, turned by witchcraft or deep magic into a vicious silver limb which ended in sharp claws with which he tore out his victims' throats. Six people had died – so far, for the general opinion was that the Night Wanderer hadn't finished yet – and they included men and women, young and old, and ranged from a beautiful young prostitute to the wealthy owner of a fleet of river craft and a mysterious recluse believed to be a wizard.

Ignoring the wilder suppositions and ideas – all the more outlandish and unlikely as the ale was consumed – Rollo concentrated on what was being said about the efforts of the men of law to catch the killer. Here, opinion was united: Gaspard Picot was only in charge because his uncle was the sheriff, he was undoubtedly as corrupt as the sheriff, he didn't know his arse from his elbow when it came to dealing with murderers and why hadn't they left Jack Chevestrier in charge?

Ah, Rollo thought. He'd been right.

Was it encouraging to know that, though? Should he now conclude for certain that Lassair was only in the man's company for her own safety?

He couldn't decide.

He returned to the deserted village, where he made a rough and ready shelter in one of the houses close to the one at the end of the track. All was quiet in that house, although he caught the faint glint of a light through the high little window. He knew he should go on watching, but he was very tired. He made a makeshift bed in the least draughty corner, and, reasonably comfortable and adequately warm in his cloak and blanket, he was soon deeply asleep.

He didn't hear Jack and Lassair go out again. Ignorant of where they were going and what they discovered, he didn't hear their return either. He slept on, dreaming vague dreams of Lassair, comforting himself, when occasionally he stirred, with the thought that she and this man were colleagues, friends, thrown together somehow and pooling their skills to try to discover who was behind the murders. She was being a good citizen, and helping the man of the law.

He fell back into profound sleep.

The next day he resumed his watch on her. It was an easy task, for she spent much of the day in a tavern on the quay, where he gathered from eavesdropping that a man had been badly beaten and she was tending him.

Rollo learned rather more than that.

By nightfall, he thought he had a fairly good grasp of what was going on. Lassair seemed to be deeply involved with this group of renegade lawmen; rightly so, he was sure, for he hadn't liked what he had found out about Gaspard Picot, and it was heartening to discover that her sound judgement had led her to align herself with men with right on their side.

Something was going to happen: long experience told Rollo that. Danger was very near, and there would be another death very soon.

He resolved to watch and wait.

Now, watching Jack Chevestrier run off down the track, Rollo was torn. Should he take advantage of the man's absence and go in to speak to

Lassair? She'd be so pleased and relieved to see him, especially when peril crackled through the air like approaching lightning. She'd leap up, fling her arms round him and say, *Oh, thank the good Lord you're here, I've been so frightened and I've prayed for you to come and look after me!*

But that was wishful thinking. She was pretty good at looking after herself, and if as it appeared she had accepted another man's protection, then she must have good reason.

And there was something else . . .

Rollo, who would have said he wasn't in the habit of being frightened of anything, discovered that he didn't dare go and declare his presence to Lassair.

Because he had no idea what he would do if she turned him away.

He was overcome with the need to move; to drown his distress in action of some sort, and just then it didn't seem to matter what.

Making up his mind, he emerged from the ruined house and set off after the man in the leather jerkin.

Eighteen

I was woken just as dawn was breaking by a terrific noise from Jack's geese. Barely awake, I stumped out of bed and, barefoot and in my shift, reached for my little knife and looked round wildly for a weapon for my other hand. Jack's house was bristling with weapons so, discarding a bow, a heavy sword that looked too old to have a good edge and a vicious knife with a curved blade like a sickle, I picked up a dagger.

Fear making me feel as if my heart was thumping right up in my throat, I ran through the main room and without giving myself time to think wrenched back the bars across the door and flung it open.

A lad stood just outside, his normally friendly face anxious and strained. His pale hair stuck to his sweaty forehead; he had obviously been running.

I sagged against the door frame. 'Henry,' I said.

His eyebrows went up in surprise. 'Oh, did I startle you, miss?' he panted. 'Sorry.'

Startle?

'Just a little,' I admitted. 'Come in.'

'No, I won't, thank you,' he said politely. The monks from whom he'd fled might have beaten him but they'd also taught him manners. 'I came for the master. We need him urgently.'

265

The fear rose up again, but now it wasn't for me. 'He's not here. Isn't he with you?'

It was a stupid question with a very obvious answer.

Henry shook his head. 'I've been keeping watch out on the quay, hiding across the path from the little passage that leads down to that young priest's workroom. Some of the others came by from time to time, but I didn't see the master.'

I was nodding even as he finished speaking. I thought I knew what had happened: Jack had gone straight to the tavern, to talk to Luke, and Henry had already been sent out to watch the passage by the time Jack got there.

I hurried back into the far room and hastily donned my overgown and my boots. I grabbed my satchel and ran back to Henry.

'Come with me,' I said. 'I know where he is.'

Along the quayside, nobody seemed to be awake yet. The taverns and the brothels were shuttered and dark, and the few boats tied up there appeared to be deserted. Word had spread throughout the fenland waterways of our town's terrible trouble and people were keeping away. It was yet another reason why Sheriff Picot ought to have been doing more to stop the killings, for the prosperity of a great many people depended on trade. Seeing the normally busy quay so quiet and empty was deeply disturbing, in more ways than one.

Henry and I reached the tavern that Walter and his men were using as their base. As we approached the entrance, I heard a strange sound which, after a moment, I identified: it was a low, steady hum of voices.

A man I didn't know stood leaning against the door. Until we were right in front of him, I hadn't noticed him, for the doorway was recessed and he was hidden in deep shadow. He stepped forward, sword in hand, but then he recognized Henry, just behind me.

'You're the healer,' he said in a gruff voice.

'Yes.'

He opened the door and jerked his head, which I took as an invitation to go inside.

I stood in the entrance to the room which Walter and his lads appeared to have appropriated. Where there had once been half a dozen of them, now their number had increased. The room was full of men, and Henry and I had interrupted their breakfast. I looked at them all – there were at least twelve of them – my eyes flashing from face to face. Some of them I recognized, for I'd seen them in the patrols and going about the sheriff's business. Some were strangers. One or two I knew from other contexts; I had treated the bearded man by the hearth for a bad back, and the skinny, black-haired one's wife had borne a pretty baby girl a few months back. These two nodded to me in recognition.

Had these sheriff's men deserted Picot and his nephew, then, and brought friends and relatives with them? Had they all despaired of the Night Wanderer ever being caught unless a better man took up the leadership? It was the only explanation I could come up with. And it was more than likely, I reflected, for, unless they were in the sheriff's pocket, they must surely prefer Jack's hard-working honesty to the Picot brand of corruption.

Jack stood over in a corner, in earnest conversation with Walter. He knew, somehow, that I was there; his head spun round and he met my eyes.

Henry, good manners forgotten now, elbowed his way roughly through the crowd until he reached Jack's side, where he began to speak, his gestures and his very stance revealing his anxiety. Jack listened intently without interrupting until Henry had finished. Then he muttered something to the boy, rested his hand briefly on his shoulder, then called the room to attention.

Into the sudden, expectant silence he said, 'It's happened. They are a day earlier than I expected, but we are ready.' He glanced around the room, and fifteen pairs of eyes turned towards him. 'You all have your orders.' He glanced at Walter, who nodded. Then, as a boyish excitement briefly lit up his face, he raised his arm and yelled, '*Go!*'

It became clear that not everybody had orders to go on the sortie. I knew without even having to think about it that Jack would tell me to stay with those who were remaining behind to guard the room at the tavern, and so I didn't give him the chance. I slipped out into the passage, crouched right down in a corner while they all filed out, then hurried after them and tucked myself in behind Fat Gerald.

Walking soft as cats, Jack and Walter led us along the quay. Soon Robert Powl's warehouse loomed up ahead; the light was stronger now, and colours were just starting to emerge from the dawn greys. Henry, at Jack's side, whispered something to him, and Jack nodded. Turning, he caught the eyes of each of the men and, gesturing, he indicated where each should stand. I slipped out from Fat Gerald's shadow and stood right up against the front wall of the warehouse, out of Jack's line of sight.

Silently, moving in small groups, the men arranged themselves so that the end of the narrow little passage was blocked off. Others stood further back, covering the possible escape routes on either side in case anyone managed to escape through the first line.

I caught movement, and close beside me one of the men, watching intently, gave a soft gasp.

I couldn't see, and I had to. A barrel stood by the wall, and I clambered on to it. I had a clear view, right over the men's heads.

Jack was advancing alone up the passage.

I was very afraid. I reached inside my satchel and touched the familiar round hardness of the shining stone. It seemed to be picking up my dread. It felt hot, as if it wanted to fight.

I looked at the door at the far end of the passage. It had been broken open. There were lights inside, quickly becoming superfluous as the rising sun lightened the sky.

I heard voices. There was a faint muttering, then someone gave a cry of delight, swiftly hushed.

I pictured the little leather purse with the drawstrings that Jack and I had left on the bench. The thieves, it seemed, had found what they came for. One of them, perhaps, had just done what I did, and spread out those seven beautiful emeralds, picked one up, held it to the light . . .

Noises from the end of the passage. Jack stood ready, and now Walter and Luke had moved up to stand just behind him. Did they feel as I did, I wondered? Did they fear for their leader, standing there alone?

Four men emerged from the workroom. I knew the brawny one and the little fellow, for they were the ones who had gone to Osmund's cell earlier. I stared at the other two, trying to see if I recognized them.

'Those are the ones that beat me up,' I heard Ginger whisper very softly from somewhere close at hand, although he used another word than *ones*; I'd never heard it applied to men before.

I studied the four men. I paid particular attention to the small man. He was my size, if a little shorter, and it seemed to me that he wasn't as broad in the shoulders as I am.

If I could wriggle down that earth tunnel which burrowed into the river bank and emerged in Robert Powl's barn, then I reckoned he could have done, too.

The man in the lead had seen Jack. His face falling into dismay, he put a hand to his sword, half-drawing it. Then he saw Luke, and Walter, and, ranged behind them and closing off the mouth of the passage, the other men.

He pushed his sword back into its scabbard, holding up his hands in surrender.

I knew then that the six victims hadn't died by his hand. Whatever I might think of the Night

Wanderer, I had to admit that it took courage – of a deeply perverted nature, but courage nevertheless – to do what he did; to go out by night, alone, to conceal himself in dark places and, when the fire in the blood overtook him, step out and so coolly, so ruthlessly, so efficiently, slay his victims.

The man who had just led his men out of the little room at the end of the passage was a coward. Jack's force wasn't that numerous; wouldn't it have been worth at least trying to get away? And what about his men? Could he be certain they too wanted to surrender? One or two might have evaded capture; I'd have put money on the little man somehow managing to wriggle his way out through the hands that tried to detain him and making his escape.

Like his companions, he wasn't given the chance.

Jack was giving orders. The thieves, it appeared, were to be bound securely and taken to the room in the tavern. Six of Walter's men stepped forward holding lengths of leather, and very quickly the captives' hands were fastened behind their backs and they were led away.

I wondered if they would ever experience freedom again. Whether they would live, even; theft was a capital offence and they had been caught in the very act. I had watched as Jack silently held out his hand for the purse of emeralds, and now he stood holding it, his expression unreadable.

The press of people around the end of the passage had cleared now, and only Jack and

Walter remained, standing close together. I sensed that this business wasn't over, and, stepping down carefully and noiselessly from my barrel, crouched behind it to listen to their plans for what would happen next.

'We have the work force,' Jack said softly to Walter, 'and now we need the master.'

'Do you think he will come here?' Walter sounded doubtful.

'Yes,' Jack said with conviction. 'I am sure of it. He is hungry for what he thinks his thieves will find here, and when they fail to report back to him he'll be driven by his impatience and his greed to come and see what's holding them up.'

Walter said softly, 'I hope you're not thinking of taking him on alone.' Jack didn't reply. 'Jack, he's dangerous!' Now there was a worried note in Walter's voice. 'He'll know you've found out what he's been doing, and given the mood in the town, he'll know he can expect no mercy. He'll have nothing to lose, and he'll probably—'

Probably kill you. Was that what Walter had been about to say?

Jack didn't let him. 'He's too clever to come anywhere near this place if he sees you and your men lurking, even if they do try to disguise themselves as innocent bystanders going about their daily business,' he said lightly. 'He has to feel that it's safe for him to come right into the room, and, with any luck, pick these up.' He held up the purse of emeralds. Walter must have looked doubtful, for Jack said with sudden roughness, 'Dear God, Walter, we have to make an end of this! Let him walk into the trap, where he'll find not only the prize but also me. You and the others can advance once I've challenged him, and bear witness to his crime.'

'But if we—'

'If he sees you and the others before he's picked up the emeralds, which he will if you're anywhere around, because he's perpetually suspicious, very observant and far from stupid, he'll instantly go on the offensive, demand to know what you're all doing there and say he's had word that the room at the end of the passage has been broken into and has come to investigate.'

'But you—'

'*Enough,*' Jack said in a sudden flash of anger. 'You have your orders, Walter. Obey them.'

I pushed myself further back behind the barrel. I peered out as Walter strode past. He looked furious.

I was very afraid. I knew I shouldn't be there. If I were to be spotted by the man Jack was waiting for, the whole exercise would be in ruins. I didn't dare think what Jack would say to me if everything came to grief because I'd just had to watch.

Walter and his men had all melted away. I knew they must be quite close but even so, I couldn't spot them. They were good, I had to admit. Could I, too, creep away? I might be able to avoid being seen by anyone if I kept right up against the front wall of the warehouse, still in shadow. I was just making up my mind to risk it when I heard someone coming along the quay.

With all that had happened since the racket of Jack's geese had wakened me, I'd vaguely thought that the morning must now be quite advanced. But when I looked out from behind the barrel, I saw that the light remained pale and thin, the sun was only just appearing above the horizon in the eastern sky, and the quay was still deserted.

A man was coming along towards Robert Powl's warehouse. He was ill at ease, frequently turning to look behind him. He walked on his toes, clearly not wanting to be heard.

He was tall, with a hard-lined face, dark, close-set eyes under heavy brows and a shaven head. He was dressed in dark garments, the swing of his heavy cloak denoting fine cloth and an excellent cut. He had a hand on his sword hilt, and that hand bore a ring on the forefinger: a large stone set in thick gold. The low sun glinted on the bright green gem.

I knew who he was and I trembled with dread.

This man was Gaspard Picot, and he was the sheriff's nephew, the man who had been put in charge of hunting down the Night Wanderer when Jack had been thrown out. Not only had he failed to catch the murderer, he had also taken ruthless advantage of his unique position for his own ends. He might have had the four thieves do the dirty work for him, but his was the intelligence behind the thefts.

The blame lay squarely on his shoulders.

I wondered what his uncle the sheriff would do when he was told.

I watched, hardly breathing, as Gaspard Picot came to the mouth of the tunnel-like passage. He peered down it to the door at the end. Then he looked over both shoulders and up and down the quay several times. I crouched still as stone.

He made up his mind suddenly and strode up the passage. He pushed at the door and it opened. He paused, perhaps disconcerted to find it unlocked. Then he went inside.

I couldn't stop myself: I crawled out from the shelter of the barrel and went on until I could see inside the place that had been Osmund's workroom.

Gaspard Picot picked up the small leather purse. Opened it. Tipped the emeralds into his hand, then put them back, drew up the drawstrings again and put the purse inside his tunic.

He had turned to come out again when I heard Jack's voice. 'Put them back,' he said calmly. 'They do not belong to you.'

I don't know where he had concealed himself but it was clear that Gaspard Picot hadn't seen him, for, hearing those words, his face went pale.

Very slowly, he turned towards Jack, standing just behind him.

I wasn't fooled by Jack's quiet tone. I knew what was going to happen. There was poisonous venom between these two men: much more at stake than this matter of the theft of the emeralds. It was, I realized, to do with betrayal of trust. Gaspard Picot had been put in a position of authority in the town, but, far from honouring that position and carrying out the duty placed on him to protect the townspeople, keep the peace and uphold the law, he was using it to make himself rich. His corruption went deep. I could sense it in him, as if it were a pool of something foul secreted beneath the costly garments and the gorgeous jewels.

Jack – good, honest Jack; out of memory I heard Gurdyman saying, *Jack Chevestrier is a better man by far than his master the sheriff, and is decent, honest and capable* – was his polar opposite.

And now Jack stood alone, facing a ruthless enemy poised like a snake about to strike.

I wanted to warn him but I seemed to have frozen.

But Jack was ready for him.

I had seen Jack's icy fury before. I'd watched him, out in the wilds of the fenland, and seen what he'd done to the hired murderer who Gaspard Picot had sent to kill him. I'd seen him wrench Picot's arm up behind his back, so violently that it was a miracle he hadn't dislocated the shoulder. I had believed he was going to kill both of them, for he had overcome them and had them at his mercy. But he didn't; he had left them, bound and helpless. He must have been confident they would either manage to free themselves or be rescued.

But this time I knew it was different. This was the second and final conflict between them, for this time the fight would be to the death.

They were in a confined space and swords would be no good. I saw Gaspard Picot reach for his dagger and, quick as lightning, Jack did the same. Both were right-handed; both had a blade in one hand, the other empty.

They circled each other, briefly coming together in an attack which had the violence of two stags

276

clashing head-on, wrestling, each trying to disarm the other. Then they fell back, both panting.

I saw something glinting on Gaspard Picot's left hand. I thought it was his gold ring.

But it wasn't gold, it was silver-coloured. It was steel.

Gaspard Picot carried a concealed knife up his left sleeve, and he had just slid it down into his hand.

Before I could scream out a warning, he leapt on Jack. I thought it was all right; I thought Jack was ready for him, for it seemed he had knocked the left hand and its blade away.

They were clutched together again, their deadly embrace unyielding, and I heard Gaspard Picot cry out. He sprang back, then leapt up on to a bench and launched himself on Jack, knife in his right hand aimed straight at Jack's chest.

But Jack held up his own knife, arm extended, and as Gaspard Picot descended on him, his own momentum drove Jack's blade straight into his throat.

He fell, on to the bench, then down to the floor. Blood poured out of his neck, and he was making terrible gurgling sounds. He lay on his back, then, as the struggle for air became more desperate, began to thrash about, left, right, left.

Now others were pounding down the passage. Walter crouched at Gaspard Picot's side, then he looked up and said swiftly 'We all saw what happened, Jack. A whole band of people were witness, and all will swear you acted in self-defence, and he attacked first.' Fat Gerald stood behind him, Ginger, Luke, Henry and a man I didn't recognize crowding in behind him. If they were afraid Gaspard Picot was going to leap up and run away, they were wrong. Gaspard Picot was dying.

After what seemed quite a long time, the awful bubbling sounds ceased. Walter reached down and drew a fold of the luxurious cloak over the white face. 'He's dead,' he said.

One or two of the men uttered a response. Someone even said, 'God have mercy on him.'

Jack didn't say anything.

Cold suddenly, I leapt to my feet and flew up the passage. Jack was sitting down beside Gaspard Picot's body. He, too, was deathly pale. He had a hand under his leather jerkin, inside his tunic.

I took him by his shoulders and laid him down. His eyes closed, fluttered open again, closed. I wasn't sure he had recognized me.

I put my hand inside his undershirt, pushing his away.

I felt the fast pulse just beneath his skin. Felt the blood pumping out between my fingers. Something detached and professional took me over. I unfastened my satchel with my free hand, took out a thick wad of soft fabric and pressed it very hard against Jack's chest.

At the back of the crowd – which was rapidly growing as news of the drama spread along the quayside and off into the town – stood a fair-haired man with dark eyes.

He had been watching for some time and had seen every move made by the two men at the far end of the passage. But now he had eyes only for the young woman who knelt with the wounded man's head in her lap. She was pressing down on his chest with all her strength but already there was a pool of blood soaking into her skirts.

It seemed as if some of the men at the back of the crowd didn't yet understand what had happened. 'We'll have to swear to it that Picot struck first,' someone said, too loudly. 'Jack will require all of us to confirm he had no option but to fight back.' Then, when nobody answered, the man said in a doubtful voice, 'He *did* strike first, didn't he?'

The girl cradling the wounded man heard. She looked up, and the fair-haired man saw her face. She screamed, '*Look how he's bleeding!*' and held up her hand, soaked red. 'Of course he struck first! He had a second blade, hidden in his left sleeve, and Jack didn't see it.' She was waving her hand now, as if demanding they all look. 'What further proof do you want?'

Now others were kneeling round Lassair and Jack, forming a protective, concealing group, and the fair-haired man could no longer keep her in sight. He didn't need to. He had seen her expression, heard that terrible fear in her voice because she thought the man was dying right before her eyes and there was nothing she could do to hold on to him.

It told Rollo all he needed to know. He turned and walked away.

Nineteen

Gurdyman sat by the hearth in Mercure's house. Dawn had broken and he was alone, for Hrype still had not returned and Mercure was, as so often, out in his workroom, where Gurdyman suspected he had been all night. There was a sweet smell in the air, which Gurdyman thought was burning apple wood. He was tired, strained; he could still feel Hrype's fury in the little room, for all that many hours had passed since his abrupt departure. Gurdyman fancied he could see the anger as jagged, brilliant blue lines that cut across the soft early light.

He slipped into a daydream, on the edge of a doze. He had hardly slept, and he knew such states were easier to enter when the mind was fatigued. He thought about Hrype, and the dislike of Lassair that ate into him. *He is jealous of her*, a calm voice said in Gurdyman's head.

Then his mind slowly filled with images of Lassair. She was in deepest distress and he made an involuntary movement, as if his body had already made the decision to find her, help her, support her . . .

But he didn't move.

The sweet woodsmoke smell intensified. Gurdyman's mind relaxed. He saw shapes, coalescing into vague human form. A tall, pale figure, black-shrouded, which slowly melted and re-formed.

Some time later – he thought only a short time had elapsed, but then he noticed the sunshine outside, although, strangely, that observation seemed to go as soon as it had come – Gurdyman woke. Mercure was bending over the hearth, stirring something that spattered in hot fat in a shallow pan, and an appetizing, savoury smell filled the air.

Gurdyman looked at him, still confused. *I was more deeply asleep than I imagined*, he thought, *for I know I am awake, yet I am disoriented.*

Mercure turned to him, smiling. 'I have been neglecting you, old friend,' he said. 'Now I intend to make up for it, for I am preparing eggs and black pudding, and we shall sit by the fire together and speak of the long years of our acquaintance.' He paused. 'Where is Hrype? I am cooking for him, too, so perhaps we should call him?'

'He's gone.' Gurdyman was mildly surprised that Mercure hadn't noticed.

'*Gone?*' Mercure spun round, and Gurdyman caught a glimpse of his expression. But then Mercure smiled, and, in a tone of casual interest, said, 'He comes and goes according to some deep and complex plan of his own, that one.'

'Indeed he does,' Gurdyman agreed. 'Just now, I suspect he is somewhere out in the wilds, quite alone, for I told him some truths about himself that I do not think he wished to know.'

Mercure nodded. 'Ah, but it is ever our lot, my old friend, to see beyond the vision of normal men, and, when we relate what we see, our words are seldom accepted in the spirit in which they are delivered.'

'Hrype is far from being a *normal* man,' Gurdyman observed. He knew exactly what Mercure meant by the word.

Mercure looked at him with interested eyes. 'So it is as I suspected,' he murmured. 'We proliferate, do we not?'

Gurdyman watched him. *He looks weary beyond endurance*, he thought with a surge of pity, *as if his work demands more of him than he has left to give.*

'Sit and eat,' he urged. 'I worry about you, Mercure. Working alone as you do, you have nobody to regulate your days.'

'I manage well enough,' Mercure replied.

There was silence for a while as they consumed the hot, savoury food. Then Gurdyman said, 'Hrype will, perhaps, visit the town. I hope for news, for I am anxious to return. I have been grateful for your hospitality, Mercure, but if the danger is past I wish to be back in my own home.'

'Say rather back at your work, my old friend,' Mercure said with a grin. Then, raising his head, his large dark eyes on Gurdyman, he said, 'But please, do not go yet. Think what became of Morgan and young Cat.'

'I do, constantly,' Gurdyman said. 'However, you forget that I too have my young adept, and I have the strongest sense that she is in danger.'

'Danger,' Mercure echoed. 'It is all around, yes.'

A soft humming seemed to start up. Gurdyman shook his head, wondering if it originated inside his own ears. He glanced at Mercure to see if he had noticed, but he was calmly carrying on with his meal.

Something was happening.

Gurdyman felt as if his limbs were slowly turning into soft wool. He slumped back against the wall, relaxed, drifting into a trance. Mercure seemed to be similarly affected: his eyelids were drooping and his empty bowl fell from his limp hand and rolled away. Somewhere in Gurdyman's head a warning note sounded. As if a part of his mind fought whatever was overcoming him and his companion, he saw an image of Lassair, and she had tears on her face and an expression of dread in her eyes. Then he saw a tall, stooping figure in a dark hooded cloak, and when the figure of horror turned to stare at him, its face was dead white and it had dark holes for eyes.

Gurdyman struggled. He saw Mercure fall over sideways, gently, a smile on his face, and curl up, surrendering. Gurdyman struggled against the enchantment. Lassair was in terrible danger and he must find her, go to her, use the mighty power of his lifetime's accumulation of strong magic to fight off whatever loomed over her and keep her safe.

He managed to get up on to his knees. Then the humming suddenly intensified, so that the whole of the little house seemed to thrum, and he fell back. His eyes closed, and the trance took him.

They took Jack to a small cell off the room at the tavern which Walter and his men were using.

He was alive. That was as much as I or anyone could say. I didn't let myself think about how much blood he had lost. Could a big man go on living when he had been so gravely depleted?

In my panic, as we settled him on a narrow cot, I kept looking round for someone to tell me what to do. I had never taken charge of a really serious case. There was always Edild, calm, serene, quietly watching me and guiding me when I went wrong or didn't know what to do. Gurdyman, too, knew so very much more than I did about the human body and how it works, and while I might not have had his reassuring presence when I tended severe injuries and diseases here in the town, he was always there for me to talk to, giving his advice and explaining how he would have set about the appropriate treatment.

I realized quite soon that the only person telling me what to do was me.

Furthermore, the others – Walter, Ginger and their companions; the kindly and anxious man and wife who ran the tavern – made it perfectly obvious that they were looking to me to save Jack's life.

I bathed and cleansed the wound so that I could see just how badly hurt he was. Gaspard Picot's treacherous little blade had gone into the big muscle in Jack's chest, just to the left of his breastbone. Had it gone in straight, it would have pierced his heart. It went in at a slight angle, and so he still lived. He was very well-muscled and it was probably that which had saved him from instant death, for at that angle the blade wasn't long enough to reach the heart through all the muscle.

Gurdyman had explained to me the theory of the Arab doctors who taught him when he was young, to do with how blood goes round the body. They said it went in little tubes, some leading away from the heart and some returning to it. If that was right – and my own observations told me it was – then I was guessing that the knife thrust had torn one such tube inside Jack's chest. If the blood stopped before he lost too much, he would live. If the wound was too big to mend itself, he wouldn't.

I stitched him together as best I could. Both my teachers are wonderfully nimble-fingered, and neither is satisfied with me unless I perform as well as they do. With Jack's blood still pumping up under my hands, I compromised, sacrificing a bit of neatness for speed. I hoped it was the right thing to do, and I prayed, harder than I'd ever prayed for anything, that it was.

Some time in the middle of the morning, I realized that the bleeding had slowed. The pads pressed to his chest were still colouring red, but slowly now, as if the blood was only seeping. Jack was still unconscious – luckily for him he had been all the time I was sewing the wound – but once or twice he stirred slightly. I knew I must get him to drink, and I asked the innkeeper's wife to have clean water ready. Delighted to have something to do, she rushed off and presently returned with a huge bucketful.

I smiled involuntarily. She seemed to think I was nursing a fully-grown horse.

The day went on. I managed to get a small mug of water into my patient. He felt cold, as the afternoon waned, and I asked for a fire. He still felt cold, so I got on the little cot beside him and took him in my arms.

I hadn't realized that it was night until I felt a warm hand on my shoulder. Turning quickly round, I saw in the soft light of the fire in the little hearth that a grey-haired priest stood over the bed.

'I am Father Gregory,' he said quietly. 'I am the infirmarer at the priests' house, and I came to offer my help.'

'Oh!' Quickly I sat up, carefully pulling the covers up over Jack and straightening my gown. 'Thank you, how kind.'

'We all like Jack,' he said solemnly. 'He is a good man.'

I tried to gather my thoughts to explain to this kindly man what had happened, what I'd done to help, how Jack had been all the long day. But my mind was a blank. I looked up at Father Gregory, shaking my head. 'I'm sorry, but I can't seem to think,' I said.

He took my hands and raised me to my feet. 'Go and rest,' he said firmly. 'I will sit with him.'

'Will you—' I began.

I didn't have to finish. 'Of course I will,' he said.

The tavern-keeper had made up a bed for me in a corner of the main room. I walked carefully between other sleeping bodies and sat down on it. A candle had been left burning to help me find my way. I was about to stretch out and try to sleep when I heard someone approach.

It was Ginger. 'I found this, miss.' He was holding out a little bag made of soft fabric. His face was wretched; I realized how much he and the others cared for and depended on Jack.

I held out my hand. 'What is it?'

'I don't know,' Ginger said, 'I haven't opened it. It fell out of your satchel when you were – when you tended the master.'

I took it from him. 'Thank you.'

He nodded. Then he said, 'How is he?'

'He's sleeping and so far he isn't feverish.' It was all I could say and no answer, because what Ginger was really asking was, *Is he going to live?* and I didn't know. 'There's a priest with him,' I added, in case Ginger thought I'd left Jack alone.

'Aye, Father Gregory. He's all right, he is.' He smiled. 'Get some sleep, miss. You look all in.' He nodded again, then crawled away.

I knew I wouldn't be able to close down my racing, panicky mind, so I thought I might as well investigate the little cloth bag. It was the object I'd found in the secret hiding place in Osmund's cell, when Jack and I went to leave Robert Powl's token.

Jack. Fit, whole, healthy. And now he—

I shut off that thought before it could undermine me.

I opened the neck of the little bag and tipped the contents out into my hand. A length of thin silver chain slithered and settled in the hollow of my palm, and there was a pendant suspended on it.

A pendant on a silver chain . . . Why did that strike a note of memory?

I bent down closer to the light of the candle flame and studied the pendant. It was a round silver coin, or so I thought at first. Then I saw that it had a strange design etched on it, unlike that on any coin I'd ever seen. The lines were worn with age but I could see what they depicted. It was a strange figure made up of a man and a woman, half and half, wearing one crown, their disparate feet standing on the back of a two-headed dragon's back.

I had seen that image before.

Silently I beat my fist against my forehead in frustration, trying to make my mind work. It was terribly important – somehow I knew it was – but I couldn't find the connection. Something I'd seen, or been told . . . But I was so tired, so worried, and I was only keeping despair and a flood of tears at bay by sheer will power.

I lay back, the pendant and chain clutched in my hand, and tried to relax. I seemed to hear Gurdyman's voice, intoning the chant he uses to enter the meditative state. Oh, how I wished he was there with me.

Perhaps the fervour of my wish conjured up some element of my beloved teacher; I don't know if that is possible. If anyone was likely to hear my desperate need and respond, though, it was Gurdyman.

All at once my mental turmoil began to ease. I closed my eyes, and I seemed to feel a cool hand on my forehead; someone was reassuring me, telling me everything would be all right, although I didn't know who it was. I didn't exactly hear words spoken; it was more a thought, put into my head. I welcomed it.

And in that dreamy state everything clarified. I knew where I'd seen that strange image before: it was the subject of a painting in Osmund's workroom. It had been beautifully done, and I could see in my mind's eye the rich blue of the man's knee-length robe, the soft pale folds of the woman's gown and the faint glitter of gold of the single crown on the two heads.

I think I must have slept for a while.

I opened my eyes to daylight. And I remembered where I'd heard mention of a pendant.

Gerda had worn a pendant on a thin silver chain. Jack had found that out when he went back to Margery's to find out if Gerda had been robbed. The pendant had been missing from her body when she was found, but it hadn't been worth much – the girl called Madselin had told Jack it looked ancient, and was worn very thin – and nobody had bothered to find out what happened to it.

Not of any great value, and we'd all forgotten about it. Other people may have had an excuse for that, but I hadn't. I knew it was important, the moment Jack mentioned it. The question *What was on the pendant?* had leapt into my mind from somewhere and I should have gone on asking it till I got an answer.

How on earth, I wondered, did it come to be in Osmund's cell? Was he – could he have been – one of her clients? But no, he was training to be a priest! *Priests are men*, said a solemn voice in my head.

I had to go back to Margery's. Jack and I had been before and talked to the other girls, but perhaps we hadn't asked the right questions. I got quietly out from under my blankets, tiptoed across the room and, taking a deep breath, went in to Jack.

Father Gregory sat beside him, still as a statue save for the fingers on his rosary. He opened his eyes as I came in. He smiled. 'The patient is sleeping,' he whispered. 'He has been restless but he is quiet now.'

I leaned over Jack. He was deathly pale and very still. I put my hand on his forehead. He was cool. I watched his breathing. Steady, deep. I put my fingers to the pulse beating in his throat. It was fast, but not as rapid as it had been yesterday.

'What have you got there?' Father Gregory asked. I still held the pendant in my other hand. I held it out to him.

He studied it for some moments. Then he said, 'Animus and anima.'

'What does that mean?' I had tensed.

'The male and female principle,' he said, still staring at the pendant as if he found it hard to tear his eyes away. Finally he looked up. 'It is an ancient symbol, representing the union of the two sides of human nature. Don't ask me any more' – he held up his hand as if physically to ward me off – 'for such matters are evil and forbidden, and I must neither speak nor even think about them.'

His mouth said the words, but I read a different

message in his wise old eyes. A message that said, *You should go on asking, for it is knowledge, and no knowledge is intrinsically evil.*

I said, 'Will you sit with Jack a little longer, please?'

He nodded.

As I ran along the quay towards Margery's establishment, I was thinking hard. Animus and anima. It was, I now realized, what I'd seen in the shining stone when Jack and I discovered Morgan and Cat. The words, like symbols, had flashed out at me, but I'd had no time to absorb them. Like far too many other things, they'd gone to the back of my mind and become overshadowed.

But they weren't overshadowed now, they were the one thing I couldn't stop thinking about. If Father Gregory was right, and that strange design represented animus and anima, then it was what we had all been looking for, since it appeared to link Gerda with both Morgan and Osmund: it connected three of the victims.

But *how*? Gerda didn't have a secret workroom, and she wasn't a magician or a magician's apprentice. She was a prostitute; her parents were dead, her kin all dispersed and either unable or unwilling to take her in, which was how she ended up at Margery's.

I had reached the firmly closed door of the brothel at the end of the quay. From somewhere within, I could hear someone busy at the wash tub; a woman's sweet voice, raised in song. I went round behind the long building and came to the laundry, where a plump woman with red cheeks and even redder hands was bending over a tub, elbow-deep in soapy water.

'I need to see Margery,' I said. 'It's urgent.'

'Come back later,' the woman said with a grin. 'When she's awake.'

'It's about Gerda.'

The name acted like a spell. Instantly the woman stood up, wiped her hands on her apron and led me inside the main building. We went along the passage to where Margery sat up in bed, not asleep but combing out her hair.

She recognized me, but, before she could speak, I held up the pendant.

Her eyes widened. 'Where did you get that?'

'It's Gerda's, isn't it?'

'Yes. Give it to me!'

I closed my hand on it. 'It was found in the cell of the young priest, the Night Wanderer's fourth victim,' I said. 'Did he visit Gerda?'

'A priest?' She shook her head. 'No. I'm not saying such a man doesn't have recourse to girls who do what mine do, but he'd hardly be likely to frequent a well-known place like mine.' She said that with a small show of pride.

'And you don't think Gerda saw him without your knowledge?'

'I know all my girls' clients.' It was said with utter certainty.

I clutched the pendant tightly in my hand. 'Could it – the pendant – have been a gift from one of her clients?'

Margery shrugged. 'I suppose so, but it was a poor gift if so. She was worth better.'

'Could she have bought it or' – I hesitated – 'stolen it?'

'She didn't steal it!' The suggestion made Margery angry. 'And I don't believe she bought it. Show me again,' Margery commanded. I held it out to her. 'Yes, it's just how I remember. But look: it's obviously ancient. The pendant itself is a bit bent, and the etched pattern is blurred with long wear. It was worn thin, see?' She pointed. 'I reckon,' she said slowly, 'it was some old family thing that had been handed down. Gerda would have treasured it, even though it had no value, because it was all she had to remember her parents and kin by. She was an orphan, you know.'

'Yes,' I said absently. I was thinking about possibilities: in particular, whether someone in Gerda's lost family had been connected with magic.

And quite how I was going to find that out, I had no idea. Return and talk to the girls, once they were up? But I'd done that before, and they'd been able to tell me very little.

I turned to go. 'Thank you for your time,' I said.

'Wait,' she said. 'How's he doing?'

I shrugged. 'He's lasted the night and he isn't feverish.'

She met my eyes. Both of us, I'm sure, were thinking the unsaid word: *yet.* 'You take good care of him,' she commanded. 'Worth saving, that one.'

I was outside, just joining the track that led back along the quay, when I heard someone behind me. Someone called my name in a sort of whispered shout, and, turning, I saw the skinny blonde girl with rats' tail hair and greasy skin who had been so scared by the Night Wanderer legends. She still looked terrified, and as she held out her hand to stop me, I saw that she had bitten her nails so harshly that the tops of the fingers bulged out over what was left.

'Hello, Madselin,' I said.

'Hush!' she hissed, although I hadn't spoken loudly. 'Come over here, where we won't be seen or overheard.' She grabbed my sleeve and pulled me over behind a half-ruined boat shed.

We stood in awkward silence for a while, and I found her wide, frightened gaze disconcerting. Also, I wanted very much to get back to Jack. 'What do you want with me? I said, perhaps too impatiently, because her lips trembled and tears filled her eyes. 'Sorry,' I said quickly. 'How can I help?'

She seemed to gather herself together, as if for a tremendous effort, then said, 'I heard you just now, talking to Margery. I had to come after you! I should have spoken up before, should have told what I knew, but I was too afraid.' The tears spilled over her eyelids and ran down her thin cheeks.

I took her cold hands in mine. 'What should you have told?'

'I heard them, see!' she burst out, wringing her thin hands in distress. 'It was the night before – before she died.' Madselin swallowed a sob. 'I was out with – well, never mind who it was, but he likes to do it in the open air when the weather allows and it was mild that night. Anyway, he'd finished his business and was away back to his wife and children, and I was making my way back to Margery's, and I *heard* them!' She looked pop-eyed at me, as if I should have known.

'Who did you hear?' I asked, fighting my desire to shake her.

'Gerda and him! They were having a row, I reckon, and both of them were angry, yelling at each other. I wasn't eavesdropping,' she added hastily, 'you could hear them a mile off! Anyway, I was quite close, so I stopped and watched, and I saw it all, though I didn't let them see me.'

'What was the row about?' I could have asked her who the other person was, but I had a feeling I already knew.

'He was so furious with her! Kept saying again and again how she was really sinful, and how wrong it was in God's eyes to live the life she did, and how would the lord Jesus feel about her defiling her flesh? He was trying to persuade her to leave Margery's and move into the little room he was renting as a workroom. It wasn't much, he told her, and not very comfortable, and he wouldn't be able to get her much food, but she'd be honest, and she could make her confession to his old priest and do her penance and God would forgive her and receive her back.'

'What did she say to that?' I asked when Madselin paused for breath.

'She said, not bloody likely!' Madselin answered with a feeble grin. 'Then he started going on about how she could help him in his work and be useful to him, only I didn't understand that bit, when you think what she did and what he was.' She frowned. 'But it sounded from his tone as if he really needed her.'

'And she still refused?' I prompted.

'Oh, yes. Told him he could disapprove all he liked but she was happy at Margery's, because they were kind to her and they didn't try to bully her. She said she didn't mind the old girl – Margery, I mean – and she really liked the other girls, and *they* were her family now.'

I thought about that.

'Then he reached forward and stuck his hand down her gown, and I wondered what was going on,' Madselin continued, 'but he was just pulling out the pendant she wore, on its chain. *I've been good to you! I gave you this!* he yells at her, shaking it in her face' – Madselin's voice rose dramatically – 'and then she pulls it up over her head and thrusts it at him. *You can have it back!* she cries. *It's old and it's nasty, and I* hate *it!'*

'And he took it?'

Madselin nodded. 'Yes! She flung it at him and stalked off, and I watched him pick it up. He looked so sad,' she murmured. 'I felt sorry for him, even though he'd been unkind to her.'

'And she was killed the following night,' I said slowly, half to myself. I thought that perhaps, at last, I was starting to understand why.

The Night Wanderer, it seemed, had believed her to be something she wasn't; something of vital importance to Osmund's secret, other life . . .

I should have thought more carefully before I spoke, for Madselin was weeping in earnest now, the hands with their poor bitten nails up to her face in a hopeless attempt to hide her distress. 'I *know*,' she sobbed, 'and I should have said what I'd seen, only I was so frightened! I thought he'd come back and do for me, too, if I spoke up!'

I put my arms round her and hugged her. 'I don't think it would have made any difference,' I said. 'And you were scared, like we all were, and nobody is at their best when they're frightened.'

She seemed to take comfort from that and her sobs slowly subsided. When she was sufficiently calm, I walked with her the short distance back to Margery's and saw her safely inside.

Then I hurried back down the quay.

I kept hearing Madselin's voice when she told me what Gerda had said about the other girls: that *they* were her family now.

I thought about what I'd first been told about the Night Wanderer's fourth victim: *he was an outsider, new to the town, studious, quiet, kept himself to himself.* New to the town . . . And Gerda, they'd said, wasn't a local girl but had come to here after the deaths of both parents. She'd been the youngest child, still at home when the older siblings had gone, and none of those siblings could take her in when she was left alone.

She and Osmund were brother and sister.

Osmund had frequently been late for the offices and had been known to go down to the river. We knew about his workroom, but going there wasn't the only reason he absented himself from the priests' house. He used to slip out to meet his sister.

He hated what she did for a living but couldn't supply the necessary support to get her out of it. Perhaps he felt guilty that he couldn't offer her a home; that her being a whore was at least in part his fault. Who could say?

He had been trying to persuade her to become his assistant. His adept; his Soror Mystica; his sister in the great work, just as she was in the flesh and in the blood.

But she was afraid and unwilling. She had been killed, and then, only a few days later, so had he.

I was almost back at the tavern. I was running now, my satchel bouncing on my hip. Suddenly it felt as if a shock had run through me. I skidded to a halt, put my hand inside my satchel and felt the shining stone, almost too hot to touch.

The compulsion to look into it was irresistible. I ran to the line of warehouses, slid between two of them and took out the stone.

I had never known it so urgent. There was no waiting for murky darkness to clear; no patient following of the brilliant green and gold lines that seemed to lead the eye into its mysterious heart. The vision was right there and it felt as if the stone was hammering it into my head.

It showed me Gerda and Osmund. It showed me Morgan and Cat. Then, in clear detail, it showed me myself and Gurdyman.

Its message was devastatingly clear, but still it forged on. I saw the four victims throatless, bleeding, lifeless. Then, in an image of total horror, Gurdyman and I lay on the stone floor of the crypt, and we, too, had no throats.

Nausea rose up and overwhelmed me and I vomited and retched until I could bring up no more. Then, more frightened than I'd ever been in my life, I fled.

Twenty

Hrype sat cross-legged before the small fire he had lit. He had been walking for the greater part of the last two days and nights, if the furious, driven striding on his long legs through wood and field and around marsh and fen could be called walking. He knew, if he was honest with himself, that he was fleeing from the truth, for it was extremely unwelcome and uncomfortably painful.

Earlier, he had woken from a brief and restless sleep. He had sought shelter in a hay barn, tunnelling into the fragrant hay like the rats and mice who kept him company to lie in the grip of dreams of violence and horrible images. Waking, he had believed he detected the ring of truth in the nightmarish dreams, and, steeling himself, he had found an isolated place and lit his small fire. He had taken his rune stones out of the bag and spread out the cloth on which he always cast them. He was finding it difficult to put himself into the right state for reading their message. Closing his eyes, he forced his mind to detach. To elevate into that strange realm where the spirits waited, and from which, if you were lucky, they might deign to communicate.

He cast the runes and looked down.

The first thing he saw made him smile grimly.

300

The powers that ruled his life, it seemed, were intent on showing him aspects of himself he preferred normally to ignore. First there had been Gurdyman, earnest, deeply concerned, brave in his determination to stand firm in the face of Hrype's increasing anger and make him hear the truth. Now the runes were following where the old man had led, for what Hrype read was the combination of symbols that he suspected meant Jack Chevestrier, and beside them the ones that implied a tearing away of smoke screens; a confrontation with the true nature of something, or someone.

Slowly Hrype nodded, as if indicating that he accepted the message.

I have always found it hard to trust Jack Chevestrier, he admitted to himself, *because, certain as I have been from the start that Gaspard Picot is involved, in the thefts and perhaps the killings too, I convinced myself that Chevestrier too is crooked and corrupt. Both men work for the sheriff – Gaspard Picot is the wretched man's own kin – and I allowed that to persuade me.*

But now he accepted that he had been wrong. The stones told him so. Moreover, seeing the truth displayed so clearly before him, he realized that he had allowed his antipathy towards Jack Chevestrier to cloud his vision.

Hrype dropped his head in his hands. He was ashamed. He was a seeker after the truth. He prided himself on his clarity of vision; his ability to rise above the petty sentiments and emotions of ordinary human beings and courageously stare the truth in the face. In the space of two days,

301

he had been shown to himself for what he was, and the pain was intense.

He removed his hands and looked down at the runes again, for he had got no further than the first message before being overcome.

He stared. Rubbed his tired eyes, stared again. What he thought he read couldn't be true; surely not!

He did something he very rarely did, for the powers that drove the rune messages didn't like having their word doubted. He gathered them up, held them tightly in his hands, prayed to his gods for help and guidance, shook the stones hard and once more cast them on to the sacred cloth.

The message was there; and this time it was expressed even more forcibly.

For a few moments, Hrype couldn't move. He muttered, 'I have been blind. *Blind!*'

Then, in terrible haste, he gathered up the stones, hurriedly performed his ritual thanks and made his reverence, then stowed them away in their bag. He stood for a moment undecided. Where should he go? He could help – he knew that, for the runes had told him so – but where was he most needed?

The answer sounded in his head, clear as a bell on a still day.

He ran.

I was running as fast as I could, but the effort was enormous; as if I was straining against a rope holding me back. I was heading not for the tavern and Jack, where I longed to be, but in the opposite direction.

Everything in me wanted to go back to him. He was my patient, he was very badly hurt, I ought to be beside him. I didn't admit that I also loved him; I didn't know quite what I felt, only that running away from him was hurting like a stab in the heart.

He has Father Gregory with him, I told myself. I have not left him untended. *But—*

I didn't let the protest form.

I ran on. I was over the Great Bridge now, diving into the network of alleys behind the market square. I had come this way often with Jack over the past few days and didn't have to think about my route, which was hard because it freed my mind to think about him instead.

Stop.

I reached the narrow passage I knew so well. I stopped to listen, but there was no sound of footfalls. If anybody had been pursuing me, I had lost them. I walked on.

And, too soon, I was at the front door of Gurdyman's twisty-turny house.

The door opened as I pushed it. I went inside.

So terrified had I been that I would be met with the real-life version of what I saw in the shining stone that it was quite hard to accept that he wasn't lying there before me with no throat.

I stepped carefully along the passage. 'Gurdyman?' I called softly.

He was standing in the little inner court. The sun shone on his dome of a head, and his bright blue eyes softened as he saw me.

'Lassair,' he breathed. Then, anxiously, 'You are unhurt?'

'Yes! And you?'

'Oh, yes.' He was staring at me, puzzled. 'There was something . . .' He broke off. 'I have been staying with a very old friend,' he said, and I was quite sure it was a last-minute substitute for what he had been about to say. 'He lives in a little house on a patch of higher ground out in the marsh, almost an island. It is reached by a stretch of narrow causeway that is so well concealed that it is all but impossible to find. This secret dwelling is on the fen edge, to the south of the great bulge that you walk around to get from your village to the town. It is a small and perfect house, right out in the wilds, and you cannot find it unless someone tells you where it is. My friend built it himself, many years ago when the need for solitude overtook him and he began to walk away from the world, increasingly deeper into his studies. It has a magical sort of name, but that must remain hidden.'

I tried to take in what he was telling me; *why* was he telling me? 'Is that where you've been?'

'Yes. Hrype said I should go, for this town was not safe for one such as I.'

'Because the Night Wanderer was killing other magicians' – in my mind's eye I saw Osmund, and then Morgan and poor, pathetic Cat – 'and Hrype thought you'd be next.'

'Precisely that,' Gurdyman agreed.

But something was wrong with that. 'You disappeared the night Jack and I saw Osmund being slain,' I said slowly. 'He was the only wi—' I had been about to say wizard, but I stopped; I've always thought Gurdyman disliked the word.

'He was the only one like you who had died, then, for Robert Powl, Gerda and Mistress Judith did not spend their private hours in magic work-rooms.' Gurdyman didn't answer; he just went on looking at me. 'You *knew* more would die,' I whispered. 'Didn't you?'

'I believed it, yes.'

'How could you have left them to their fate? Morgan, and Cat! He tried to protect his master, you know. His body was found flung across the old man's, but it didn't help either of them.'

Gurdyman saw my distress and held out a hand to me, but I ignored it. 'Child, do you not think I tried?' he said, an edge of anger in his voice. 'I railed at Morgan with all my strength, trying to impress the horror of what I had seen just ahead, but to no avail.'

'You could have—'

Gurdyman drew himself up. His anger increased, and just for an instant it felt as if a flame was brushing my skin. It hurt. '*Ow!*'

'I'm sorry, child, but you are losing yourself in your own emotion, and, while your urge to demand retributive justice for Morgan and Cat is admirable, you need to know the truth. Morgan refused to leave his home and his work, and Cat refused to abandon her.'

'Him,' I corrected automatically.

There was utter silence. Something crackled momentarily in the air.

I couldn't take my eyes off Gurdyman's.

'The name, in fact, is Morgana.'

I felt my jaw drop. 'He – she – Morgan was a *woman*?'

'Of course,' Gurdyman said shortly. 'Since Cat was quite clearly male, his magician had to be female. Always there must be the opposites, the poles, the two sexes. Animus and anima,' he added.

I sank down on to the bench that stands by the wall of the inner court. 'Why did she pretend to be a man?'

'She was brilliant, and her powers were great,' Gurdyman said. 'The world – even the world of like-minded souls – was perhaps not quite ready to accept that such a leading light could be female.'

Animus and anima. I took out Gerda's pendant and silently gave it to Gurdyman. He went pale. 'Where did you get this?'

So I told him. Trying to be brief, I told him everything that had happened since he left.

When I finished, he joined me on the bench. 'It begins to add up,' he murmured.

But I barely heard. I had been thinking about the night he disappeared; the night I thought I saw him and Hrype, down in the crypt, only when Jack arrived with a light – oh, Jack! – there was no sign of either of them.

'Were you really there that night?' I whispered.

He knew exactly what I meant. 'Yes,' he said. 'Hrype had come to fetch me and we were on the point of leaving when you turned up. Hrype was convinced the forces of the law would soon break in – that's who we thought you were – and that was why I'd—'

'That's why you tidied up the crypt,' I interrupted, 'to make sure there was nothing incriminating to be found.' *Nothing*, I added silently,

306

that would give away who and what you are, for that knowledge is very dangerous.

'Yes,' he murmured.

'How did you do it?' I had to know. 'One moment you were there – I *saw* you – and then you weren't, yet you couldn't have got out because I was standing at the foot of the steps, and Jack was coming down right behind me.' It was conceivable that Gurdyman and Hrype might have squeezed past me without my feeling their presence, but they couldn't have got past Jack. He was too broad.

Gurdyman was looking at me, his head on one side. 'Do you remember what I told you about this house?' I shook my head. He had told me many things, and I wasn't in any state to run through the store of my memories and extract the right one. 'I said,' he went on softly, 'that this house of mine holds many secrets, and that you would come to know about some of them, although some would remain hidden.'

'Is this a secret I won't know?' I whispered.

He smiled gently. 'Not yet, child, for there is no need.'

'But—'

'Enough.'

My mind was roaming wildly, throwing up possibilities. Did he mean there was another exit from the crypt, one so well hidden that I had no idea it was there? One that, perhaps, only revealed itself when there was desperate need? Oh, but that was impossible, surely, even for Gurdyman, unless—

Quite gently and firmly, he stopped the thought.

I found I just couldn't pursue it; it had ceased.
Just like that.

I stared at him. He looked so normal, sitting
there in the sunshine, his wonderful, gaudy shawl
wrapped round him, his blue eyes twinkling
benignly. For a moment I doubted everything.
He was just a rotund, absent-minded old man,
and the rest was all in my imagination.

Presently I said, 'You came back. Does that
mean it's safe now?'

But he frowned, his face darkening into anxiety.
'Oh, no, child, it is very far from safe. I came
back precisely because of that; for the peril
reaches its climax now, and we shall have to
fight it.'

Something suddenly struck me. I sat up straight,
looking around. 'Where's your friend?' I
demanded. 'The one you were staying with, in
the house with the magical name?'

Gurdyman looked down at his small, plump
hands, folded in his lap. 'I do not know.' He met
my eyes. 'Something happened this morning; an
enchantment, I believe, affecting both my friend
– his name is Mercure – and me.' He frowned.
'I believe I perceived something I was not meant
to see, and then some power overcame me and
obscured the sight.' Now he looked pale. 'I
believe that power might have emanated from
the Night Wanderer.'

'*Oh!*' My hands flew up to cover my mouth,
muffling the sound.

'I do not know where Mercure is,' Gurdyman
repeated, 'for he was not there when I was
released from the spell and came back to myself.'

I had an image of him, out at his friend's house. Waking from trance, or sleep, or enchantment – whatever it had been – and finding himself alone. Desperate with worry for his friend, yet leaving the lonely, isolated house to return here.

Gurdyman nodded, as if he followed the line of my thoughts. 'I am indeed very anxious for Mercure, but he is powerful, and wise, and better able to look after himself than almost any other.' He reached for my hand, briefly holding it. 'My greater fear was for you.'

I stared at him. While it made me feel warm with pleasure that he should care about me in this way, at the same time I was filled with dread because Gurdyman, whom I'd come to think of as inviolable and omnipotent, had just admitted to anxiety and fear. If a magician of his quality was afraid, what hope was there for the rest of us?

'What should we do?' I whispered.

'We shall go down into the crypt,' he said firmly, 'where I have in mind certain defences which I shall begin straight away to—'

He was interrupted by the sound of footsteps coming slowly, draggingly, along the passage. Both of us spun round.

An old man in long robes was creeping towards us. He was very white in the face, as if he had suffered a severe wound or a dreadful shock. His dark eyes stared imploringly at us. His garments – musty black, or perhaps a deep shade of brown or grey – were dirty, and the flowing skirt of his robe was torn into tatters down one side. He clutched the remnants to him, perhaps in a pathetic attempt to preserve his modesty and hide his pale and bony legs.

With a soft exclamation, Gurdyman removed his shawl and held it out to the shuffling figure, helping him to wrap it around his narrow hips. He guided the old man to the bench by the wall, encouraging him to sit down. Over his shoulder he said, 'A restorative for our visitor, I think, Lassair, if you would be so kind.'

I couldn't take my eyes off the old man.

He was—

'Lassair?' Gurdyman prompted. 'Mercure needs your help.'

I hurried inside to the kitchen, lowering the pot of water closer to the fire in the hearth and then quickly mixing honey with pinches of the soothing, calming herbs for a comforting drink. So that was Mercure. Gurdyman had said he was powerful, capable of looking after himself, but he didn't appear so now. He looked as if he'd just suffered some frightful attack.

It didn't take much imagination to work out who had attacked him. He was Gurdyman's friend, and I was in no doubt that he performed the same sort of work. So had Osmund, Morgan and Cat, and all three were dead. And that horrible line of rips in Mercure's robe could easily have been done by a set of sharp claws.

The water was boiling and I quickly made the drink. Hurrying back out to the court, I handed it to the old man, who thanked me with a nod.

Silence fell. Mercure sipped at his drink, but made no sound. I was just thinking idly that it was unusual for somebody to consume almost boiling liquid without slurping at it when I became aware of a low, soft humming. I was going to make some comment – to ask Gurdyman what it was, to question, perhaps, if it was some strange bird – but then the impulse, and the curiosity, left me. It was a nice sound. I smiled, and the humming intensified. My legs felt weak – what a lot I'd done recently! No wonder I was so weary – and I moved backwards so that I could lean against the wall.

I was looking at one of the late-flowering blooms in the little flower bed, thinking how pretty it was, how intense the colour, when Gurdyman said, his voice oddly strangled, 'Lassair!'

'It's no good, you know, my dear friend.' Mercure's voice was like liquid silver, and I thought it was the most beautiful sound I'd ever heard.

'*Lassair!*' Gurdyman's, by contrast, sounded like the coarse croaking of a hideous bird. 'You must— *aaaah!*' Abruptly his words choked off, and he put both hands to his throat.

Oh, dear. He seemed to be in some sort of distress.

That flower was *so* pretty!

Somebody else was humming now, in a higher octave. It was quite sweet, and blended well with the deep, powerful vibration now flooding the inner court and bouncing off the walls. With faint surprise I realized the new sound was coming from me.

Mercure and I were humming together, and the music was quite enchanting.

I turned to face him. It wasn't a conscious move; I had no choice. I looked right into his deep, dark eyes. They were like wells in the pale face. I straightened up into a long, thin reed and poised to dive right down into them.

But at the very last moment, something held me back. I could see Gurdyman, still trying and failing to call my name and capture my attention, but the enchantment held him mute.

It must, then, have been another's voice that yelled, over and over again, *Lassair! Lassair!*

It was the voice of a man in his prime, loud, vibrant with strength, desperate with fear for me and full of terrible warning.

It was enough – just – to make me pause.

Mercure laughed softly, a sound so sweet that I yearned towards him. 'Ah, but you resist!' he said gently. 'I am pleased to see it, Lassair, for it demonstrates, if demonstration were needed, that I am right in my choice.'

His *choice*?

He stood up and moved closer to me. He was no longer stooped and cowed. He was straight and tall, and it occurred to me that he wasn't an old man after all . . .

He reached out a long, graceful hand and touched my cheek. I leaned towards him, yearning, longing. His raised arm had parted the neck of his robe a little, and I saw he wore beneath it a medallion on a gold chain. My eyes were drawn to it and I saw the image etched into the gold.

A human figure composed of man and woman, half and half, wearing a single crown.

I managed to pull my gaze away from it and

312

met his stare. For an instant, before he changed, I saw right into his eyes, and they were black holes that opened into a pit. But then he smiled, his eyes were human again and compelling me, drawing me, towards him.

'I see you recognize the symbol,' he said, his breath like a soft, fragrant breeze against my cheek. 'The male and female must both be there, and I have striven to achieve union within myself, without the aid of pupil or Soror Mystica. Morgana had her Cat, Gurdyman has you' – for a moment his gaze seemed to reach right inside me, as if fine cords emanated out of his eyes to enter into mine – 'but I believed I could manage fusion alone.'

He winced and slumped briefly, as if in memory of some awful pain. Then, recovering, once more he focused himself on me. 'I have been working these many long months – years – to bring full life to both sides of myself, the female and the male, but I have not succeeded, and I must conclude that what I have striven for cannot be achieved.' He made a strange gesture then: he wrapped both arms around himself, at the level of his ribs, and squeezed very hard.

It looked as if he was trying to hold himself together.

'It is not meant to be, I think,' he said ruefully. 'My experiments have made a great rift, and although I try to put my two selves together again, I am no longer myself.'

I ought to have been curious. I ought to have been bursting with frightened questions, for he spoke – in that calm smooth voice – of things that were far beyond anything I'd ever learned; far beyond, surely, what men should even think of attempting.

But I stood, silent and docile, like a lamb awaiting the blade.

'We who do the great work allow the fools who share this precious earth with us to believe what they see as our goal,' Mercure went on. 'For them to view us as covetous men and women seeking to make gold out of lesser metals suits us well, for it disguises our true aim. Not that we expect outsiders to see the huge importance of this aim, for who but we value the refinement of the soul?'

He kept his eyes on me, holding me as if I were in chains.

Then suddenly he clutched at himself, and my healer's experience told me he was in dreadful pain. At the same instant, I had a slight disturbance in my sight; it seemed, in the space of a blink, that he altered. That the guise of a benign old man tore, and something else looked out.

Before the terror could burst out in a long scream, he had me – and perhaps whatever lurked inside him – back under his control.

'I have erred, Lassair,' he whispered, and the agony made his voice shake. 'I tried to suppress my dark side; to bring it under my own control and then release it back into myself. But dark sides are not amenable to our control. Mine, at least, is not.' He sighed, and now I could detect that his breath reeked; that it was foul and corrupt with some dread matter.

'I have altered my soul's true nature by what I have done to myself,' he murmured – I noticed

314

that he was trembling, his whole body shaking as if he was in the grip of some sort of fit – 'and I am forced to admit, at the last, that I cannot achieve my uttermost desire alone.'

Now he turned on the full force of his glamour, and I felt it descend on me like a glittering cloak. 'You shall come with me,' he said – it was more like a chant – 'and we shall go to my house on the island, and I shall destroy the causeway so that we are for ever alone, my Soror Mystica and I, and we shall unite our bodies and our different essences – our very souls – into the ultimate.'

He raised his hand, began to back away, and I followed.

But our route to the door was blocked. Somebody stood in the passage.

Hrype said calmly and firmly, 'She will not go with you, Mercure.'

Mercure spun round and, again, I had that glimpse of something terrible beneath the disguising robes.

But his voice was still sweet and so seductive.

'Oh, I think she will,' he said.

He moved so quickly. He lowered his right arm, seemed to reach deep within his voluminous garments, then raised it again.

It was no longer a human arm.

The forelimb was bright, shining silver, and the hand was the paw of a savage animal, with long downward-curving claws that glittered sharp as blades.

One of those dread claws had a small chip on the tip.

He made an inarticulate, bestial sound and lunged at Hrype. He swung the clawed limb, and I heard the whistle as it descended down through the air.

Hrype stepped aside.

Mercure, his own momentum forcing him on past Hrype, turned and tried again. But just as the raised claw was about to home in on Hrype's throat, a hand caught it from behind.

Twisted it, bent it, caused Mercure to roar with pain as his shoulder dislocated.

He looked wildly around, and his dark presence seemed to fill the narrow passage so that I could not see who had stopped his murderous attack. Then he gave a great cry, and, the pain making him retch, he drove his claw of an arm up towards his own throat and tore it out.

He must have died almost instantly. Released, all the strength – his strength – left me and I fell to the ground. I felt arms around me, and Gurdyman's voice in my ear whispered words of comfort, reassurance.

I looked up. Hrype stood over us, and I couldn't read the expression on his face. He seemed different, but I did not know what had changed.

But there had been someone else . . .

Mercure had had the ascendancy, for Gurdyman and I were already under his spell and Hrype surely could not have held out for long. Another's hand had grabbed Mercure's wrist, and that action had saved us all.

My eyes flew past Hrype, trying to look everywhere at once, searching, searching.

And then I saw him.

Behind Hrype, leaning against the stone wall of the passage, stood Rollo.

It felt like much later, but only a short time could have elapsed, for although the body of the Night Wanderer had been removed by some of Sheriff Picot's men, his blood was still wet on the floor of the passage.

Gurdyman and Hrype had disappeared down to the crypt. Rollo and I sat in the inner court, and the sun shone on us.

He had told me how he'd been watching me for days. How he'd gone out to Aelf Fen and overheard what I'd said to Sibert about being safe with Jack. Guarded my footsteps as I returned to the town, aware that there was a grave threat and wanting to keep me from harm.

Watched me with Jack.

Seen me as I cradled his head in my lap, taken in every detail of my expression as Jack's life blood soaked into my skirts.

He didn't actually phrase it like that, but I knew what he must have seen.

'Do you love him?' he asked me now.

'No. *Yes.* I don't know.'

Rollo smiled briefly. 'That covers every possibility,' he remarked.

I truly had no idea what I felt. I was numb with shock, for I had just been under the spell of an exceptionally powerful man who had bent me to his will as easily as if I'd been a blade of grass. I'd seen him take his own life, right before my eyes. On top of that, as if it wasn't enough, I was exhausted and I wanted to be with Jack because I knew he was in grave pain and perhaps he was dying, and here I was, half a mile or more away from him, and it hurt so much I couldn't bear it.

I took a deep breath. Rollo had every right to ask me to explain, and I must do my best.

'I love you too,' I said. 'As well as Jack, I mean.' Normally *I love you too* is the response when someone has just declared their love for you, and I had no idea how Rollo felt about me now. 'When you went away, I had no idea when I'd see you again, although you promised you'd come back and I believed you.' I paused. He didn't interrupt – for which I was very grateful – and after a moment I went on. 'I'd had every intention of waiting for you, and it wasn't too bad, really. But then I met him – Jack – and I liked him, because he's a good man doing a hard job in a town that's dirty with corruption, and—'

Of all things, an image of Jack's geese floated into my head. Those guard geese, that he kept because he lived all alone and there were a lot of men who would rather he was dead because he spoke up for honesty and decency and the weak and the helpless, and he was never going to accept the right of powerful men to override all those things just because it made them rich.

That attitude, in a town where the law was corrupt and weaker men chose the easy path over the tough one, created a lot of enemies.

My hands in my lap were wet and I realized I was crying.

'Rollo, he's so very lonely.'

Rollo's arms were round me, but there was

318

comfort and kindness in the close hug, and, just then, nothing else. Thankful for his presence, for his strong heart beating against me, I surrendered to all the pain inside me and wept.

He went away.

'I'm not going far,' he told me firmly, 'or, at least, not as far as I went last time.' He smiled at some private thought. 'But there's something I have to do, and now seems a good time.' He took my hand, holding it in a brief, hard grip. 'Your man here is hurt, and I don't think you can think of anything but that at the moment. If you find you love him, you can tell me so when I come back.'

He turned away.

'I'm sorry that—' I began, but he stopped me.

'No recriminations, Lassair,' he said. 'I've been away a long time, and I sent you no word. If you got lonely, and took comfort in the love of another man, then the responsibility is as much mine as yours.'

He was being very fair. It was nice of him, I reflected, to say *responsibility* and not *blame*.

I looked at him, at the blond hair now threaded with strands of grey, at the dark brown eyes with unfamiliar lines around them. Wherever he'd been, it hadn't been easy. He had suffered, and I read it all through his lithe body.

I loved him; there was no doubt of it.

But all I wanted to do was go to Jack.

So that's what I did.

Down in the crypt, Hrype and Gurdyman heard the slamming of the door.

'She has gone back to Jack,' Gurdyman said.

'She cannot do anything else,' Hrype replied. Then, after a brief pause, 'Do you detect it too?'

Gurdyman nodded. 'As soon as I saw her.'

'Does she know?'

'No.'

The two men fell silent.

Then: 'The other one has gone too,' Hrype said. 'And that is wise of him, since at present she is given over entirely to the care of the injured one.'

'It is also kind,' Gurdyman said with a faint note of reproof, 'since to add to her burden by forcing her to decide between the two of them would be cruel.'

'You think the Norman is *kind*?' Hrype demanded. 'It is not a word I use when speaking of his sort.'

'And you are too blinded by your prejudices,' Gurdyman flashed back. 'In any case, both men are Normans. Lassair has the ability to look beneath that, and see them for what they really are.'

Hrype opened his mouth to give a stinging retort, but then he closed it again.

After a while, Gurdyman said, 'I believe that since both Lassair and Rollo have gone, and their private conversation is therefore over, we may return upstairs.' He led the way up the steps, Hrype following.

'Where will you go now?' he asked as, in the passage, Hrype turned towards the door.

Hrype looked at him for a long moment. 'I'm going back to my village.' He laid a slight emphasis on *my*, and Gurdyman smiled faintly.

320

'As I walk along, I shall be thinking of the right way to say what I must say to Froya.'

Now Gurdyman's smile was wide and delighted. But he spoke with careful restraint, for Hrype was a proud man. 'I am glad, my friend,' he said.

As if that short exchange was more than enough, Hrype abruptly changed the subject. 'What happened to him? Mercure, I mean?'

Gurdyman sighed heavily. 'I do not know,' he confessed. 'I think perhaps it was indeed as he said himself: he tried to work alone, and somehow, in trying to seek out his female side and treat it as a separate entity, he disintegrated his soul and couldn't put it back together.' He shook his head. 'Mercure used powerful substances,' he said darkly. 'He was experimenting extensively with cinnabar, that is obvious, and it seems that all three of them – Mercure, Morgana and the young priest – believed that some combination of quick-silver and emerald might yield a deep and awesome result.' He shook his head. 'Morgana and the priest, however, appear to have been more cautious and circumspect, but I only begin to suspect some of the poisons Mercure must have ingested. Such potent and frightening substances must be treated with a great deal more respect than he showed them, in his desperate need, for they can have terrible consequences and drive a man deep into madness.'

He paused, a thoughtful expression on his smooth, round face. 'And yet, despite the terrible and corrupt uses to which he ultimately put his great talent and skills, we must surely admire him. Somehow he perfected the ability to change

321

his appearance, taking on the Night Wanderer guise with dead-white face and holes for eyes, but I fear it must have taken huge amounts of concentration and magical energy to maintain it. He had depleted himself savagely, and the image he presented right at the end' – he hugged himself, as if feeling the blast of a sudden cold wind – 'was incomplete. He had begun to shake almost ceaselessly, and bits of his true self appeared through cracks in the facade. As, indeed,' he added, wrapping his shawl more closely round him, 'parts of the darkness were appearing through when he tried to present himself as Mercure.'

It seemed to Hrype that, just for a moment, a cloud of blackness floated in the passage. Then it dispersed.

Silence fell.

Hrype said after a while, 'He began his killings with the slaughter of the rat, the cat and the dog, I imagine, in order to introduce the belief that he was indeed the Night Wanderer, returned to haunt the town and embark on the same sort of terror that he had carried out before.' He paused, frowning. 'I understand why he had to kill Morgana and Cat and the young priest, for they were working towards the same ends, and I imagine he wanted no competition.'

'I believe that is so,' Gurdyman agreed cautiously, 'although it is hard to say, when someone is so far gone into insanity.'

'But what of the others?' Hrype went on.

'The first victim brought into the town the rare and costly substance that the great work required, and the apothecary's widow sold it in her shop. Mercure was simply stopping anybody else getting their hands on it.'

'And the little whore?'

Gurdyman frowned his disapproval at the word. 'Gerda was Osmund's sister. If we could question Mercure as to his motive in killing her, I believe you would find that he thought Osmund was about to recruit her as his mystic sister; force her to adopt that role as well as being his blood sister.'

Hrype was shaking his head, a wry smile on his face. 'How can you possibly know they were brother and sister?'

Gurdyman shrugged. 'Margery told me. We are old friends, and I have known her for years.'

Rollo strode out of the town to the stables where he had left his horse. He found the sturdy mare turned out in a field, where she stood nose to tail with an intelligent-looking grey gelding which stared with interest at Rollo.

'Sorry, but I'm taking your new friend away,' he said to the gelding, gently pushing aside its questing nose.

He tacked up his mare, paid the proprietor what he owed and set off on the road south.

He couldn't think about Lassair.

He planned to go back across the Channel, make his way to the court of Duke Robert of Normandy and sell, again, what he had learned at such cost in Constantinople and beyond. If he couldn't have what he wanted – and how much more he wanted it, now that it appeared he couldn't have it – he might as well use his time profitably and earn some more money.

He thought of the humble little dwelling of the wounded man, out in the empty village that would once have thrummed with life while the Conqueror's workforce built his castle. He thought of the palatial house he intended to build for himself one day, when he had finally got travel, adventure and risk out of his blood and was ready to settle down.

He realized that, of late, he had been planning his house with Lassair in mind. How foolish that had been, when she wasn't the sort of woman whose heart could be won by riches.

Despite his firm intentions, he was thinking about her.

Ruthlessly he shut off the images and began a mental list of everything he had ever heard concerning King William's brother.

By evening, Jack seemed just about strong enough to risk moving him, although the process worried me deeply. But the little room off the tavern was no place for a badly wounded man. With the death of the Night Wanderer, the town was rapidly returning to normal – normal coloured by vast relief, joy at the end of the terrible anxiety, quite a lot of revelry and a great deal of drinking – and the tavern-keeper and his wife, understandably, wanted to encourage trade and not turn it away because the place had to be kept quiet so Jack could rest.

They liked and admired him, but business was business, and everyone had a living to earn.

Walter, Ginger, Fat Gerald and young Henry carried Jack on a makeshift bier, along the quay, over the Great Bridge, down the path beside the castle and through the deserted village to his house at the end of the track. For the first part of the walk, we'd had to dodge revellers spilling out of the taverns, determined to make the most of the lifting of the curfew and many of them clutching mugs of ale and already well on the way to insensibility.

It was a great relief to reach Jack's house. Once the geese had set up their terrible racket and stopped again, it was quiet out there.

The four men gently lowered the bier and together, with me helping, we moved Jack on to the bed. He was half-conscious and he cried out in pain. Henry shot a swift look at me, and his eyes said accusingly, *Can't you do something?*

Fat Gerald was already making a fire and Ginger had gone for water. I opened my satchel and took out my packets of herbs – they wouldn't last long, I'd have to go out for more very soon – and mixed the right ones in a mug. I met Henry's anxious gaze. 'As soon as the water boils,' I promised, 'I'll make the medicine.'

I would mix it strong. Jack needed sleep – it was probably the only thing that would mend him – and I would make quite sure he got it.

The men stayed long enough to check that the fire was going well, the water was coming to the boil, that I was adequately supplied with food and firewood and had everything else I needed. Finally they left. Walter, pausing to turn in the doorway, said quietly, 'Don't let him die.'

I felt something lurch inside me. *Die*. Oh, don't even say the word . . .

I met Walter's steady eyes. 'I will do my best.'

He grinned, very briefly. 'Reckon that'll have to do, then.'

I went outside on to the track and watched them walk away.

Then I went back to my patient.